Wardens of Starlight

A Soulmark Series

Rebecca Main

www.RebeccaMain.com

www.ViaGraphia.com

Table of Contents

AMETHYSTS OF THE AZTECS

- Chapter 1 -

Relics line the walls of the atrium. Sacred hammers and swords. Vinewood wands and staffs of yew. Rings of amethyst, pearl, and pewter. Each with their own unique history and power. Some forged by gods of old. Others by those of new. I'm still learning them all. The Wardens of Starlight seems to have an almost endless supply.

Five months into my training as a Starlight Warden and I have only just finished learning the upper level of relics housed in the atrium. Five months since I was reassigned from the Stellar Warriors and sent here, to the Banks Facility. The Starlight Council had called it a blessing. A righting of a wrong. I've lost count of how many people told me that I was lucky to be reassigned as a Starlight Warden. After all, among my kind, women weren't seen as "well suited" for the call of a Stellar Warrior. No. They are much better suited for other trades. Trades such as Shadow Scouts or Occult Scholars. Even a Weapons Master is better suited for a woman than a position among the Stellar Warriors. Or so everyone thought.

My fingers itch to toy with the butterfly knife hidden snuggly beneath my belt and sweater. Not a year ago, I had proven myself worthy of the elite group of warriors, yet one mistake and I had been kicked to the curb. Banished here instead.

Guilt coils heavily in my stomach.

It had been more than a mistake. It had been a tragedy. A massacre. And the blame for it could only be put on my shoulders. Maybe they'd been right to strip me of my warrior status after all.

"Are you listening, Callie?" Still lost in my thoughts, I let my head bob carelessly along. The triplets who occupy the atrium with me continue to speak, seemingly satisfied with my assurance. Then, an elbow smashes between my sixth and seventh rib.

"What was that for?" I wheeze, rubbing the offended bones. Nova sends me a smirk, her heavily lined eyes sparkling with mischief.

"Let's just say I had a gut feeling you weren't listening," she replies. I let out an unladylike snort.

The triplets are known for their "gut feelings" and uncanny ability to understand the power of the Borealis and the relics we keep safe. Most find their shared ability off-putting, but I didn't mind one bit.

"We're only trying to help you, Calliope," Noelle gently scolds. "Your final exam with the head warden is only a few weeks away."

"And she will not go easy on you," Naomi affirms, eyes large and doe-like. A wistful sigh falls past my lips. How unsurprising. Felicia Metzart is tougher than diamonds and smart as hell to boot. She expects no less than the absolute best from those under her tutelage, and I'm no exception.

The Starlight Wardens are the keepers of magical relics, but more importantly, they're the handlers of starlight. Only the Wardens are allowed to harness the mystical power sent forth from the sun—Borealis Matter—to infuse into our weapons and make them unimaginably stronger. Only the Wardens know the vast secrets and knowledge of the world's hidden relics. Daggers that can cast a single un-sealable cut. Brooms that allow the rider to sift from place to place in the blink of an eye. Liquid gloves that can tame any flame. It is an honor to be among them.

Too bad my heart belongs to the warriors. Those who fight and kill the dark supernatural forces littering the earth.

"I know. I know," I finally lament, toying with the velvet cloth that drapes the altar we stand around. The rich fabric is out of place among the sleek white walls and glass display cases that houses the relics.

Noelle lets out a distinct *humph*. "Daydreaming about your time with the warriors won't do you any good now, Calliope." I send her an unimpressed look, enjoying a bit too much the way her cheeks color in embarrassment. "Your thoughts and talents are better put to use here than with them anyway. Don't you have your degree in astrophysics?"

"Yes," I confirm begrudgingly. *Not that I wanted to*, I think bitterly. Why JJ was allowed to go straight to his apprenticeship instead of having to run the ramparts of higher education is still a mystery to me. A niggling voice in my head croons a familiar tune; it's because he is our parents' favorite. I wouldn't be surprised if it's right. JJ is everyone's favorite. Including mine.

"Just because we don't risk life and limb to fight the monsters underneath the bed, doesn't mean we aren't cool," Nova teases. We share a smile.

"Oh, we're *cool* all right. We're stuffed in a glorified igloo up here in the middle of nowhere, Alaska. Reading books and dusting shelves all day. Oh lord," I groan, "we're librarians."

The three sisters wear matching expressions of disdain. "Librarians are cool," Naomi insists, fiddling with the glasses perched atop her head. My bluster deserts me as I take in the slump of her shoulders. Of all the Stavok sisters, Naomi is the most sensitive.

"Librarians are cool," I concede.

"Hell yeah, they are!" Nova agrees. We share another smile. I spent most of my time with Nova. Whether studying dusty tomes or showing her how to handle my butterfly knife properly. We always seek each other out in the small fortress. Noelle rolls her eyes, smoothing a hand over the tight ponytail she typically sports as she fights down a smile. Nova continues, "Let's not forget we get access to the best shit. Did you know Felicia keeps the Baltic ivory harpoon head on her for 'safe keeping'? *At all times.* If that isn't a perk, I don't know what is."

"I do like that we get to wear our bracers all the time." The iron cuffs that adorn our wrist are etched with intricate spirals and notches. When activated by the wearer with a purposeful twist of the wrist, the etchings fill with a pale green luminescent light—the sacred power of the Borealis. The power increases both our strength and speed to almost supernatural proportions, but only the Wardens are permitted to wear the bracers at all times.

"What was that?" Naomi asks, mouth modestly agape. The conversation dies as our ears perk to catalog the faintest hint of movement or disturbance in the air. For a tense moment, my breath catches before Noelle shoots her sister an annoyed look and relaxes.

"Nothing, Naomi. You must be hearing things," she says. Naomi flushes, but her eyes dart nervously toward the sliding glass doors that lead into the atrium.

"What did you hear?" I ask.

Naomi flushes brighter and tugs the glasses off her face to clean them, a nervous habit of hers. "I just thought I heard a pop." While her face is downturned, I spare a look toward the other sisters. They wear matching frowns, but Nova's seems to set itself deeper as her head cocks to the side.

"I don't hear anything," she finally says, stance relaxing. I mirror her movement. My shoulders relaxing from their stiff pose. I hadn't heard anything either, but the glass doors of the room are thick. Bulletproof-thick.

"Me either," Noelle agrees, gently patting Naomi on the shoulder. The youngest of the triplets flushes and places her glasses back upon her crown.

"Maybe something was dropped in the hallway?" Noelle opens her mouth to reply—no doubt to offer some half-hearted and thoughtless agreement—when a second *pop* occupies the moment. My gut clenches, and once more the atrium fills with roaring silence. The cool metal of my knife digs into my spine as I shift and walk toward the door.

"Where's Nathan?" *Where indeed*? The hallway is unusually empty, though protocol dictates at least one guard should be stationed at the end of the hall to patrol its length.

"Something isn't right," the triplets respond in unison. A tingling sensation flashes across my scalp and down my spine. An eager restlessness is quick to follow through my nerves and muscles.

Lights flash from overhead. They blink red in unison three times, pause, then repeat. That alarm sequence means only one thing.

"Wolves," I hiss. A sharp twist of my wrists outward and the bracers ignite. "Nova, get the dragon skin and balaclava. Noelle and Naomi, unlock the cases," I order stepping back from the doors.

"Who put you in charge?" Noelle gripes, though she does as she's told. I may not have seniority when it comes to the Starlight Wardens, but my fighting experience is far greater than the sisters'.

My eyes don't stray from the empty corridor. There is a fair chance the wolves won't make it this deep into the facility. There is also a fair chance that Nathan is dead.

"Here." Nova presses the dragon skin armor into my arms, along with a modified balaclava. Our eyes meet for a split second just before the room goes dark.

Chances are the wolves have made it past the outer web, the first level of the facility, which means there's only one more floor between them and us.

I slip on the armor, which wears like a duster. It falls just above the knee with a slit in both the front and back to allow the wearer better movement. It fits almost as well as the bracers and protects better than the strongest Kevlar. By the time the generator sputters to life, I'm slipping the balaclava over my face and we can all see Nathan's body lying awkwardly at the end of the hallway, a pool of red ballooning around his head.

"What's your poison?" Nova asks. I glance at the sisters to see what they've chosen. Naomi holds a yew staff, Noelle a crossbow with silver darts, and Nova sports two souped-up .44 auto mag pistols. My fingers ache for the butterfly knife in my pants, but I gesture to the bone harpoon.

"Predictable," she taunts. I hold my hand out expectantly. The auxiliary lighting is nothing more than mediocre fluorescents, but they are enough. Minutes tick by as we wait impatiently for an attack, but the only thing to note is Nathan slowly bleeding out.

"Did you hear that?" Naomi asks.

No, I think, *just the sound of my heart in my ears.* Or the slight creak of the floor as Nova shifts restlessly from one foot to the other and the soft whisper of fabric as Noelle adjusts the crossbow in her hold. My eyes drift to Naomi. She is entirely at ease, her body loose, the staff griped only just enough in to keep it standing, eyes closed.

"What do you hear?" I breathe, tilting my gaze back toward the glass doors. The triplets give pause.

"Currents," Naomi answers.

"Electricity," Noelle corrects softly. The fluorescent lights begin to spasm, and one by one burn out. Thankfully, our bracers provide more than enough illumination.

"Fucking wolves," Nova mutters disgustedly as the steady hum of electricity comes to an end all around us. I find myself nodding in agreement. Why is it that every beast and demon chooses to fight in the dark?

Figures emerge, eight in all, and approach the doors.

"W.E.S.T. formation," I order softly. "Naomi, take the south position. Noelle and Nova, flank middle. Trigger point is me." The triplets move quickly and silently to their places as I set myself firmly in the lead point of our diamond shape. The door opens, and a man with raven hair steps cautiously into the glow of our bracers. He sports a lazy smile and a cut on his brow.

"Now, now," he murmurs, "no need for any more bloodshed. We're just here for a teensy, insignificant piece of jewelry. A ring, as it would happen." Something clicks, and a thin flashlight illuminates more of the room. It scores the walls in pursuit of the ring.

"No piece here is as you describe," Naomi responds without inflection. The wolf turns a wayward glance over my shoulder toward her before following the line of the flashlight.

"I stand corrected," the man replies. I note the way his gaze lingers on the south end of the room and stiffen.

"Leave," I command. "You desecrate this sacred place with your mere presence." The man shifts, placing both feet wider apart as his hands form fists at his side.

"That's not very nice," he comments, voice heavy with contempt.

"You're a mongrel," Noelle says.

"A beast," Naomi adds.

"A dog," Nova snarls. She fires at the floor. The bullet lodges itself an inch from his toe, but I'll give the wolf some credit for he doesn't spare it a flinch.

"Woof," he snarks back as something rolls between his legs. A cloud of smoke blooms from the rolling canister and into the heart of the atrium. It fills the room quickly—too quickly—and in seconds we are wreathed in a filmy white haze. Nova fires into the doorway. The sound of splintering glass and tearing flesh bear the brunt of her blind attack.

"Naomi! Fall back to the—"

"On it!" she replies before I can finish. If it's a ring they are after, the southeast section needs to be guarded.

A fist plants itself in my stomach before another thought can dart through my mind. I lurch backward, the force of the hit taking my breath and doubling me over. I clutch the harpoon tightly in my right hand and thrust it up and forward into my attacker's side. The figure in front of me lets out a throaty, masculine growl.

I yank the harpoon back, swinging it about to smack him across the face next, with the light of my bracers to guide me. He hits the ground a second later, and I feel a dark thrill of excitement rush through me. It feels almost sinisterly good to take down my opponents.

My breath sounds heavy in my ears, despite the commotion around me. For a brief second, scenarios and outcomes of the battle whir through my mind. There is no telling how many guards and Wardens have been taken out already on the upper levels, so I must assume the worst; we are all that's left to guard the relics. The bleak thoughts drive my fortitude and thirst of blood.

They'll retrieve their precious ring over my dead body.

I slash my harpoon to the left at the sound of feet. It catches on a body, and I ram it forward with relish. A raspy gasp follows as I yank the head out, then swing the harpoon in an arc to my right. It cuts through the thick smoke but nothing else. My feet shuffle backward, ears straining to hear the next oncoming threat. Another step back. I spin on the balls of my feet and swing the harpoon out to catch another enemy. Nothing.

Action blares behind me. Luminescent green streaks the smoke in jabs and thrusts. Some pause midair, strained and quivering, before forced left and right. There is no time to hesitate.

Instinct guides me as my other senses go into overdrive to compensate for my weakened sight. My harpoon strikes and latches on arms and legs, the press and pull of each motion dragging me closer and closer to the real fight. It feels as though the harpoon is an extension of my body. With each hit, my body surges and feints away, and I can't help the grim smile that lights upon my face as I take another punch to the gut. Then one to the face.

There it is again. The spike of adrenaline. The thirst for pain, whether to inflict or receive it, surges inside me without pause. Something inside me craves the fight. An irrational, adrenaline-laced rush I can't ignore. *A darkness inside me*, I think as I strike out with the blunt end of the harpoon to jab at the wolf behind me. *A darkness I have lost control of once before.*

Something smashes against a glass display case. Or somebody. The empty click of Nova's barrels sound, followed quickly by a startled cry that is unmistakably Naomi's. I favor the weaker sister and dart to Naomi at the southeast end of the room, promptly tripping over a body and falling onto the glass-laden floor.

"Ouch! Watch it," a very feminine reprimand yelps from the ground. I suck in a deep breath and maneuver quickly into a crouch, diving forward into the body. She lets out a cry as we crash into the ground, squirming viscously and banging her hands against my chest as I fight to claim her wrists. "Get off you *bitch*!" she cries.

The sprinkler system activates above us, reacting to the smoke at long last. The woman beneath me sputters in indignation as the water doses us. Giving me the perfect opportunity to capture her hands. She struggles weakly against my hold. It's almost pathetic how weak she is against me. Almost too weak.

My breath catches in my throat, a sudden horrible realization stunning me.

"You're not a wolf," I pant, releasing her hands as if they burn.

The smoke is slowly dissipating around us, and I can make out the fright across her features. But only barely. I scamper off her, a thousand dreadful thoughts slashing through my mind, but one screams above all others: *not again.* Memories unleash themselves upon me with ruthless intent.

—A scared and broken girl clinging to my leg and the last remnants of her humanity. A plea for sanctuary tearing past her blood-soaked lips—

—A secret and betrayal. The strange nuance of hope that things will be all right—

—Human bodies torn to bits and pieces spilled across a chapel floor. The small child feasting on the steps of the altar. My mercy. My mistake—

—The blinding lights of the Auroral Bastille cast down upon me as I answered to the Councils accusations. Falling to my knees at their sentence and wondering how I could have been so wrong—

Something bashes into my back, knocking the air from my lungs. I fall forward. The raven-haired man helps the blonde up off the floor, pulling her into a dramatic kiss.

"Are you all right?" She nods, sparing me a wide-eyed glance. "Do you have it?" She nods again, and the man sounds off a shrill whistle.

No. A sharp burst of panic startles me into action, the feathering darkness pooling inside of me goading me back into the fight.

Stay low, my instincts tell me. *Use your environment to your advantage.* My harpoon lays somewhere behind me, but weapons coarse the ground. A jagged piece of glass is clutched in my hand in the next instant, and I slam it into the wolf's foot. He lets out a howl of rage, limping backward and dragging the girl with him.

I stagger to my feet as he rips the glass from his foot, my eyes frantically scanning the room to see most of the wolves retreating and the sisters regaining their ground. A knee surges into my line of vision too quick for me to process and knocks me solidly under the chin. Pain erupts inside my head as I crumple to the ground, my equilibrium further stolen by a heavy blow to my cheek. A final kick to my side leaves me grounded and watching in agony as the wolf and girl sprint away.

"Follow them!" I manage to order, watching as Nova and Noelle give chase through the darkened hallway. Sturdy arms wrap under mine to haul me up, tugging me forward as I take in a few strangled breaths.

"Are you all right?" Naomi asks. I nod and push her away, stalling at the doorway as a rogue idea swims into my head. We needed more bodies to take on the wolves, and I know just the place to get them.

"Stay behind and keep guard," I tell her, turning back around and running to the back of the room where a hidden panel leads to a passageway.

"Where are you going?"

"To fight fire with fire." I throw a quick grin over my shoulder as I pick up my harpoon and the bloodied shard of glass from the ground. Then, I'm running as fast as I can down the passageway to the back of the Banks.

RETRIBUTION

- Chapter 2 -

My heart is hammering by the time I reach the cages. I cast a wary glance to my left and right, searching for the figures I know to be racing away. Gunfire sounds relentlessly from the Banks, which means not everyone is dead. *Thank God.*

It's late at night, sometime close to midnight, but with the Alaskan summer, that hardly means a thing. In truth, it's barely dusk. As I approach my destination, the dogs we keep bark eagerly from their kennels. I race to unlock their doors, letting them all take a good whiff of the blood-caked shard of glass and harpoon.

"Take a good whiff of that, Dakota," I instruct as the lead dog makes its way to the front of the throng. "*Gehen*!" *Go.* The large malamutes and huskies bark and bristle with enthusiasm. "Attacke." I snarl the German command just before unleashing them into the bright night, the cage door swinging open with a *clang* as they rush past me. The night air presses through my armor into my skin, but the biting chill doesn't hamper the heat coursing through me. It invigorates me. Fuels the flame of my desires. Though the summer months are coming soon to their end, the nights still bear a slight chill in the air this far north. *It is a fine night to hunt*, I think as I chase after the dogs whose barks and hollers fill the air.

Fire with fire. They certainly won't be expecting this.

The dogs intercept the wolves just as they reach a stash of motorbikes hidden amongst the trees. Several are already equipped with drivers geared up and ready to make their grand getaway. I tighten my grip on the primitive harpoon, feeling the pulse of the Borealis skirting across the surface of its shaft. I adjust the pace of my run, swing my arm in an arch, and release. The harpoon sails ahead, the length of rope attached to it spindling behind. It pierces the arm of some slender wolf, and victory flushes through my veins. Catching the rope midair, I skid to a halt and rewind the rope between my hand and elbow. Once it's taut I give a hearty yank. The wolf stumbles sideways and gives me a look between horror and anger. Its eyes flashing gold in the night.

The wolf yanks back, but I bear down. Heals digging spitefully into the earth. I just needed to hold out a bit longer, until reinforcements—

A body slams me into the ground out of nowhere. I move with the momentum, tumbling forward with the strong arms wrapped around my waist. My feet find purchase on his side, and I push out of his hold, rolling away to tuck myself into a crouch. He mirrors my position, a dark scowl on his features as he pulls himself slowly into a standing position. The bounty of his muscles ripple across tattooed flesh. I cast a rueful glance to the side where the rope lays forgotten.

"I don't want to kill you," he tells me in a husky baritone. I scoff as I mimic his posturing, slowly beginning to circle him. He's much larger than me, somewhere around 6'3" to my 5'9", and with his hair trimmed short, the cut of his jaw seems all the harder. Deep caramel eyes dig into me in assessment, but with my dragon skin armor and modified balaclava, there isn't much for him to see. His eyes linger over my chocolate hair and eyes—eyes which hold the faintest hint of an angle due to my Native Alaskan heritage. His jaw clenches, the muscles of his neck cording slightly as his gaze flickers down then back up. *Men.*

"I can't say the same," I tell him, taking my butterfly knife out. It flashes open with a mere sleight of hand into my palm, and I take a moment to savor its familiar weight. His scowl deepens, and his fists rise defensively. I bare my hands low and wide, ready to attack with the knife, held in possession of my right hand.

We meet in two easy strides, my hand lashing out to deliver a cut to his forearm. He takes the hit with good grace, angling away and throwing a punch before I can retreat. His fist catches my cheek. But it glances off as I swerve back. The wolf presses on, and I force my knife into a more defensive position. I duck the next blow and skirt inward, stabbing at his ribs and hitting my mark. But not without receiving a blow myself. We go on for what seems like ages. Blocking and pressing. Hits landing or steering too wide.

He's good, I credit to myself, *a little too good.*

He moves with military precision, unafraid to press forward even as my knife keeps marking his skin. My foot catches, and a look of shock passes over both our faces as I ungracefully pitch to the side. He's on me in an instant, knocking my blade from my hand and thrusting me against a tree. His hand a sudden vice around my neck.

I struggle to break his choke hold, my feet kicking forward with little effect. He draws himself close, pressing into me and blocking my lower assault. The warmth of his breath skirts across my cheek in heavy puffs as I attempt to strike his face. I aim for his fighter's nose, slanted slightly to the left, the point is moot. I am fighting a losing battle. Black spots emerge in my vision as I struggle to breathe. A tightness ruthlessly grips at my chest. There is no relief from the pain, and it's quick to spread throughout my body. He wears a look of... pity? Sympathy? Either way, it rouses in me one last push. My hands grab his forearm, nails digging viciously into the arm that holds me captive.

His frown returns. The pressure of his grip increasing just a fraction. *Just enough.* My hands slide down the length of his forearm, one hand falling away completely. The other barely holds on, trailing across his skin like some gentle caress. Our eyes lock and the world stops as my fingers brush past my worst fear.

Oh no.

I'm engulfed in a whirlwind of sensation. My lungs begging for breath as my hand clenches around its purchase. It is unlike anything I have ever known, and all from a singular touch. A storm folds over my vision, the creeping darkness fractured by spears of lightning. Something aches inside of me. My soul crying out for more as my eyelids flutter closed.

A startled gasp breaks past his lips as he stares at me aghast. For the briefest of moments, I dare to think I see his eyes flash gold.

"You," he breathes, eyes wild as he takes my wrist and pulls my hand away from the mark on his arm. His *soulmark.* The sensation of warmth—of electricity and fire—departs in an instant. Almost painfully so, I realize when my body shivers at the loss. My heart *aches.*

The wolf tugs me forward, and like some damsel, I crash into his chest, staring up at him in muted horror. He pulls off my balaclava, staring down at my face with such intensity I dare not move. His eyes roam down the slope of my nose and high-cheekbones before settling on my full lips.

"You."

I find my nerve at long last and shake my head, pulling back to no avail. "No." *No, this can't be happening.* Yet, the soulmark that lies upon my hip seems to sear itself deeper into my flesh, sinking itself into my blood and bones. *This wolf doesn't wear just any soulmark*, I think with dismay, *he wears* mine. There is no other way to explain what I feel when I touch his mark. And we both know it. This… *this beast*, is in possession of the other half of my soul, and for all intents and purposes, *is* my soul mate. My deepening horror draws the blood from my face. *This can't be happening.*

"Where is it?" he asks almost frantically, eyes darting over my form as I continue my struggle.

"Let me go," I beg, feeling a wave of fear tear through me. This can't be happening. If anyone finds out about my soulmark, I will be banished. Exiled. And if they find out I have *found* my soulmark… I rip myself out of his hold, calling on the strength of the bracers like never before. He gapes at my retreat for but a moment, before a steely look crosses over his features.

"Come with me." The husky timbre of his voice drops an octave. A promise lingers at the edges of his posturing. He stretches out a hand. My heart, the traitorous thing, skips a beat. Before I can deign to reply, a sharp crack sounds in the air, and he stumbles sideways, grasping his arm with an angry scowl. My head whips to the side. Nova stands on the back of a motorbike, Noelle in the driver's seat speeding toward us.

"Run," I whisper harshly, eyes never leaving the sisters. I don't dare look back at him, but I can hear his hesitation. Nothing sounds for a long pause, and then the forest floor crunches beneath his hasty departure. I drop to my knees just as the twins near and Nova jumps off the bike, the mysterious man already lost in the dense woods.

"Are you all right?" Nova drops down in front of me, her hands skating over my body to check for injury. They slip upward to cup my face, her fearful gaze cataloging every bruise.

I nod numbly, fighting the urge to cry as Nova rests her forehead against mine. *What am I going to do?* I draw in a shaky breath and let Nova help me stand and guide me to the bike. She speaks soft assurances near my ear as her sister rounds up the dogs. I lean into her hold in hopes of staving off the memory of his touch. But it's no use. No use at all.

+++

The Council and various members of the Stellar Warriors arrive at the Banks Facility roughly two hours after the attack to take stock of events. There had been only two deaths, but over a dozen people had been injured. Apparently, the wolves had relied heavily on tranquilizer darts and KO gas to gain access to the facility, and the Council was not pleased. They chose to gather in the observatory to hold their summit and collect information. It held just enough space for the Alaskan branch of the Council, all eleven members, plus a few extra.

"I wish they would hurry up," Nova complains. She sports a nasty black eye, made complete with a popped blood vessel that stains her sclera a vibrant red. Her sisters and I fair better, though we all sport some variation of black and blue across our bodies.

Naomi nods her agreement, but it's Noelle who responds to her sister. "I need a hot shower."

A hot shower. A warm bed. Some kind of laser removal treatment for the blasphemous mark on my hip. I still feel some strange phantom reverberation from our earlier contact. Small flashes of euphoria send little bursts of electricity throughout my body when my mind draws his face into focus. That handsome face with its cross demeanor and slightly crooked nose. Or his arms stacked with muscles and lined with ink. Or the way he seemed to tower over me. He exuded masculinity effortlessly, and there was no denying the fact that my body took notice.

"Callie?" My gaze snaps to Nova and her expectant expression.

"Sorry, what did you say?" I ask, giving a small shake of my head to rid myself of my reflections.

"Are you all right?" It's not the question she had been asking by the way her voice softens, and I catch the similar look of concern her sisters cast me.

"Just upset that they got away with the ring," I respond with a sigh. *Some Wardens we are.* As upset as I am to have been unable to protect the relics, I carry an altogether separate worry in my heart. What if the Council deems me unfit to serve the Wardens of Starlight at all? Will they rest the blame for tonight's events solely on my shoulders? Will they count this as my second strike?

"It wasn't your fault, Callie," Noelle tells me firmly. "The odds were against us. We were outnumbered, and the attack was planned. This isn't the first time the Banks has been attacked, you know."

"But it is the first time they've been successful," Nova counters.

"That's not true," Naomi corrects lightly, adjusting her glasses carefully so as not to rest them on the cut across her nose. "Three years ago, that rogue group of Eldritch Witches attacked and stole the Wand of Sorrow. A select group of Wardens and Warriors hunted them down and brought it back."

"Yes, but the Wand of Sorrow meant something to them. It held significant meaning. With it, they could control the shadows. Those wolves stole the Amethyst of Aztec ring. What the hell would they want with that?" My clipped rebuttal stops further protest. "I don't get it."

Nova frowns, mouth opening to speak when the iron doors finally open. We file in silently. The Council arranges themselves in a semicircle with three chairs sitting slightly farther forward than the rest. In the chairs sit Sterling Hall, Karen Baker, and Joseph Sawyer—my father.

"The Council is now prepared to hear your testimony regarding tonight's events. Noelle," Mr. Hall has his pen poised to take notes, "begin."

"The testimony would best be given by Ms. Sawyer," she responds. A murmur of discontent arises from the Council. "Ms. Sawyer took the lead position in response to the attack. She should give testimony."

"Very well," he says, voice neutral and pen still poised. "Ms. Sawyer, when you're ready."

I take a fraction of a step forward and begin, relaying the evening's time line in succinct detail. After completing my version of events, the Council turns its unnerving attention back to Noelle. She explains what occurred when she and Nova separated from the group. Then Naomi gives her account. After answering a multitude of questions, the Council dismisses us to review our testimony.

"Do you think they'll demote us?" Naomi asks, her nerves naturally frayed. The Council had directed most of their questioning toward the youngest Stavok, making their displeasure clear at her lack of action. My intervention on her behalf had done nothing to help.

"No," I tell her, my hand reaching out to give a reassuring pat on her shoulder. She gives me a small smile and shrugs out of my touch. I don't take the minor slight offensively. The Wardens of Starlight aren't known for being affectionate, even in such paltry measure. "They don't gang up like that if they intend to demote or reassign you. At least not in my experience," I say, fighting down a small swell of shame that surfaces at the mention of my past. "It's more pointed. Plus, only one member of the Council will address you. I think we'll be fine."

"We'll be reprimanded," Nova offers, and I nod in agreement. The reassurance does little to relieve Naomi's tension.

"You may enter," a cool voice calls as the door cracks open once more. We enter again, faces devoid of any emotion.

"After reviewing the events of this evening, the Council would like to remind the Starlight Wardens of the Banks Facility of the following: first and foremost, that you vowed to forfeit your lives to protect the Relics of Terra. Yet here you stand, all in one piece," Mrs. Baker remarks, a patronizing lilt to her voice. "Second, that leadership is based on seniority"—I keep my eyes trained on the wall behind the Council's head, well aware of their harsh regard—"unless otherwise sanctioned with Council approval. Lastly, the Starlight Wardens act as a cohesive unit. Wardens do not act alone in their duty, such as scouts or warriors, but as a team in all efforts. I trust this reminder will not need to be issued again?"

We give a clipped, "Yes, ma'am," in return. Mrs. Baker lets out a small sigh and leans back slightly in her chair.

"The Council would also like to commend the Wardens on their ingenuity. We recognize the unusual and difficult circumstances you found yourselves in; faced with a lack of support in an unstable environment, while being outnumbered threefold. You managed to take down four wolves in total and, by your accounts, injured several more. As such, we give further commendation to Ms. Noelle and Nova Stavok for the forethought of using tracking bullets in their pursuit of the attackers, and to Ms. Sawyer." My spine straightens as I look Mrs. Baker in the eye. "Releasing the dogs was a rather clever idea. One that paid off. Furthermore, the Council recognizes your quick thinking and leadership benefited the night's events instead of hampering them." *Gee, thanks.*

"Thank you," I reply, tipping my head toward the Council. She returns the nod and shuffles the papers in front of her.

"Now, onto the next matter: the retrieval of the ring." My heart skips a beat. If the Council has any sense, they'll choose me to go out with a small guard of warriors to retrieve the ring. Or better yet, they'll send me alone. I possess the knowledge and training of both Warrior and Warden, and can retrieve the ring without distraction. It will be like killing two birds with one stone.

I roll my shoulders back, chin lifting an inch. It has nothing to do with the fact that I would be able to do a little reconnaissance on the side. Find out more about the hulking specimen of a man who bore the fang that is our soulmark. Nothing. At. All.

"—which is why the Stavok's will go in two days' time to retrieve the ring," Mrs. Baker finishes.

"Wait—what?" I receive a collective of frowns at my outburst and feel myself color.

"Calliope." My father's voice rings heavy with indignation, and I bow my head.

"My apologies, I only thought—"

"Your thoughts are not what was asked for, Ms. Sawyer. In fact, before you so rudely interrupted, we were about to explain what is expected of you while your cohorts are away." I maintain my submissive stance, though a wave of resentment and unease takes hold. "You will stay behind along with a personal guard of Stellar Warriors to guarantee the safety of the facility and partake in your final examination with the head warden in a week's time. Additionally, you will catalog all the relics to assess the full damage of tonight's offense. Stavok's, you'll be briefed tomorrow with more detail regarding the retrieval of the ring. You're dismissed."

My shoulders sink as we exit the observatory and head down to the second level of the facility to our rooms. So much for my plans.

SECRETS TO KEEP

- Chapter 3 -

"I can't believe they don't want me to go," I bemoan, "or that I have to take this stupid exam, weeks early. As if being reassigned wasn't bad enough, now this? It's like throwing salt in an open wound. I have the training of both a warrior and a warden. I'm more than capable of handling this assignment."

Nova raises a brow. "And my sisters and I aren't?"

I run the butterfly knife over my knuckles in quick repetition. "I didn't say that," I tell her flatly, my eyes tracking her movements as she places another shirt into her duffle bag. "You're very capable of going out on assignment, but they're not even sending warriors out with you."

"We've all been trained in the art of combat, Callie," she reminds me tersely. I relax my rigid position and fold the butterfly knife closed in my palm.

"I know," I respond, voice placating and smooth, "but you've never been out in the field. This is the most experience you've had facing supernatural creatures, right?" She nods with a forlorn sigh and zips her bag closed. The triplets are two years younger than me, and though their training is just as extensive as mine—even more so as Starlight Wardens—they couldn't match my skill as a warrior.

"That doesn't mean we aren't ready for this."

I let my silence linger, flipping the knife back open and over my knuckles. "I just think—"

"—that you would be better suited for the mission. *I know.* But that doesn't mean you're right." Her words bring me to a standstill.

"Excuse me?" I ask incredulously. Nova crosses her arms over her chest, her waist-length hair catching in the action.

"Listen, Callie. Noelle might not have noticed because she was driving, but I saw that wolf almost take you *out*." I swallow the sudden lump in my throat, ignoring the discomfort I suddenly feel. "Just when I thought you were about to lose consciousness, all of a sudden it looked like you were about to break your back… and then he let you go. His face looked shocked. *You* looked shocked."

"You were at least a klick away, Nova," I respond irritably, feeling my calm reserve waver. "How could you have possibly seen?"

"I had a scope on the assault rifle." The color drains from my face as I look away.

"He was shocked because I got a grip on his radial nerve and sank my nails into it."

"He said something to you after. What was it?"

"Some parting words about 'fighting like a girl.'"

The weight of Nova's regard feels like a ton of bricks. I fight to keep an outwardly calm composure, meeting her dark eyes unflinchingly until she unwinds. Nova offers me a small smile.

"I hate it when they do that. Can't guys come up with anything clever?" I let out a forced chuckle.

"Apparently not."

"You're sure everything is fine? I get why you're upset about not being chosen, but you seem more amped up about it than I expected you to be."

Nova comes to sit next to me, her thigh and the length of her arm pressing infinitesimally into my own. The truth crawls at my throat. Nova is my closest friend, and if I'm honest with myself, she is the one person who might not shun me for finding out my secret. The thought carries a strand of hope with it, and I allow myself to lean into her side, taking comfort in her steady presence.

"Can you keep a secret?" I ask quietly, eyes darting nervously to the half-open door of her private quarters.

"I am an expert at keeping secrets," she says with a slightly breathless quality to her voice. I cast her an uncertain glance, noticing the way she leans in closer.

"He didn't let me go because I pinched his nerve. And he didn't make some sleazy, predictable comeback about me being a girl."

"What happened, Callie?"

I worry my bottom lip, surprised to feel a nervous tremor run down all the way to my fingertips. Nova's hand brushes against my own, taking hold of it with a reassuring squeeze. "He wears my soulmark," I blurt out. Nova's grip tightens. Her widened eyes meeting my own as her lips form a small "O."

"He wears your soulmark?" she asks rhetorically. "As in, you have a *soulmark*?" The blood recedes from her face as her gaze falls downward to our joined hands. I give the faintest squeeze in response, holding my breath for her next words. "Oh, Callie."

"It's not like I planned it," I tell her defensively, trying and failing to pull my hand from her grip.

"I know that," she bites back frostily. "You don't get to choose if you have a soulmark or not. You're either born with it or not. I can't believe you never told me before now." My expression goes slack.

"What?"

"I thought we were friends, Callie. More than that even… *shit*." Nova screws her eyes shut and releases me.

"I'm sorry, all right. You are more than just a friend—you're like a sister to me. But you know the consequences I'll face if anyone else finds out I have it." My voice strains at the end, the harsh reality of the Wardens of Starlight's predictable retribution stabbing me squarely in the chest. Banishment, if I'm lucky. Death, more than likely.

"I would never tell anyone," she tells me earnestly, eyes lifting to meet mine. "I know how the Council would react. They'd tear the mark from your flesh with their bare hands, then banish you from the community for having it in the first place. Anything connecting a warden so *intimately* to the supernatural is forbidden."

"Anything connecting a warden to the *supernatural* is forbidden," I respond flatly.

"Where is it?"

I let out a brief sigh. "It sits low on my hip. It's always been hidden by my underwear, so I've never been too nervous about anyone spotting it."

"Wouldn't your parents have noticed it when you were young?"

"The shape only became more distinct as I got older. By the time I was eight, it was fully formed, and I didn't need my parents to give me baths anymore," I joke weakly.

"Right," she breathes, swallowing visibly as her gaze darts curiously to my waistline. "Can I see it?"

"Close the door." Nova rushes over to shut it while I stand slowly and unbutton my pants, tugging the zipper halfway down. When she returns to stand in front of me, she places her hands expectantly on her hips, but there are patches of red stealing up over her throat and cheeks.

"Hurry it up," she says jokingly. "I don't have all day."

I fold down my pants on the left side, pushing down my panties an inch as well. The mark is in sharp relief against my tan skin but doesn't look remarkably out-of-place due to the number of tattoos on my body. Nova reaches out before I can protest and runs her fingertips over the slightly raised skin.

"Does it hurt?"

I shake my head and step away from her gentle touch, redoing up my pants. "It's just like a birthmark," I mutter.

"A birthmark that just so happens to have an identical twin on some maniac wolf that also happens to house the other half of your *soul*." Nova takes a large breath after her mini-rant.

"Exactly." We share weak smiles.

"That's why you wanted to go on the assignment?"

My head bobs. "Partly. I still stand by everything I said, but yes. It is partly why I wanted to go—not to be with him. Obviously. I mean he's a lycan for goodness sake. I don't actually plan on going through with the binding process." A semi-hysterical laugh bubbles forth. "That would be insane. I would be exiled, and then for good measure, they would send someone to assassinate me for daring to humiliate the cause in such a way."

"I don't think they would do that...," she hedges. When she catches my unimpressed look, she lets out a hoarse laugh of her own. This one carrying a more honest tune. "They'll just kill you." We both burst into laughter at the gallows humor, the bent-at-the-waist-clutching-at-your-sides kind of laughter. When we finally trickle down into giggles, she takes my hand once more.

"It'll be fine," I tell her, though the words feel sour on my tongue.

"He's your other half. He was made for you," Nova scolds me lightly, "and you were made for him."

"Didn't we just go over the whole 'they'll kill me' thing?"

Nova squeezes my hand before letting go and taking a step back to begin pacing the room. "What were you going to do if you were assigned?"

I sigh and shrug pathetically. "Just observe. See what he's like from afar, I guess."

Nova frowns at my apathetic response. "That's all?"

"I already told you I don't intend to do anything about the mark, or anything equally as stupid." Her frown remains. "What?" I snap, feeling my defenses rising. "You and I both know the Council has my future neatly planned out for me."

"You mean Mrs. Baker and your dad?"

"I'll finish my training with the Wardens, stay for a few years, and then start my study as a council delegate."

"And marry Wyatt," she adds with surprising bitterness. Wyatt Baker, Mrs. Baker's only son. A founding family just like my own. A sinking sensation dwells in the pit of my stomach. Wyatt and I had dated years ago but ended things when I started training as a Stellar Warrior. *It wasn't part of the "plan,"* he had protested to no avail. The Baker women always held positions on the Council, and Baker men always held positions as Head Stellar Warrior. *Not the other way around.*

I give another helpless raise of my shoulders. "It is what it is." Unless I find some way to validate a life without Wyatt to my dad, or forge a new path on my own.

Her lips purse unhappily as she stops her pacing, her hair swishing dramatically to the side. "And you're positive it's him? That the wolf is your soulmark?"

There's a sort of desperation in her tone, a pleading, but I nod my head along sadly.

"You said you saw it yourself. I touched his mark and the reaction was instantaneous."

"All you did was touch it? You're sure he didn't seal the mark? Or anything else?"

"I'm positive," I tell her with more confidence than I feel. "There are words that have to be spoken while the soulmark is being touched for the sealing to happen,"*—at least that's what our books on the subject say—*"The same goes for the other two steps; the marking and binding of the soulmark. Words are said. The soulmark is touched."

"And once all three steps are completed, the sealing, marking, and binding, your souls are joined as one," Nova finishes, staring off into the distance. I feel my stomach turn uneasily. So the books say.

"But he didn't say anything," I persist. "And *I* didn't say anything. So we aren't sealed."

"And what I saw?" Nova questions somewhat cautiously.

"Shock and awe," I offer after a moment's hesitation, the truth spilling forth. "One second I'm on the verge of passing out. The next, we're both hit with a tidal wave of emotion. It was like being swept up in the sweetest storm as it rained down this tremendous heat and—" *desire* "—fullness," I finish lamely.

"Fullness?" she asks dubiously.

I nod fervently. "It's hard to explain," I tell her, opening and closing my butterfly knife as I begin to pace as well. "It was as if I could feel this all-consuming *feeling* in every part of my body."

She raises an eyebrow, arms slow to fold over her chest once more as her lips twitch upward. "Feeling?"

I blush. "Not that kind," I lie.

"Right." She snorts and goes to sit on the bed by her bag. "Well, if you want, I can do some covert reconnaissance on him for you? Find out the basics.

Name, age, history, medical records. You know, just the basics."

The weight of my secret lifts fully from my shoulders, and I give a breathy laugh. "That would be," I pause, thinking of the right word and coming up empty, "nice."

Nova gives me a small smile in return, one that doesn't exactly meet her eyes as she pats the spot beside her. "You've got it. Now, show me that knuckle trick again."

+++

It's late, and the triplets left hours ago. The remnants of my displeasure linger in my muscles and mind. I appreciate what Nova is doing for me, but I still can't stem the jealousy I hold, or the stifling notion that things are falling into place, just as my father has planned.

My fists careen into the punching bag with ruthless efficiency, the bracers I wear enhancing my force and sending it nearly off its hinges. I grasp onto it, steadying the bag as I pant from my exertion.

"You're in a fine mood tonight, Calliope," comments a familiar voice from behind. *Wyatt.* I frown at the bag and keep my back toward him. His light footsteps echo in the empty gym until he comes to stand by me. I cast a wary look his way.

"What do you want?"

His eyebrow arches scrupulously while his gaze ventures the length of my body. I tense, but he sends me an easy smile, relaxing his stance and shoving his hands into his pockets.

"Need any help?" His eyes flick to the bag and then to my bracers. "You'll knock it off if you keep going at it like that." I nod begrudgingly. There's too much adrenaline in my veins to stop now, and the whole purpose of coming to the gym is to tire myself out, so I can sleep tonight. Wyatt moves to stand behind the punching bag, placing his hands securely on it.

"One-two, weave, weave, two-three," he instructs me, voice dropping any lilting amusement in favor of something more serious. *Jab, cross, double weave, cross, hook.* I nod and bounce on my feet, taking in several deep breathes before going into the combination. Even with Wyatt stabilizing the bag and providing resistance, my hits push him and the bag back.

"How about something more… challenging?" I ask, stepping away from the bag after completing a repetition. Wyatt peeks his head out from behind the bag to study me.

"How long have you been going at it?"

I shrug. "Maybe forty minutes?"

He frowns. "And you want to keep going?"

I nod and put my hands back up in front of my face, bouncing once again on my toes. He gives a small shake of his head.

"Fine. Lead front kick, one-two, lead side kick, back kick." I catch the gleam in Wyatt's eyes and feel a grin tinker at the corner of my lips. That combination is more of a challenge.

Wyatt knows just how to push me—which is both a good and bad thing. With Wyatt I learned to push past my limits, exceeding my expectations time after time with him at my side. He gave me the confidence to believe in myself, but he also knows how to take that confidence away. Wyatt knows exactly what buttons to press and triggers to pull to bend me to his will.

My left foot nails the side of the bag with a sharp *smack*. As I plant it back on the ground, I twist myself around to deliver the back kick with my right. *Smack.*

"Feeling stressed?" he asks.

I feel my concentration waver for a moment, and my lead front kick doesn't land nearly as well as the previous. A frustrated air issues past my lips. *Jab.*

Cross. Am I feeling stressed? I move with the bag, toggling from side to side before launching into my side kick and twirling into my back kick with vicious accuracy.

"You know you can talk to me, right?"

I scoff, sending him a look that displays my skepticism. Talk to Wyatt? Never again will I let this man in on my innermost thoughts. My feet shuffle backward and forward as I find my pace again, speeding through the next interval with concentrated breaths. All the while his eyes are on me, staring me down in a way I'm much too familiar with. I'm lucky Wyatt never thought twice about my fanged soulmark. To him, it was just another tattoo among the many. A moon on the back of my neck. A trident down my forearm. A shield on my shoulder blade. A dozen other tiny insignificant markings to hide the one that meant the most.

"I'm fine," I tell him through gritted teeth, pushing on. The punching bag rattles with each hit of my fists and feet, Wyatt's small grunts of effort providing infinite satisfaction.

"Right." He snorts, pulling back and signaling me to stop. He shakes out his wrists, eyeing me with a small level of disapproval. "How about you fight against something that'll give you a real challenge?"
I take a couple of steps back, my breath coming in deep gasps as I attempt to catch it. "Are you suggesting yourself?" I ask dryly.
He gives a confident smirk in return, popping the knuckles on his right hand. "We both know I can give you what you want," he says, a husky edge to his voice. Not bothering to wait for my response, he strips off his shirt and goes to grab the hand wrap and a set of gloves. "No bracer power," he comments over his shoulder. "Just us. One on one."

I flick my wrists with purpose, and the luminescent light sinks back into the iron bracelets. If he thinks he can beat me, he has another thing coming to him.

"Ready?" I ask after he's taken a few minutes to warm up.

He gives a brief nod and circles forward. At first, we both pull our hits, dodging and feinting as we take up the violent dance. In no time at all, our movements become quicker. Harder. There is a comfort in this act with him. At least to me, there is. It touches the part of my soul that craves the fight, that yearns to inflict pain. My darkness; an all-consuming feeling of feral rage, that dominates me as I lose myself in a fight. It is considered a curse among our people, a blemish on one's sanity, but if I'm honest, the soulmark feels more damning.

Wyatt takes my hits with good grace, waiting me out patiently as I work out my aggression on his body. It doesn't take long for me to feel fatigued, which is of course is when he comes at me.

I should have seen it coming. I should have learned by now—should have remembered—that he knows me. He knows how I move and how to read my body. He can expertly predict what I'll do next and how to take advantage. Wyatt works his way meticulously inside and under my guard. Throwing hammer-sized blows to my torso until he all but levels me with an uppercut. I fall to the ground, sideswiping my feet out in retribution. His body lands close to mine with a startled grunt.

"I thought we were boxing, not kickboxing," he grumbles good-naturedly, nudging my calf with his foot.

I pull off my gloves to rub my jaw. "Good hit," I begrudgingly offer, hauling myself up onto my feet.

"Want to go another round?" He's up on his feet a second later, following me to the other side of the room where I put the boxing gloves away.

"No."

"How about a different workout?" His voice tumbles into that husky tone again, the one he so often likes to use to coax me into submission. An echo of feelings long since lost shivers their way up my spine as I recall our old "post-workouts."

"No," I tell him firmly, tossing my hand wraps into a laundry basket and briskly walking away. He jumps ahead of me, slamming his hand out against the wall to block my path. "I'm not getting into it tonight with you, Wyatt," I practically growl, rearing back my fist to deliver a swift punch to his arm. As if expecting this reaction, he uses my momentum against me and pins my arm against the wall.

"Were you always this feisty when we were together?" he asks with a charming smile, eyes smoldering with intent.

I snap my head forward, hoping to catch his nose with my head-butt, but he lets out a bark of laughter and slams me back against the wall instead. His forearm and elbow dig into my clavicle. A noise of frustration passes my lips as my eyes dart to the side.

"What do you want, Wyatt?" I growl.

He loses the smile, leaning forward until his forehead rests against my own. "You know what I want, Callie. What I've always wanted." I keep my eyes to the side, not daring to look into his honey-colored eyes. "You. Us."

"Don't."

"You've been avoiding me."

"I was reassigned," I remind him blandly, keeping my face expressionless as he trails his fingers along my neck, tracing the bruises. "I've also been busy. Besides, there's no need to avoid you. We aren't together anymore. We haven't been for years. There's no reason for me to see you."

He lets out an indignant scoff. "Ours is a small community, Calliope. Besides, after last winter. I—"

"Last winter was a mistake," I bite out, pinning him with a hard look. His fingers stall on the side of my neck. And I don't care if our Native Alaskan community is small.

"Apparently it was a mistake worth repeating," he tells me, all false charm and barbed words. "What was it, a dozen times? More?"

My palm rams into his lower sternum, and he lets out a grunt, pushing into me harder until our bodies are pressed tightly against one another. His head dips, and he nips near the bruises on my neck. I let out a startled gasp and go rigid.

"You can't run from me, Calliope. We were always meant to be together, and now that I've been assigned as part of the extra guard for the facility, we'll be seeing a lot more of each other."

"You didn't," I protest, rearing to the side and away from the soft pull of his teeth and lips.

He meets my horrified look with half-lidded eyes. "I spoke with our parents, and they approved."

I bite the inside of my cheek, fighting off the sharp sting of emotion that suddenly rises within me.

"Don't be that way, Calliope," he tells me tightly, his features hardening. "There's no need to get worked up about this. You and I both know—hell, everybody knows that we were always going to end up together. Save the theatrics, all right? You're acting like a child."

"Fuck you," I spit, stumbling backward farther. Wyatt reaches out for me, but a well-placed kick leaves him doubled over at the waist. He lets out a pained whine.

"Callie—" His glossy eyes send me a glare that promises vengeance.

"Save the theatrics, Wyatt," I deliver coolly. "You're acting like a child." As I walk away, a strange tightness surrounds my heart. Quite suddenly the idea of being bound to a wolf seems far more appealing than the alternative.

ONE STEP FORWARD, TWO STEPS BACK

- Chapter 4 -

Proctor's Knife...
Hamelin Pipe...
Obsidian trident...
Eight sets of poisoned-tipped pilum...
Ammit Amulet...
Enchanted coral necklace...

Cataloging the relics is a shit task. What makes it even more shitty is the fact that we're shorthanded and relic storage totals three floors. I'm assigned the atrium—by myself—and I'm on the fourth day of the monotonous task. The cherry on top? Only one display case out of the hundreds that lined the walls had been smashed open and its contents removed. All other displays were left untouched in the assault. On every level. Yet protocol dictates a complete catalog of the relics.

Chains of the Wasted...

Sanctum's Collar...
Two sets of Spring Jade rings...
Five sets of Chameleon bracelets...
A dozen Daylight rings...
Vagrant's Whip...

I understand the reasoning behind the task, but that doesn't mean I like it. On the upside, the cataloging proves to be a great aid to my studying. I'm sure I passed my oral exam with Felicia the other day. Too bad there's no one to share in my hypothetical accomplishments. The triplets have been gone a little over a week so far, and between carrying out miscellaneous tasks to secure the Banks Facility, cataloging relics, and taking my oral exam, I'm feeling extremely restless.

Harpe Sword...
Ophelia's Kestros...
Onyx Bident...
Bone Sword of Shadows...
Tigre Claws...
Caster's Diadem...
Phoenix Fire Elixir...

The Council finally departed yesterday. They left behind more guards and Stellar Warriors. They'd also left behind instructions for newer, stricter protocols. Not that I'm privy to the changes. They are "above my grade," as my father put it.

"Are you almost finished?" I look down from the ladder I'm perched on. It's Felicia Metzart.

"Yes." *Thank God.*

"Thank God," I hear her mumble under her breath as she flips through some pages on her clipboard. Her glasses already rest low on the bridge of her nose and slide forward even more as she scribbles something down. "We're behind schedule thanks to that little attack while I was away, which means your written exam is going to be moved forward." She shakes her head with an exaggerated huff. "So"—she gives her pen a decided click and peers up at me—"since your oral exams went well, I'll need your assistance in some of my tasks before you take your written portion."

"Of course," I respond.

"Perfect. Finish up here, and then meet me at the observatory. Now that the Council is finished setting up shop in there, I can do my work. I'm assuming you read yesterday's memo about the solar flare?" I nod my head. "Good. The upgraded solar panels collected enough of the flare to finish the backlog of relics needing Borealis Matter impartation. And because the backlog is two weeks overdue now, the imparting process will be unstable. Hence, more hands are needed for the process. Your hands, to be specific."

"Seriously?"

"Since this will be your first time participating in the imparting process, I'll walk you through it with a non-relic. That way you can get a real feel for how it's done."

"*Seriously?*"

She sends me a glare, not at all amused by my genuine bewilderment. "I don't like repeating myself, Sawyer. We'll impart the Borealis on that butterfly knife you keep on you. Meet me in the observatory in ten." She walks away, flipping through her papers as she goes. The sharp click-clack of her heels sounds loudly in the tiled hallway.

It takes a long moment for the significance of the offer to sink in, and then I'm scrambling down the ladder, hesitating a beat later when I reach the last step. If I'm being offered the opportunity to work with Felicia, then that means I'm on track to become her protégé, which means being one step closer to becoming a master in the field and eligible for a spot on the Council.

"Damn," I whisper, gently knocking my head against one of the rungs of the ladder.

Partaking in the imparting process is a coveted role among the Wardens. Only a select few are allowed to handle the Borealis Matter and the instruments used to impart it into the relics. It's a job that requires meticulous precision and steady hands, since imparting too much could change the relic's natural disposition to dark matter. Too little, and its power can't be harnessed.

There's also the issue of residual Borealis Matter escaping into the contained environment and sinking into those who are imparting. In the wrong hands, the Borealis Matter can be used to make anyone superhuman in strength and speed, and who knows what else. This is the real reason why the process was entrusted to so few people. And I just made the list.

There's not much time allowed for me to dawdle heading to the observatory, but I find my feet dragging under me regardless. Did Felicia really mean to take me on as her protégé? What about seniority?

"Finally," Felicia remarks, tucking a strand of mahogany hair behind her ear as I enter the room. "Let's get going. We don't have all day."

The observatory houses a large aperture telescope that takes up nearly half the room. The other half is a combination of mirrors, filters, and crystal-like pieces of machinery that collect and store the Borealis Matter. It's hard to believe just a day ago the Council had taken up the space.

"Watch me," she instructs. "Metals, earthen, and precious stones all have different procedures. Set your blade on the table here."

I slip the knife from the back of my pants and place it on the table gently. Felicia clears her throat, eyeing me pointedly as she begins to press a combination of buttons from left to right. It follows a simple enough pattern, diverting only once to flip a switch near the bottom right of the machinery.

"Roll up your sleeves and dip your hands into the resin over there. Make sure it's up to your wrists. It will help with the handling of the knife once the imparting is complete. Since it's not a relic, we won't be imparting much, somewhere around 220BM." I can feel my eyes widen and my face pale, though I feel a stir of excitement. That kind of power is almost equivalent to that of an electric fence.

"Yes, ma'am," I breathe, stepping eagerly over to the barrel of resin she speaks of. "Felicia?" I ask tentatively, dipping my hands into the cold liquid carefully.

"Hmm?"

"Why exactly am I here? Why I am helping you?"

Felicia gives me a look of confusion, pocketing her pen and setting down her clipboard. "Your father came to me, along with a few other members of the Council"—*Mrs. Baker most likely*—"and they expressed to me their interest in you taking on more responsibility."

I plant a false smile on my face, heart sinking as my suspicion is confirmed. There went the last of my hopes for planning my future myself. "I understand."

"Do you?" she asks, voice wary as she watches me pull my hands from the thick liquid. I nod. Felicia frowns at me, though it feels heavily of pity. "Listen, I know all about your history, but this is a great opportunity for you. You might not find the work here as action-intense as your old role, but it is stimulating. With that being said, the private fellowship under me is yours. Don't let me down."

"I'll do my best."

"Good," she says, approaching me and the basin. "Miles, stay on at the directory. I'll be helping Calliope on deck today." The older gentleman sets himself up behind a large U-shaped desk full of knobs, switches, and screens. Felicia pushes up her sleeves and dips her hands into the resin, eyeing my knife with unveiled interest.

"It was a gift," I tell her, "from my grandmother."

"I know all about your grandmother," she responds with a kind smile, the one that people usually wear when the subject is broached. Grandma Lynn was a fierce woman and a legendary Stellar Warrior. She died fending off a cluster of sirens from her team. The butterfly knife had been hers. "Maybe the knife should be considered a relic."

Felicia lifts her hands from the resin and strides toward the table. She has an eager look on her face as she peers down at the knife.

"What do we do?"

She sends me a brilliant smile. "First, we activate our bracers." I nod, and my bracers illuminate a second behind Felicia's. "The lasers will create a small-scale celestial sphere around the knife. It's our job is to maintain the sphere as the Borealis lashes out in small bursts and streaks. We use our hands to block these outbursts and guide them back onto the sphere's surface. Miles, adjust the lasers to a fifty-degree angle and dial the increments in ten."

"Will it hurt?"

Felicia shakes her head, sparing me a grin.

"Does it hurt Miles?"

"Nope!" he calls cheerfully from his seat, sparing me the same grin as Felicia. A nervous flutter of anticipation starts in my stomach.

"Don't worry," she says with a soft laugh, "you'll be fine. More than fine. Just follow my lead. Toward the end, the streaks will come more rapidly, which is one of the reasons why the bracers must be engaged. The whole process should take about ten or fifteen minutes."

I let out my nerves in a stream of air and mirror Felicia's stance: hands raised to my chest, palms facing outward, legs shoulder-width apart. A look of rapt focus comes over Felicia's features in the next instant; then she sends a decisive nod to Miles. The whirl of the electronics and machinery hum to life and a strange static fills the air. It lifts the hair on my arms and back of my neck. Another second passes by, and a concentrated stream of light erupts from the lasers, hitting the knife at each end. It lifts into the air, the lasers slowly ticking upward as a growing sphere of transparent golden light grows around the blade. It stops at chest level, the sphere no bigger than a foot in diameter.

"Ready for phase two: Borealis Matter Impartation." The whirl of machinery whines louder, with the delicate hum of electricity skirting the edges of my hearing. The sphere changes color, a delicate turquoise tinted more green than blue. The same color that floods through the etchings on our bracers. A wisp of blue light curls upward from the top of the sphere, and Felicia reaches out a hand to gently smooth it back over the curve.

"Will they all be that small?"

She shakes her head. "They grow a bit bigger and produce faster as the process continues and the voltage increases. You'll take the ruptures on your side and the top of the sphere. I'll take my side and the bottom. Understand?"

I lick my lips in anticipation and nod, waiting with bated breath for the next wisp to appear. It rises near the right side of the sphere, and my hand darts out eagerly to meet it. I suck in a harsh breath as a trill of energy skates across my nerves. My fingers gently flatten the wisp back along the sphere, though they have a distinct trembling quality to them as they pull back. The energy cuts abruptly from my fingertips and sinks past my muscles into my bones. Another harsh breath careens past my lips as the afterglow leaves me feeling *flushed*.

"That's…." I lick my lips once more, eyes darting nervously to Felicia as a blush rises to my cheeks.

"Intense?"

A somewhat strangled laugh surfaces from me as I nod my head. A wisp lashes out tantalizingly near the top of the sphere, and I smooth it down, noting this particular strand takes slightly more persuasion. It levels me with the same current of energy as the last. It pulses through my body in short bursts. *Like miniature supernovas*, I think.

"Yes," I finally say, noting that the wisps and tendrils snaking out are increasing in frequency. They snap at my fingers, licking up my palms and delivering their pointed shocks. The resin that coats my hands begins to darken. Spider-like veins spread and spill across the protective coating with each lash of the Borealis. Soon a light sweat builds at the back of my neck. My breath comes in short, soft pants as my hands are set to work in tandem to corral the excess matter. A buzzer sounds from somewhere behind, and the workings of machinery slows down to a calm hum. The sphere recedes. The knife returns to the table's surface, and the lasers turn off.

My body is strung with power. It courses through my veins and brings about a heady sensation. Every movement I make sends a small thrill up my spine. I can feel it all. My muscles stretching. The shift of the air against my skin. How ridiculously ablaze I am.

"No wonder not everyone is allowed to do this," I say. "People would be lining up out the door to get their shot." Felicia and Miles laugh. I cave instantly and join in. *Holy shit.* "That's better than sex," I insist, walking with Felicia to a sink on the far side of the room to peel off our used resin.

"Sweetie, if you think that's better than sex, you've been having sex wrong," she tells me matter-of-factly. "Don't get me wrong, it is a rush. And it will give you a major high, but there's no payout. No… release, if you get what I mean. It'll just leave you feeling on edge until you can figure out a way to take the edge off."

I find myself coloring, eyes skirting to the observatory doors where I know Wyatt and Tucker stand on guard outside. My mind wanders back to a time when Wyatt and I were still together. The sex we had, had been great, but it lacked something. *Intimacy. Meaning.* Two something's, apparently. Toward the end of our relationship, the dynamic between us had changed. After I applied to train as a Stellar Warrior, Wyatt had gone to great lengths to express his displeasure. It showed in the way he treated me in the bedroom. The dominance of his actions left me feeling small and used, like he was trying to put me in my place.

"Ready to go again?" Felicia asks, walking over to the barrel of resin.

"Of course," I tell her tightly. She flashes me a knowing smile, though she interprets my mood incorrectly. Miles fetches the butterfly knife from the table and places it in a glass cylinder filled with a red liquid.

"Then let's get started on the rest of the relics."

+++

It takes close to six hours for us to make our way through the relics. All that remains is an ancient Viking Thunder round shield. Felicia insists on a break before we work on the last item, and I sigh in relief. My T-shirt has long since been stripped off, but the camisole I wear underneath is soaked. Even Felicia has stripped down to a workout tank and shorts, both of which were hidden beneath her lab coat.

"You look a bit wound up, Callie," Wyatt whispers jovially from behind me. The smug undertone of his voice reverberates across my bare shoulder and elicits a shiver down my arms. "I suppose the rumors are true about the imparting process."

"You're not supposed to be in here," I tell him a mite breathlessly while tossing away my empty water bottle. He steps into my line of vision, a satisfied smirk on his face.

"If you'd like, I can help you let off some steam. I don't mind being your... punching bag, so to speak."

"That's unnecessary," I tell him sweetly. "I can work it out by myself. You're not much company wise."

Wyatt's smirk drops, and the color rises on his cheeks. "I wouldn't let this fellowship position go to your head. The only reason you have it is because my mother insisted."

"And my father," I add. "I'm aware."

"As long as you know who put you there," he says, rolling back his shoulders and taking on an unaffected air. The words bring an uncomfortable pang, but knowing he's only saying these things to upset me makes them somehow easier to handle.

"Don't you have somewhere to be? Like somewhere far, far away from me?"

He reaches out a hand, but I sidestep the touch. The movement is abnormally fast, and the shock of it wears on his face. His hand falls lamely to his side. "You can't avoid me, Calliope. Not here, at least. There's nowhere for you to run that I can't follow."

There is a constriction of my lungs. An un-ignorable seizure of my muscles as a ripple of anger floods me. I grit my teeth against the heightened emotion, knowing full well that the Borealis Matter spurs it to such heights. Out of the corner of my eye, I can see Felicia and Miles and become aware of how quiet the room is.

"You should go," I finally tell him. Wyatt presses forward, an earnest expression coming into his eyes. His hand reaches out to me once more, but it halts when the alarm lights go off overhead. Three red flashes, pause, repeat. Wolves. Again. Wyatt turns and sprints toward the observatory door. I follow not a beat behind, beating him easily.

Wyatt's body slams into my own, my wrist crumpling between myself and the door with a small but audible crack. Grabbing me by the shoulders, he hauls me away from the door, shooting me an incredulous look.

"You're not a warrior anymore, Calliope," he grunts, yanking the door open. "Let me and the boys handle this." The door closes behind him with a snap, and a series of clicks resound throughout the room. My eyes widen in panic.

"No," I mutter, tugging at the door handle with my good hand. Locked.

"Protocol states—"

"Fuck protocol!" I snarl at Miles, snatching my hand back to cradle my left wrist. A hand comes to rest on my arm as I silently seethe. My wrist gives a painful throb. It's broken. There's no doubt about it. Felicia turns me around, a dark scowl upon her beautiful features.

"Let me see it," she commands. I present my wrist to her, and she lets out an aggravated sigh. "Come on." I follow her to one of the smaller tables scattered across the room and take the seat she offers. "Lay your hand and wrist as straight as possible. Miles, grab some medical wrap and a couple of splints from the med kit. Quickly." Felicia adjusts my wrist carefully, ignoring my hiss of pain. "With the Borealis Matter so fresh in your system, you'll heal fast. I wouldn't be surprised if it's better by the end of the night, but if we don't set this properly now, it could heal incorrectly."

Miles returns with haste to work with Felicia on setting my wrist. I purposefully ignore the knowing looks Miles shoots my way throughout the process. *Let me and the boys handle this.* Wyatt's words play in my mind on repeat. Like the most annoying song ever.

"We're going to forget this little incident occurred, understood?" Felicia's voice holds a precariously tense note to it. I nod my head stiffly. Miles offers the same response, though a tad more eagerly. "Miles, lock down all the equipment per protocol. We'll help in a moment."

Miles walks off, and I keep my gaze steadfast on the metal table, squaring my shoulders as much as I can for the upcoming reprimand. "What were you thinking?" she hisses. I let out a small exhalation, head shaking dismally from side to side.

"I wasn't," I tell her. *It had been instinctual. Second nature.*

"You're damn right," she responds. "The atrium might house priceless relics, but the observatory houses expensive equipment. Equipment that is extremely hard to come by without raising a lot of eyebrows." My head bobs. Felicia lets out a frustrated sigh. "Look at me, Calliope." I do so. "This can't happen again."

Her eyes flick toward Miles surreptitiously, and I note the way he observes us from afar. "I understand," I whisper.

"Good. How's your wrist feeling?"

I give my fingers an experimental wiggle and scrunch my nose in response. "Shitty," I admit.

"Take a few more minutes and then come watch me shut down."

"Felicia." The 5'4" woman pauses midstride to pass me a look over her shoulder. "Wolves are attacking again." The red light continues to flash above us. By this point last time, the wolves had cut the power. Why hadn't they done so again?

"I'm aware," she says dryly.

"And the power is still on," I continue, following her with measured steps.

Felicia turns to face me, folding her arms over her chest, a look of annoyance stealing through her gaze.

"I'm also aware that the power is still on. Thank goodness."

"But why?"

"*Why?*" She lets out a scoff and turns back around, walking toward a string of switches and levers running across a wall. "How should I know?"

The lights stop, and so do I.

"Great!" Felicia exclaims. "Now we don't have to continue to shut down. Miles."

"On it," he answers excitedly, quickly rebooting all that he'd turned off. I remain frozen in my stance, mind whirling a thousand miles per minute. It seems extremely unlikely for the wolves to attack again in so little time. They had gotten exactly what they came for. So why the second-round hit? Unless....

"Callie?"

They aren't the same.

"Callie?"

It's a different pack.

"Calliope!" My head jerks to the side at the sound of my name. Felicia and Miles both look at me expectantly. "Your wrist?"

I stretch my fingers. The muscle and bone are tight, but the pain has lapsed. I give a short nod of my head and join Felicia. It takes a great amount of effort to concentrate on her words, but by the time we are finished rebooting and imparting the final relic, I know one thing for sure. We have two enemies pounding on our front door. It's just a matter of figuring out who and why.

BAD REPUTATION

- *Chapter 5* -

I'm escorted back to my room an hour after we've finished the last relic. All of us are. The men who accompany us have no news to share, which is complete bullshit. I find myself pacing my room, anxiously waiting for Wyatt to turn up. Surely, he'll want to gloat. Or at least hold some tantalizing piece of information over my head, without telling me the full story. I will take what I can get.

"Knock, knock," Wyatt's voice calls as his knuckles rap against my door. The door inches open without my reply. "Can I come in?"

I usher him inside with an impatient sweep of my hand and plant myself on the edge of my bed. "Well?"

"They're dead." *Christ.*

"All of them?"

He nods, running a hand over his jaw. "Not the wolves, the dogs."

My stomach drops. "The… dogs?" Despite myself, a quiver runs through my voice. The dogs? They killed the fucking dogs? "All of them?"

"That's what I said, isn't it?" he snaps. My mouth shuts. I pale at the disturbing news. "They disabled the new perimeter alarms and took out the dogs before charging the facility. The atrium is a mess. We don't even know if they took anything or if they just wanted to cause chaos."

"Maybe both," I offer softly, mind whirling. I blink back the tears that gather along my vision. "Even Dakota?"

Wyatt takes a seat next to me, grabbing my hand and giving it a rough squeeze. "Sorry, Calliope," he mutters. I slip my hand from his hold and rub it along the back of my neck.

"Mongrels," I spit out. Wyatt's hand moves to rest on my thigh, and I let out a little defeated sigh. There is no point in scampering away like some scared rabbit.

"Your bruises are gone," he finally says after a minute, his eyes lingering momentarily on my wrist. I clench my jaw and slowly exhale.

"Borealis Matter."

Silence crawls into the space between us, broken by the squeaking of the bed as Wyatt shifts. I cast him a sidelong glance, but his gaze rests solely on the hand placed on my thigh.

"I'm sorry about earlier," he apologizes, "but you know how it is now." *Let me and the boys handle this.* I raise a shoulder nonchalantly, letting my hands settle in my lap. "Forget about it," I tell him, even though I have no intention of doing so.

"I kept thinking of you out there," he admits, leaning in closer. "I couldn't help but think if you were there by my side we could have taken down the whole lot of them." His fingernails begin to dig softly into my thigh.

"Wyatt...." My heart skips a beat, knowing precisely what he intends to do next. Knowing I'll do nothing to stop it. *But why?* A small voice cries in my mind.

Wyatt twists, his lips planting themselves against mine in stunted urgency. We tumble back onto the bed, lips slanting over each other like an old habit. But there is nothing there behind it. No spark. No feeling. It's certainly nothing in comparison to the mere touch of the mysterious wolf's soulmark, but at least it takes the edge off this need crawling under my skin. Wyatt reels back after a long minute, taking in my lackluster performance with a sculpted frown upon his brow.

"What's wrong?" I shake my head, eyes flying to the wall. *Anywhere but him.* Wyatt leans back in slowly, letting his lips run along the length of my throat before nipping at my ear. "Upset that you had to keep the darkness at bay?" I suck in a sharp breath, shoving him away with both hands. He lets out a mean laugh as he almost falls off the bed, enjoying my fury.

"Take it back," I order firmly.

"Come on, Calliope," he cajoles. "No one takes on a nest of wendigo and lives to tell the tale if they don't have that killer instinct inside them. Own your darkness."

"Get out," I command, lacing steel into my words. Wyatt hesitates before delivering a mocking bow. "The Council will be here in a few hours. I'd suggest you clean up and get ready for questioning," he says lightly.

"Why would they question me?"

He straightens, rolling back his shoulders and pinning me with a superior look. "I'm sure they'll want to question you after I finish giving my report of the events." I swallow hard, but say nothing more. He departs with a satisfied smile on his face, leaving me to stew and brood over what I might expect.

+++

The stirring sensation of the Borealis Matter has mostly passed. The proverbial "itch" scratched behind closed and locked doors. Afterward, I wait patiently for a Council crony to come and lead me away. They came. I went. And, well… it could have gone better.

"Ms. Sawyer, I had hoped not to see you so soon after our last meeting," Mr. Hall comments, shuffling the papers in front of him idly. He peers at me over the rims of his glasses. "But alas, as Mr. Baker detailed, you attempted to, and I quote, 'take charge of the situation and aid the Stellar Warriors. By force, if necessary.' In your insistence, you 'pushed and shoved' Mr. Baker—"

"That's not true," I tell the Council sharply. "Mr. Baker's account is wrong."

Mr. Hall takes off his glasses to clean them on the end of his shirt before responding, "And what part is wrong?"

"All of it." The Council breaks out into angry murmurs, and I catch my father's disgruntled scowl.

"Do explain yourself," he calls from his seat. I straighten, taking a calming breath before speaking.

"The alarm went off, and I rushed to the doors to activate the security protocols via the security panel. There was a bit of pushing and shoving, though not on my part. Mr. Baker was keen to exit the observatory and assist his comrades. I was keen on securing the observatory."

"I see," my father grumbles.

"I'm happy to have cleared up the matter. It would have been unfortunate for the Council to make a decision based solely on one report."

"And your supervisor, Felicia Metzart, can corroborate your story?" Mrs. Baker asks slyly. I give a brief nod. "How very interesting," she says confidently.

The smile I suddenly sport feels brittle. Mr. Hall opens his mouth to speak when I press on. "What's interesting?"

Mrs. Baker wears that cat-that-got-the-canary look. The one her son likes to don so frequently. "Well, I don't think it will come as a surprise to you when I say, between Wyatt and yourself, the Council is more inclined to believe the former given your... history." I swallow down the hurt that comes with her well-placed hit, the smile on my face fading. "You understand, don't you, dear? We'll certainly be sure to crosscheck the facts of the evening with Ms. Metzart and—"

"And when her version is the same as mine?" I ask. Mrs. Baker stops short at my interruption, the satisfaction waning from her smile.

"While doubtful, if your stories do align, then Wyatt will be reprimanded accordingly. However, if the inverse is true, then a reprimand befitting the situation will be applied to you."

"Which means?"

"Which means, Ms. Sawyer, you've been in front of this Council several times in the past year. All for disorderly behavior. We have been lenient thus far—"

"Lenient? The first time I made a mistake you completely reassigned me! There was no discourse to handle it," I shout.

"Enough!" my father cries, slamming his hands down on the table—one constructed of flesh and bone, the other of metal and fiber. The latter a direct result of an encounter with a ruthless vampyré. "That is enough. Your report of the evening's events has been recorded, as has your ill-mannered behavior. Go."

It definitely could have gone better, but at least afterward I was able to get some information out of the younger warriors, such as the Council's rapidly growing concern about wolf attacks and how the most recent attack is labeled as "personal."

I spin the butterfly switchblade around my fingers pensively. The feel of the cool metal running across my skin is beyond comforting, a fact I attribute to the Borealis Matter that pulses through both of us now. It has never felt more natural in my hands.

The vibration of my phone captures my attention. It's hidden somewhere among the numerous shelves along the walls.

Nova: *<<open image>>*

My thumb hovers over the downloadable link hesitantly before tapping down. I haven't heard from any of the sisters since they had left, but that's not unusual. Typically, when on mission, communication is strictly kept between the outbound agents and coordinating director. Which means the image is either a gag photo or....

The image comes through a few seconds later. A picture of a man's back. A man's bare back that is detailed with an assortment of images in black ink: a Celtic knot, a skull and compass, distorted ravens, claw marks, and paw impressions. Countless more. They do nothing to diminish the sculpted trapezius or broad shoulders that stack the body. Nor the straining muscles that compose his lats.

Nova: *<<open image>>*

I don't hesitate this time around. When the image loads, I'm greeted with the wolf's scowling face—at least half his face—as he wipes at it with a towel. His front is just as ripped as his back. And I can't help but think how well those broad shoulders fit his broad chest. Or how nice the dark hair spanning his pectorals looks. My thumb and forefinger separate on the screen, zooming in on the way said hair spears a direct path south. His abdominals aren't too shabby either. Though he doesn't sport a swimmer's trim waist, it's easy to see that he packs muscle everywhere. A fighter's body through and through.

Nova: *You're welcome.*

Calliope: *How exactly did you get these photos?*

Nova: *I snapped a few pics on the new camera. Don't worry. I deleted the pics once I sent them to my phone.*

Calliope: *You are brilliant.*

I find myself smiling stupidly down at my phone, tapping the pictures again to see the wolf—not wolf, the man, I correct myself. They don't build men like that these days. Ones who take pride in their body and know how to take care of themselves. And probably know how to take care of others just as well. I swallow past the sudden lump in my throat.

Nova: *You owe me! ;p*

To say the least. Ugh. What was I thinking letting her do this for me? It's not like I'm going to pursue anything with the man. Moreover, if her sisters get wind of the photos or our correspondence, I don't know if I can count on them to keep quiet.

A knock sounds quickly at my door. Two sharp raps and the issuer makes their way inside. I shove my phone in my back pocket, keeping a neutral expression on my face as my father shuts the door behind him. He's a tall man, with hair and goatee kept neatly trimmed. He doesn't look happy to see me, but that's not unusual.

"Calliope." I note his greeting comes out as more of a grumble than a salutation.

"Dad." I pat the spot next to me, giving him a wry look. He takes a step forward but doesn't accept my silent invitation. I feel my butt vibrate, and my eyes go wide at the sensation. Thankfully my father doesn't take note of my exaggerated expression.

"Your behavior today at the Council meeting was inexcusable. The way you act reflects upon your family, Calliope. I thought your mother and I taught you better."

"He lied, Dad," I tell him calmly. "Shouldn't he be the one getting the lecture?"

My father crosses his arms over his chest, the robotic hand fitted to his right wrist curling over his bicep. It was lost in a battle long ago, and a constant reminder of his failure. As well as a lesson he preached to my brother and me all our lives. Perhaps it's not a stretch to see why he's become colder to me after my incident with the Stellar Warriors. Perhaps he thinks I'm making the same mistake he did.

"Wyatt admitted his phrasing could have been misconstrued and corroborated your story." I let the silence linger, waiting expectantly for an apology I know will not come.

"Anything else?" My phone vibrates, the noise of the action covered by the sound of my voice. I shift in my seat and cast a sidelong glance at the door.

"Just because he corroborated your story doesn't mean I have to believe it. I know you, Calliope. Your grandmother runs through your veins more than your mother or me, but you are *not* your grandmother. You are *not* a Stellar Warrior. You're a Starlight Warden, and when the time comes, your mother and I fully expect you to become a member of the Council. It's far past time you gave up pursuits of combat and settle into a more stable role among the community. That means no more running into the fray headfirst. I didn't pay for four years of higher education so you could waste your life on the battlefront."

I quell the rush of emotion collecting in my throat. "I'm a good fighter."

"You might be a good fighter, Calliope, but you let your emotions get the better of you. That's why we like girls to take up more practical roles within the community, to avoid incidents like the one from last year—"

"When I tried to save that little girl? That incident?"

His face blooms red at my interruption. The mech hand flexes against his bicep. "You knew full well she was in transition to become a wendigo. Attempting to offer her a merciful death, letting that thing manipulate you—"

"She was still a little girl, Dad! Scared and unable to comprehend what was happening to her. Or why she craved—"

"Enough!" My jaw clenches as I stare down my father, taking in his wrath with more composure than I thought I could muster. "You let your emotions rule you, and you forgot your lessons as a Stellar Warrior. They are *beasts*, Calliope. Dark creatures set on ravaging the good people of this earth. It is our duty to protect them, and you and your damnable empathy got over twenty people killed. The price the Wardens of Starlight paid to cover up your mess was immense. You should be thankful you're still here today."

My eyes flick to the floor. "You know it was never my intention for that to happen. I was going to put her out of her misery, but not the way the others would have had it."

"Beheading is the only way to kill a wendigo."

"*I know that*," I snap back. "That doesn't mean it had to be done so cruelly or callously. She was scared—"

"She was a monster." His words are soaked in venom and make me flinch. "They're all monsters, Calliope. Or have you forgotten your teachings? All supernatural creatures are born from the blackest of flames. They are drawn by the darkest of gods. They plague this world and it is our *duty* and *honor* to destroy them before they can ruin humanity. To even question it is blasphemy." My father let's out a noise of frustration. "Stupid, child."

The utterance is delivered with equal passion as his earlier words, and I force myself to swallow down my anger. I take a deep breath to calm my frayed nerves. Then ignore the third vibration of my phone announcing another new message. "I hoped that finding the child and her nest would earn back my favor with the Council," I admit.

"I know," he says with a tired sigh. The wind seems to have gone out of him, thankfully. "But that too provided its consequences. You know what they think now."

"That there is a darkness inside of me." My shame brings a flush to my cheek. When I had gone after the child and its nest, it was with a righteous fury in my heart. Consumed by the need to avenge the innocents killed, I let myself fall into the darkness, and drew from it shamelessly to finish off my enemies.

I didn't know then that I wouldn't be able to shake the darkness from my thoughts. Or that it would haunt me in every future fight and skirmish.

"The life of a Starlight Warden suits you well," he tells me after a long moment.

"Just as the life of a Stellar Warrior fits JJ?"

My father's scowl returns, deeper than ever. "The Sawyer family plays a crucial role in our community. We always have. As such, there are certain expectations your mother and I have of you and your brother."

"Shouldn't JJ be the one to serve on the Council? He's the oldest after all." The phone in my pocket goes off once again, this time earning the attention of my father's ire.

"We sent you to school for a reason, Calliope, and it wasn't so you could question your responsibilities to this family. JJ understands"—my cell phone vibrates—"you should try to be more like him."

Hadn't I tried, though? JJ was my idol growing up. He was the one who trained me. He was the one who helped me through all my trials. I always wanted to be like him. Another message comes through.

"Sorry," I apologize halfheartedly, reaching into my back pocket to silence my phone. My father shakes his head.

"Who is it?"

There's no point in lying when he will most likely demand to see my phone. I flash him the screen briefly. "It's Nova."

"And why is she contacting you?"

"She was asking for advice," I tell him, shoving my phone back into my pocket after switching it to silent.

"Questions should go to her director, not you, Calliope."

"The field of question is outside of the director's knowledge."

My father raises both eyebrows. "Meaning?"

"Nova requested information regarding the rings previous handling and history, including previous Borealis Matter implementations and aftereffects."

"And Mrs. Abernathy wouldn't know—"

"I just spent the better part of the day assisting in the imparting process. My grasp on the subject now far surpasses what Mrs. Abernathy and a majority of the community understand."

Something like pride flashes behind my father's eyes, which I'm sure I've read wrong. Then, he is nodding his head at my firm reasoning. "Very well. Be sure to keep your communications brief."

"I will."

He leaves without another word, letting me stew in our exchange of words. It feels like I'm fighting a losing battle. At every corner, I'm met with resistance, herded back into a role I do not want. Like I'm merely a pawn on my life's chessboard. I feel trapped, looking for an escape that doesn't exist. Curling up onto my side, I take my phone from my back pocket. Five new messages.

JJ: *Dad's on the warpath—stay clear till he cools off!*

A little too late for that warning, brother, I think glumly. It's the thought that counts, and JJ is always thinking of what's best for me. Sometimes that means avoiding our father. The rest of the messages are from Nova.

Nova: *<<open image>>*
Nova: *<<open image>>*

The first image is of Noelle and Naomi huddled together against a tree trunk, reading from the same book. The second image is an unobstructed view of the wolf's face. He wears a heavy five o'clock shadow and the vague impression of a grin, the glint in his dark chocolate eyes playing into the illusion. His skin is deeply tanned, hiding the faint impression of scars around his right eye.

Nova: *Found out name*
Nova: *Keenan O'Neal*

A leaden sigh pushes past my lips. So, my soulmark has a name: Keenan. It fits him. A strong name, for a strong man. I bring the image of his face back into full focus, studying his features more intently. After minutes spent this way, I download and save the photos to a locked folder on my phone, then delete the messages, pretending like it never happened at all.

SUPERNOVA

- Chapter 6 -

Angry over the fact that she lied for me, Felicia sets me to task cataloging the relics. All of the relics. On all three floors. Even though, once again, only the atrium took the hit. The room is a disaster. Several of the display cases are shattered, leaving the floor littered with bullet casings and glass. It takes me a full two days to clean up the room properly and another day to place orders for replacement glass.

Security at the facility is oppressive. A dozen more guards are brought in with strict new clearance protocols to enforce. It's a pain in the ass, leaving me access to only a few rooms. The mess hall, the observatory, the Relic Halls, and, of course, my room. Wyatt's right. I can't run away from him, but at least the other guards are more easily dodged than my ex. They keep to a tight rotation schedule, but by seven most leave to continue rounds and patrols outside of the facility. Including Wyatt.

It's late, sometime near two in the morning, or so I hazard a guess. The halls boast few guards, and I let my music play a little bit louder than necessary.

Vagrants Whip...
Harpe Sword...
Ophelia's Kestros...
Onyx Bident...

I'm only just beginning to catalog the items of the atrium, deciding to work my way down the floors instead of up. My pen deftly checks each item as my eyes roam the relics on display.

Bone Sword of Shadows...
Tigre Claws...
Phoenix Fire Elixir...

A soft stirring of my nerves turns my gaze unconsciously back to the trio of relics. The order doesn't seem right. Something is missing. My finger draws down the list I carry, stopping on the missing item: the Caster's Diadem. It offers invisibility to the wearer, and it's gone. Or maybe misplaced? *Shit.*

"Hey."

I almost knock half the relics from the altar I'm cataloging. Naomi stands tentatively in the doorway, half her face an ugly blackish-blue. Noelle pushes past her into the atrium, her eyes bloodshot, lip split. Naomi too steps further into the room, letting the door close softly behind her.

"Hey," I respond, the words falling short on my lips as I wait for the third of their trifecta to appear. "Where's Nova?"

Noelle sucks in a deep breath, eyes filling rapidly with tears.

"She's not here," Naomi says stoically.

I take them in more fully. They must have only just arrived. Their clothes are rumpled and dirty. Their bumps and bruises fresh. Nova must be in the hospital wing, and I don't have access there.

"What happened? Where is she?"

"Our recon was going as planned. We learned their schedule. We got their numbers. We figured out the general location of the ring, but then complications arose," Naomi says.

"Complications?" The sisters won't meet my eyes. "What complications?"

Silence, and then, "There was another pack. As well as a group of witches that hadn't been taken into account. Our tracking bullets led us to the right spot, but we couldn't have anticipated the number of supernaturals in the region."

"There was an attack?" The words feel too raw in my throat. Too steeped in honest fright. A terrible intuition gnawing at my conscious. Noelle fidgets with her ponytail, her left wrist wrapped up in beige bandages. She is unusually quiet and discontent. It puts me even more on edge.

Naomi nods, a frown coming to crease her forehead. "A couple of days ago, we were reporting to Mrs. Abernathy, trying to decide if we should return or wait for more backup to secure the ring. Our connection went dead and then...."

"The wolves attacked," Noelle says, finally finding her voice. Her eyes no longer hold their glossy quality. "The second pack started firing into the other pack's territory. It was chaos, and we thought we were safe up in the tree line, but then the witches got involved. Our cover was blown and—" Noelle takes two large deep breathes, her sister busy wiping at her cheeks "—then the vampyré appeared. We were halfway out of the forest to our car, and suddenly he was right in front of us."

"A vampyré...."

Noelle nods, lips thinning. "He smiled and thanked us. Then told us we had done a good job, but he couldn't afford to keep all three of us around. That he only required one body to get the rest of the job done."

Something inside me clicks off. A numbness sets in as she continues. "He was so fast. He had her before we could even blink. And we couldn't fire without hurting her—"

"He took her?" The words sound oddly hollow coming from my mouth.

"He killed her, Callie," Noelle tells me, voice barely above a whisper.

Killed her. My head moves back and forth. The clipboard and pen fall from my hands to the floor. "No." *No.* Not Nova.

"It was a trap. The vampyré orchestrated everything. He—" Noelle continues.

"No!"

Noelle's mouth snaps closed at my interruption, and her eyes once more swell with tears. She strides forward, Naomi catching her by the arm before she can come over and—

"He turned her. In front of us. I know what I saw. I know what we saw," Noelle snarls at me, tears running down her face. "That monster turned her, and there was nothing we could do about it." Before I can make some snappy reply, she pulls herself free from her sister's hold and storms off.

"She's not really dead, is she?" Naomi nods. Her face twisting in pain as she lets out a sob. I run to embrace her, gathering her in my arms and letting my tears flow as well. "How could this happen?" I whisper, aghast.

Naomi pulls back, wiping carefully at her eyes and nose. "I think he set it all up, Callie." I stare wide eyed at the youngest Stavok. "Think about it. The wolves stole the ring for the vamp. Why else would they have taken it? He must have been there to get it from them."

I pace backward, shaking my head all the while. "That doesn't make sense, Naomi. How would he know to have attacked you then? And why would a pack of wolves steal a sun-walker ring for a vampyré? That's not even factoring in the other pack or the witches. What was their role?"

Naomi hops up onto the altar, her shoulder and back hunching as she takes in my critiques. "I don't know," she answers slowly, "but there has to be a reason for all of this. Maybe... maybe it was because of what we discovered and the vampyré wanted revenge or *something*."

"What did you find?"

"A crystal. Nova spotted it." Naomi's voice cracks over her sister's name, but she forges on. "It creates some kind of magical barrier."

I pause midstride. "A magical barrier?"
Naomi nods her head somewhat hesitantly. "That's what Nova said anyway."

"There was another attack on the facility. Just a few days ago."

"And here I thought this was still from the first time around," she replies dryly.

"Some people are under the impression that it's the same pack of wolves, but I don't think so. I think it was a different pack."

"I mean, after what we saw, I guess that could make sense. Two packs. Two separate attacks."

"So where do the witches and this vampyré fit in?"

Naomi casts a wry grin. "You're not going to believe this—the witches are working with the wolves who stole from us in the first place. The Adolphus Pack."

"Who's the other pack?"

"Noelle knows the name, it's kind of wordy and starts with a W. We called them the alpha pack and beta pack."

I run a hand through my long hair, resuming my pacing at the new information. The witches and wolves are working together and stole the ring. Meanwhile, the other wolf pack could very well be the culprit of the second attack and responsible for stealing the other artifact. So which is working with the vampyré?

"Was anything taken?"

"Huh?" My head snaps in Naomi's direction. "Oh, actually, yes. I think something did get taken. I just caught it before you came in." *And told me your sister was dead.* "The diadem is missing."

"The Caster's Diadem?" I nod my head. "Fuck." She slams her hand against the altar, sliding off and onto the ground. The burst of anger is so out of place to her usual demeanor, I almost jump. "That makes so much more sense!"

"What does?" I ask, alarmed by her sudden vigor.

"The attack came out of nowhere, Callie. One minute everything is calm along the border. I'm keeping watch while Noelle and Nova are speaking with Mrs. Abernathy. Then *bam*! Out of nowhere, this wolf gets stuck with a tree branch in the gut. It wasn't thrown. It just rose up from the ground and slammed into him!"

A nervous tremor clasps my heart. "What did the wolf look like?" I ask, going for casual and failing miserably. Naomi is too absorbed in her thought process to notice my discontent.

"Blonde. Just over five foot," she replies absentmindedly. She turns to me abruptly. "Don't you see? The other pack used the diadem to instigate the fight! A bunch of them ran out past the border to engage with the other pack, and then the witches were all flustered because of the fighting."

"Which is when you were spotted." She nods her head eagerly. "And the vampyré? How does he fit into the equation?" I ask.

Naomi slows her stride, knotting her fingers together as she begins to explain her reasoning. "Well, the vampyré wants the ring. Obviously. But the alpha pack and witches have it."

“And the beta pack has the diadem,” I add pensively.

“And the beta pack started the fight.” Our eyes meet. “And the vampyré, he thanked us. He must have been keeping tabs on all of us. Maybe he’s in league with the beta pack, and got them to instigate the fight.”

“That’s a pretty big jump,” I say slowly, but it does seem plausible. More than plausible. A surge of hope creeps into my heart. “And Nova... she really—”

“He grabbed her and forced his blood down her throat, then snapped her neck," Naomi says calmly. "She died with his blood in her system. In three days, if she doesn’t manage to kill herself, she’ll complete her transition and turn into a vampyré.”

“And then the only way to kill her will be by decapitation or an ivory stake through the heart,” I finish sourly.

Naomi sucks in a tight breath. “They’re going to hunt her down like a dog once we submit our report. They’re going to send out a faction to retrieve the ring, probably that crystal, and most definitely my sister.” A cool chill runs down my spine at the thought.

“No—”

“Yes, Callie. They will. You know it. I know it. And so does Noelle.”

I walk over to Naomi and take her by the shoulders, forcing her to stop pacing. “I wasn’t trying to disagree with you. I’m fully aware of the Council’s lack of empathy,” I respond evenly, “which is why we can’t let them hurt her further.”

Naomi stills completely, her eyes going wide. “What do you mean?”

“I mean—” I lick my lips nervously, releasing Naomi from my tight grasp. “—that we have to save her.” The idea warms me, igniting a hope inside me I haven't felt in ages. We *can* save Nova. We can take back the ring. All will be forgiven....

Naomi lets out a choked laugh. "She's already dead—he *turned* her."

"But what if we could change her back?" I cast a wary eye about the room before stepping closer to Naomi and lowering my voice. The very suggestion of my idea is insane. Hell, there's an enormous chance it won't work, but we have to try. "Vogart's Blade."

Naomi's eyes widen. The blade is rumored to reverse vampyrism in the newly turned, but the records of such acts have long since been lost. I'm not surprised by Naomi's twisted expression, knowing how absurd I sound suggesting it, but I manage to keep my own wariness off my face.

"I don't know, Callie. What if the blade doesn't work? If it does work, then wouldn't the Council have it on our best Warrior?"

I shake my head with semi-forced conviction, lips thinning.

"The relic is too powerful. The Council would never chance it being out in the field where it could be taken or lost," I reason calmly. "You can bet they've got it hidden away here somewhere." Naomi avoids my gaze, chewing on her lip indecisively. "Come on, Naomi. If there's a chance to save her—even the slimmest chance to bring her back to life—shouldn't we try? She would for any one of us."

Naomi takes a deep breath. "I think I know where to look."

+++

I'm left waiting on the relics third floor storage for Naomi to return, a small backpack resting by my feet, filled with only the essentials for our secret mission. Naomi is packing and double-checking her notes about the location of the blade, but she's nearly positive its location is here.

I find myself oddly unworried about the threat of being caught. All I'm truly worried about is securing a big enough head start before the Council becomes privy to our escapades and sends a group to retrieve us. That, and whether or not my harebrained scheme will work. *Please, let it work*, I pray. The blade is our only shot at restoring Nova. It's also the only shot I have at being reinstated as a Stellar Warrior. If this worked....

The door creaks open a few minutes later to reveal Naomi slipping in. Her face is devoid of emotion, though the black and blue about her face tells a different story. She gives me a brief nod, tossing her bag to rest near mine.

"Did you get the tablet?" she asks. I nod, recrossing my arms over my chest. The tablet holds all personnel files of the Wardens of Starlight, including our tracker identification numbers. If Nova's tracker hasn't been disabled or removed from her forearm by the vampyré or herself, then our mission will be a hell of a lot easier.

"Do you know where it is?" I ask, not bothering to hide the slip of anxiety in my voice.

"Of course," she remarks stoutly, fiddling idly with her glasses. "I confirmed with Noelle, as well." Naomi catches my startled express with a steady look, walking past me and down the center aisle of the labyrinth of relics.

"You told Noelle?" I whisper harshly, casting a quick glance over my shoulder as I speed after her. "What were you thinking?"

"I thought that Nova is her sister too. She has every right to know what we're planning on doing. Besides, we need someone to cover for us, and she will." My lips press together in a firm line. There is no point in arguing, even if I had wanted to keep our plans between us. At least I can begrudgingly accede to her reasoning. Noelle can better ensure our head start. "She said it's in plain sight. The third shelf. Aisle D4. About halfway down."

We jog over to the aisle, hands skimming the boxes and their glass lids. Everything is pleasantly clean of dust, in part because of the recent cataloging.

"I thought it was going to be harder to find," I finally say once we locate the blade, shifting uneasily from foot to foot. I can feel my anxiety building, except I'm beginning to think it might not be anxiety at all. Being in the trenches of the relics is lighting my nerve endings on fire. *Like calls to like*, I think as the vestiges of the Borealis Matter come to attention. It makes my bones feel heavy. My skin feels too tight. I'm hyperaware of the seconds passing as Naomi carefully removes the case and unlocks it.

"Chill out, Callie. I can feel the tension coming off you in waves." Naomi adjusts her glasses, wincing only slightly at the movement.

"Sorry," I say, forcing myself to take a few deep breaths. Naomi removes the blade. It's in remarkably good condition considering it is centuries old. The almost sickle-like shape of the blade looks particularly savage to me. The blade, made of onyx, is lined in quicksilver. Though the handle is of much poorer quality, it's sturdy after all these years. At least I hope it is, among other things. I curb the swell of doubt I feel, chewing on my bottom lip as Naomi tucks the blade away. "Ready?"

She nods and puts away the case, walking away with much surer steps to our gear. I'm startled back a step when she halts a foot away from our bags. Naomi turns around to face me, hair nearly whipping me in the face. I take another step back.

"Tell me the plan again," she asks a bit breathlessly, the color gone from her face. I square my shoulders and repeat the plan to Naomi.

"Nova's tracer is still active in the area you were in two days ago and—"

"I bet he left her for the wolves," she cuts in bitterly, sucking in a few sharp breaths and turning her eyes to the floor. Naomi's shoulders tremble. "That fucker."

"Hey." I reach out to Naomi, but she shrugs away my attentions. "Don't go there," I reprimand her firmly, stiffening as I shove away my lingering doubts. I needed to be strong. We only have some twenty-four hours to find Nova, and the threat of another Council meeting being called before we have a chance to leave, is too close for comfort. "We have the blade and the tablet. We'll get out of the facility, and Noelle will cover for us while we track down Nova."

"And once we find her... we stab her in the heart with Vogart's Blade and hope...."

"*And then* she'll turn back into a human. The blade only works on newly turned vampyrés. It's the last necromancer tool in existence. It will work." *It has to work.* "All right? Then the three of us will take back the ring and hightail it home."

Naomi shakes herself of whatever doubt she carries and gives me a curt nod. I nod back, and we grab our bags, striding toward the door.

"Going somewhere?" We freeze. Naomi releases the door handle slowly, as we turn to face my brother. Our expressions kept carefully blank.

"Not at all," I respond. "What are you doing here, JJ?" He walks closer, out of the aisles and into the main corridor. His approach is too casual. Shit. "How much did you hear, JJ?"

"It's quite the plan," he remarks.

"It is." We stare each other down. His hands come out of his pockets to cross over his chest. I keep mine on the straps of my bag. "JJ—"

"Do you realize how much trouble you'll be in once they find out? They might go easy on you, Naomi, but

Cal—" JJ frowns as if he's in pain. "—they're gunning for you. If you go out in the field, they might not let you back. You understand that, right?"

A tightness builds in my throat, but I dip my head in understanding. "I know what they'll do, but I couldn't live with myself if I let Nova become a chew toy for that pack of wolves. Something's going on down there. Something much bigger than the Council or anyone else knows about. We have to find out what it is and stop it."

"And Noelle is in on the plan too?"

Naomi takes a cautious step forward. "She's going to cover for us, for as long as she can. Nova's her sister too," she finishes softly.

"Okay," he says with a sigh, shaking his head. Naomi and I share a confused look. *Okay*?

"So...."

"I'm going with you," he says calmly, closing the space between us.

"You can't come with us. It's our mission."

JJ rolls his eyes at my insistence. "I'm coming. You really think you two are getting out of this facility without some kind of higher clearance? Besides, this has all the signs of a trap."

Naomi and I share another look, this one filled with understanding. "The vampyré," Naomi states. "I hadn't thought of that."

"Which is why you need me."

"She has me," I persist. "I got the same training as you."

"And I've been a Warrior longer than you and have more experience than you. This isn't a competition, Cal. If you want a fighting chance at this crazy plan of yours, then you need me." I let out a growl of frustration, rubbing my face with the heels of my hands.

"Fine. But we need to leave. Now."

"Okay," he says, breathing a sigh of relief. "Let me just grab my bag. I'll meet you in the atrium in ten minutes, then act as escort to the vehicle depot out back."

"Great!" Naomi chirps with false enthusiasm, spinning on her toes back toward the door. "Let's go." She yanks the door open wide only to reveal Wyatt's lonesome figure standing right outside. Shit.

LYING IN WAIT

- Chapter 7 -

I've lost track of time, which isn't good for Nova's time is quickly running out. It takes three days for a person to transition to a vampyré, and between the sister's travel time returning to the Banks and ours back out... we don't have much time left.

Naomi is incensed with the addition of Wyatt to our group, but there is nothing to do about it. With no way to prevent him from coming, our only choice is letting him tag along. Wyatt's saving grace is commandeering a bush airplane to get us as far as Fort McMurry. Wyatt even paid off the pilot to take the remainder of the day off to extend our head start.

Signs for Calgary are appearing more and more frequently out the window. Hopefully, that meant another pit stop soon. The back seat of our hijacked utility van isn't exactly comfortable, especially considering I'm sharing it with Wyatt.

"Are you going to keep glaring at me for the rest of the ride?" he murmurs, lip quirking upward even as his eyes remain closed. He sits opposite me in the back, legs spread out in a wide V.

"Yes."

One eye opens. "You'll get wrinkles," he informs me.

"I'm hardly concerned," I hiss back. "Now, be quiet. Naomi is trying to sleep."

"I'm trying to sleep too, but you keep glaring at me. I'm afraid you're going to murder me in my sleep or something." I'm tempted too. His other eye opens at my adamant expression. "What?"

"Why did you insist on coming? I mean really, why? Your whole story back at the Banks was total bullshit. Who were you trying to fool saying you liked Nova?" I scoff, and Wyatt straightens at my curt tone.

"I do actually like her," he tells me with a scowl. "At least out of the three of them. Noelle's too uptight. Naomi is... weird. Nova's by far the most tolerable."

"You're a dick," I inform him, "and you didn't answer my question. Why did you insist on coming along?" His gaze darts almost worriedly to the front seat where JJ drives and Naomi rests beside him. Then he's shifting and moving to sit right next to me. "This seems unnecessary," I mutter under my breath.

"I came because of you," he tells me, voice low in my ear. My eyes look in the rearview mirror and catch JJ's hard gaze. He doesn't like that Wyatt came either. "Do you realize the amount of risk you're putting yourself in to save someone who is beyond saving? She's a vampyré now, Callie. There's no way between all this travel time her seventy-two hours aren't up. She's one of them. It sucks, but it's the truth. Your little Hail Mary pass with the blade isn't going to work. We don't even know if it works."

"You don't know that," I hiss back.

"Doesn't matter," he replies. "What I know is that the Council has plans for you. For us. And this plan of yours could get you killed."

My breath catches in my throat. "Plans?"

I cast a sidelong glance his way, watching as color rises to his cheeks. "I've made my intentions clear, and we both know our parents hope you'll serve on the Council one day. So, if I have to follow you across the country to try and save your friend—and mine—then I will. I won't let anything out there hurt you, and I'll help make sure we all get back. I promise." Wyatt catches my eye, and what I see makes my heart clench uncomfortably. *Hope.* It's going to be a long ten hours to get to Branson Falls.

+++

"The tracer is sounding off roughly twelve klicks southeast of our position, and it's on the move," JJ tells us, scanning the tablet, his eyes lifting to flick through the dense forest sporadically. Wyatt hovers nearby, rifle perched in his hold while two more guns rest on either side of his hips. Naomi and I are finishing adjusting our dragon skin armor and weapons. The tension in the air builds around us. We've navigated the van deep into the forest, courtesy of a dodgy unused road clogged with fallen branches and littered with ditches. We're lucky the van made it so far in, but even so, seven and a half miles—twelve klicks—will take a long while to cover.

"Well," Naomi says, "what are we waiting for?"

JJ leads the way, setting a steady pace through the foliage. Naomi and I take the middle, ready to hold ranks at the side if necessary, while Wyatt brings up the rear. The first hour and a half is made in silence. There are no breaks. No shared looks of contrite concern or weariness as we traverse the mountainous terrain. The trek would have felt more difficult if not for the canopy of leaves and the cool breeze winding its way through the branches. As it is, the dragon armor isn't exactly breathable fabric, but going without it isn't an option.

"Target is changing direction and heading west," JJ announces, pausing only slightly to tuck away the tablet and change our course.

"Toward us?" Naomi's optimism saturates her words, her head whipping about surreptitiously.

"Yes," JJ answers, voice clipped. We continue onwards silently, trekking through denser shrubs, along the alpha pack's boundary lines. When the little red dot signifying Nova stops some two klicks away, he has us do so as well. Naomi pulls out the topography map from her pocket, her finger running along a hand-drawn line through the forest.

"We're coming up to one of our old tree posts," she says. "It's almost a kilometer west of the alpha pack's boundary line."

"Which means we're in the beta pack's territory?" She nods at my conclusion. "Yes, but the packs don't start manning the boundary line until at least three klicks north from here. We should be in the clear for now, but we should stay alert. There's still active wildlife in this area. Both predator and prey."
Predator and prey? Just which are we? I cannot help but think that we are walking a perilous line between the two at the moment.

"Do the wolves wander?"

Naomi shakes her head, folding and pocketing the map once more. "They typically stick to a schedule."

"And you said they would patrol outward from what coordinates?" Wyatt asks.

"47°38'51.9"N 115°14'30.0"W," she says smoothly. "More wolves will be coming since nightfall provides better coverage for them."

"You didn't tell us that their patrol size increased toward nightfall during the brief," I respond, surprised and a tad miffed at her casual delivery.

She gives a short shrug, not bothering to meet any of our eyes. "I didn't see what difference it would make. I know the area. I know the schedule. We'll stay out of their way." She takes a quick glance at the tablet in JJ's hand. "She's moving again. Toward us. Faster."

Naomi walks off without another word, trying to take the lead. JJ catches up to her in two long strides, whispering something as they continue walking.

"She should have told us," Wyatt grunts, shuffling forward to stand by me.

"How many more do you think are going to come?" I ask quietly.

"I don't know," he says slowly, "but I think we should have brought more guns." We watch as Naomi and JJ come to a stop ahead of us, heads huddled together over the tablet.

"Probably," I remark sarcastically. Wyatt nudges my arm, a sort of grin trying to steal its way onto his face. "What?"

"Just like old times, eh? Out in the field. The odds stacked against us." I roll my eyes at his nostalgia, though I don't deny the comfort of familiarity it brings about. "Tell me something. Did you come up with this plan just to get Nova back, or was there some part of you just dying to get back out in the field one last time? Whatever the cost?"

I suck in a harsh breath. "Fuck you."

He lets out a bark of laughter. "Oh, come on! Not even just a little bit? I know how the anticipation always got you riled up before—"

"Would you just shut up? That isn't why I came up with the plan. Nova is my friend. My best friend. She's loyal, and she's good, and she didn't deserve this. We have the power to reverse it. So, why shouldn't we?"

"You know why, Calliope. We don't know if the blade works, and even if it does, it's too dangerous to have outside of the Banks Facility. In the wrong hands, it could start a war." I avoid his gaze, managing to take one step forward before Wyatt places himself in front of me. "You get that, right?"

"Of course I understand. I'm not an idiot."

"Says the girl who brought her brother and friend into warring wolf territory with a fledgling vampyré on the loose. Oh, and let's not forget the Eldritch Witches on patrol as well. This is a suicide mission if I ever saw one. One the Council would never have approved of… but hey, if you can manage to pull this off and get the ring back? Then maybe the Council won't banish or kill you. They might even reward you for your daring and ingenuity. Reinstate you as a Warrior. But I bet you already thought about that, didn't you?"

Heat gathers and spreads across my neck and cheeks. "Drop it, Wy," I order icily, unable to bring myself to deny his observations.

His hand reaches out and grips my wrist tightly. "I know you, Calliope. I know how you think. I know how you act. I know all about that darkness inside of you. Because you and me? We're two sides of the same coin." He lets his words sink in, but my mind drifts traitorously to an image of Keenan. His stern face and anxious plea the fateful night of our meeting. If anyone is to be my other half, isn't it the mysterious wolf? "You didn't just come here to save Nova and get the ring back, and we both know it. You can't honestly believe the Council will reward you for this suicide mission, even if you pull this off. At least not without all of our support and testimony." I catch the meaningful look on his face and feel a pit of worry develop in my stomach. "And if you don't pull this off, you'll need a lot more than that."

"I'm aware of the consequences I might face—"

"Are you? Really? Because if you don't, we all know what consequence you alone will face." *Death.* "Though, with the right persuasion, you could find yourself allowed to stay, at the very least." I go to reply, lips opening to administer a callous retort, when I see the glint in his eyes. His grip intensifies. "My family holds considerable weight with the Council, Calliope. More than yours or the other two founding families. Marry me, and you'll come to witness it firsthand."

"Wyatt—" His name cracks on my tongue as he pulls me back into his chest.

"We could have done this properly," he tells me heatedly, eyes suddenly wide and wild. "But you've cut that option to shreds. Marry me."

I shoot a desperate look over my shoulder at JJ and Naomi. They remain near one another, backs hunched and heads dipped forward. I swallow the lump in my throat. Feel my hummingbird heartbeat pulse all throughout me.

"We can't possibly get married," I finally say, eyes still locked on the other two. His fingers gently persuade my chin to the side, to face him fully.

"We need only a Warden's light and blessing to sanction a handfasting, plus a witness. We have both."

"We also need rings," I respond, tugging out of his hold. Wyatt pulls a cloth out of his pocket and unwraps its contents. "Wyatt," I breathe, closing my eyes as I shake my head. "We can't get married."

"Two rings, a witness, and a Warden. We've all we need. You just need to say yes. After all this mess is taken care of, we'll conduct the ceremony on the plane on our way back. It's the only way they won't find a reason to banish or kill you. Just think about." His hand reaches out faster than I anticipate, cradling the back of my head and pulling me forward into an earnest kiss.

"Keep your hands to yourself, Baker," JJ barks. I take two steps back in hasty retreat, hand flying to my lips as I stare aghast at Wyatt. His mouth trims into two thin lines, his eyes meeting JJ's in a menacing glare. "We're not here so you two can rekindle your relationship. We're here to help Nova and secure the Amethyst of the Aztecs. Understood?"

Wyatt grunts and straightens. "Understood." JJ's hard gaze lands on me.

"I understand."

Naomi touches JJ's arm, pulling his attention back to her. I catch the frown upon her brow, the worry etched plainly across her features as she steps toward him.

"What's going on?" I ask. Naomi nervously adjusts her glasses.

"Nova's movements are becoming sporadic," JJ tells us.

I look back to Wyatt, taking in his expression of the news. He too can tell something is off between the two. "So, is she headed away from us?" He shakes his head. "Then what's the matter?"

"She's still moving toward us, but faster than before. Much faster." There's unspoken meaning in the short sentence. Much faster? More like too fast. Not humanly possible fast. Our seventy-two hours is up. There is no other explanation for a target being able to move at such high speeds. "She's coming in at us in a strange pattern though. She'll arch one way, then dart another."

"But she's still coming toward us?"
He nods, then motions for us to gather closer. "Wyatt will take trigger point," JJ says, slipping to position himself at the back while Naomi and I once more take position in the middle. Wyatt slowly leads us forward by JJ's instruction, and a strange hush falls over the forest. It will be predator against predator should we encounter Nova, and the thought does not bode well.

Though my eyes should be tracking for movement, I can't help but steal glances at Naomi. Vogart's Blade is still snug in its sheath on her hip, but Naomi looks ready to exchange the gun she holds for the blade in a second flat.

Something catches my eye in the distance. A blur of movement too fast for the human eye to catch.

Wyatt raises a fist, and the group comes to a halt. "How far away is the target?" Tension pricks at my skin while we wait for JJ's response.

"Less than one klick. Hold position. Wyatt, at the ready."

"Ready. Will shoot on command," Wyatt answers. Naomi's head whips to the side to stare at him in shock. "Shoot? We're not shooting Nova. What the hell, JJ? This isn't the plan." My gaze darts across the darkening plain. My swirling, fluttering nerves skipping into overdrive as the group loses focus. Another movement. This one far off in the distance and accompanied by a shuddering of branches along a row of bushes.

"We're not going to kill her, Naomi. Wyatt's gun is loaded with—"

"We're not shooting my sister," she snarls, effectively cutting him off. "End of story."

"Listen—"

"No, I won't fucking listen! You listen to me."

"You guys," I hedge, gun poised and at the ready to cover my side if necessary, "we need all eyes out on the ground. We're in wolf territory, remember?"

Naomi growls her frustration, "Are you seriously agreeing with them?"

"No," I snap back, frustration and aggravation clear in my voice, "but I'm also not willing to leave us unguarded. And I seem to be the only one who—" A sharp crack sounds in the air, stealing all of our attention. And anything within a mile radius.

All eyes turn in shock to Wyatt, the crack of his gun still reverberating through the air. A strangled cry rears from Naomi's throat as she staggers forward. I roughly pull Wyatt back, receiving an undignified grunt in response. Heart hammering in my chest, I seek out Nova's figure in the fading light. Some 500 meters away, a deer wavers on its feet. A muted bleat echoes through the air as it buckles to the ground.

Naomi's fist drives into the side of Wyatt's face, her body twisting and adding to the weight of her punch. Wyatt stumbles, hands releasing the rifle to cup his jaw. "Jesus, Naomi! It was just a deer."

"It could have been Nova!" she shouts back. "You piece of shit, that could have been her!" Naomi launches forward once more, but I'm quick to step between the two, hands held high in surrender.

"Everybody needs to calm down," I speak softly, letting my hands lower slowly.

"That could have been Nova, Callie." I don't dare look over my shoulder at Wyatt, though I'm dying to deliver the same punch.

"I hit the deer with a tranquilizer. If you would have let JJ finish explaining a minute ago, instead of flying off the handle, you would know the rifle is loaded with two tranquilizer darts made for vampyrés. That deer will be out until tomorrow." Naomi's face is flush with anger, but her eyes scream uncertainty.

"That could have been Nova," she breathes harshly, unwilling to back down. "You would have shot her with a tranquilizer?"

"She's still a vamp, Naomi," JJ cajoles. "We're deep in wolf territory, and that deer is apparently wearing your sister's tracer."

"What?" I ask wide eyed. He nods, jaw clenched tight as he shows us the tablet. *Oh no.* The red dot remains at a standstill 500 meters from us. He stows it away and picks up his weapon once more. I trickle of apprehension digs into each vertebra along my spinal column. "Why would a deer have her tracer?"

"*How* would a deer have her tracer?" Naomi asks, voice hollow with dread.

"Resume formation," JJ orders. In strained silence, we do as we're told. Wyatt spits out a thick curdle of blood as he snatches his rifle from the ground. He passes both Naomi and me an icy glare, but the point is moot. My Beretta M9 feels heavy in my hands as I direct the muzzle northward, a swell of adrenalin taking place of my apprehension. The Borealis Matter only heightens the sensation as I survey the growing shadows. There is still little chatter from the inhabitants of these woods, which means a predator still lurks nearby.

"Fall back," JJ commands softly. Naomi stiffens, casting a helpless look my way.

"But—"

"No buts. We planned accordingly for this scenario earlier. We stay at the ready, all of us, and fall back to the van." Cautiously we backtrack, JJ resuming the lead trigger position. A mile into our trek, JJ turns on a small flashlight attached to his belt. It's only half past nine, yet already it's startlingly dark. *We most certainly aren't in Alaska anymore*, I think. And the once helpful canopy now works to our detriment, spoiling the last vestiges of light as the sun sinks past a distant mountain peak. Thankfully, the walk back passes more quickly than our way out; JJ's pace to credit.

When we make it back to the van, weapons still at the ready, an uncertain calm takes hold. Naomi lets her gun drop to her side, the tension she carried all throughout our journey back dropping from her with a crestfallen look.

"Remind me again, what scenario is it we just experienced? Nothing happened out there. We could have still found her somehow."

"That tracer didn't place itself on the deer, Naomi," he says flatly, though some regret lingers about the edges of his tone. "The movement of the deer was too scripted up until the end. Too easy. It had all the signs of a trap. I couldn't ignore it. Besides, without the tracer still actually residing in Nova, the chances of finding her fall considerably."

"And we're not out of danger yet, Stavok," Wyatt adds, opening the side van door and placing his tranquilizer rifle inside, then his side guns. "This is still wolf territory, and we're bound to catch notice if we stay out here much longer."

"But it wasn't a trap," comes her biting response, refusing to remove her belt or armor when Wyatt holds out an expectant hand. "Nothing happened, JJ. Nothing. We could still—"

"No," JJ says harshly, all manner of civility gone from his demeanor. He wears the role of Stellar Warrior like some indifferent mask. Like I used to. No trace of emotion in body or voice. This is simply a job that cannot be done, and casualties won't be risked with the odds so high against us. Wyatt lets out a small noise of frustration when Naomi crosses her arms and turns to me.

"This was your idea, Callie. Back me up on this; we can't just leave. What about the ring? What if we used one of our tree posts to scout for just a day? We could keep an eye out for Nova and execute a plan to get the ring—"

"You want to take back the ring, then go out looking for your sister again with a pack of wolves and witches hot on our trail? All the while in the contested territory of said wolves?" Wyatt asks sardonically, walking forward, hand still outstretched. "Brilliant plan. Now hand over your weapons. We keep to protocol and catalog all items."

Naomi removes her guns, shaking with anger. Wyatt rolls his eyes to me as if to say, "See what I have to put up with?" But all I see is a girl coming to terms with the loss of a sister, finally succumbing to grief after my false hope crumbles all around us. There will be no retrieving the ring. No returning Nova. And I will face the consequences of my failures once again. Forced to marry a man I know I can never love, and lose the respect of my people for my rash decisions.

I catch the look of sorrow and resignation on Naomi's face and clench my teeth. *No.* We can't give up. We can't leave it like this. The blade has to work. Wyatt ticks something off on a clipboard from the van, setting aside Naomi's guns. JJ undoes his belt and armor, tossing them in the van and rubbing a hand over his head.

"Your gear, Callie," he says, somewhat tiredly, but I find myself shaking my head. He stiffens at the action, shoulders rolling back and face tightening. "Your gear, that's an order, Warrior." I shake my head more firmly, stepping back as the faintest hint of adrenaline kindles in my blood.

"I'm not a Warrior anymore, JJ. Besides, I won't be *anything* if I don't stay and finish this. We all know that." I let my words settle, catching the varying reactions of everyone: JJ contrite, Naomi cautiously optimistic, and Wyatt furious. "If I go back without something to show for all of this, then I'm better off out here anyway. The Council will have my head for taking the blade and coming up with this plan, not to mention all the expended resources. Naomi, give me the blade. I'll finish this."

Naomi takes in a shaky breath, judging the distance between us, as well as Wyatt and JJ's alert stances. Both lunge forward when she grabs the knife and throws it to me. I catch it out of the air easily.

"Dammit, you guys," JJ curses, pacing backward. "This isn't the time for—"

"Calliope, we talked about this," Wyatt says calmly, taking a tentative step forward. "You don't have to worry about the Council."

JJ looks uncertainly between us. "What does he mean, Cal?"

"We agreed to wed on the plane ride home," he tells JJ. The forest feels uncomfortably quiet at his announcement.

Despite myself, I feel a tepid heat fill my cheeks. "No," I reply, straightening my spine, "you proposed the idea of marriage as a solution. I didn't agree with it."

"It's the only way, Calliope," he snaps. "Don't be stupid. This is the wendigo Church Hill all over again, at least that's what everyone will think. Now give your brother your gear back and get the fuck in the van!" His temper flies from zero to sixty in no time, echoing through the trees. It clears any remaining wildlife from the vicinity—not that there's much to begin with anyway.

The hair at the back of my neck stands to attention as I watch JJ stop. His head ticking to one side. Our eyes clash as his earlier words drill into my head… *all the signs of a trap*. Naomi and I flick our wrists at the same time, bracers igniting. The boys go tense, their weapons out of reach.

"I have an idea," a voice drawls. "Give me the blade, and in return, you can have my newest pet."

Nova pitches forward from behind the van, a quiet "oomph" sounding from her lips before she crashes to her knees. Hands tied behind her back with thick black rope, she keeps her head bowed forward, but it hardly disguises the state she's in. Her clothing is soiled with both dirt and blood, along with most of her skin.

The other vampyré steps out from behind the van in stark contrast to Nova. He's dressed entirely too nicely for the situation at hand, wearing dark slacks and a pressed long-sleeved shirt rolled to the elbows. Both of which are tailored to his long and lean body. The vampyré's silver-stained eyes are startling against his alabaster skin and high cheekbones, and they watch us with a bored expression. He looks as if he's some modern-day aristocrat. Maybe he was in his human life.

The moment before us hangs in suspense before we snap into action. Naomi darts forward, and I too, to stop her. With my arms locking around her waist, I swing her behind me. Knowing she'll only try once more to reach her sister, I do the only thing I can think of; I turn and stand at the ready with Vogart's Blade held threateningly at Naomi, leaving me exposed to the threat at my back.

There's only a second for me to spot JJ and Wyatt. Wyatt is the only one among the two to snag a gun, while JJ angles back to be nearer to the van. Fight and flight wage war inside of me. I'm poorly positioned—we all are—which make the logistics of both fighting and fleeing a challenge. A tendril of unease winds around me when the shrubbery around us begins to rustle.

"I'm sorry," Nova says quietly, voice cracking at the end. "I—"

"Hush," the vampyré commands. Nova's teeth snap together with surprising force, enough to fill the small clearing with the sound. "Good girl," he delivers smoothly. "The sire bond is a most curious thing, don't you agree? The will to disobey any command is nonexistent." His lips curl into a malicious smirk.

"*Bastard*." The word issues from Naomi's mouth with a foul vengeance. She holds a rigid stance with fists clenched at her side, her bracers burning bright.

"I can assure you, madame, I am not." I can practically hear the smile in his voice. "Your sister and I have had many enlightening conversations over the past few days. About guardians and ancient relics. About you and your friends. I assume the young woman presenting her back to me is the infamous *Calliope* and the lovely blade in her hand is Vogart's."

No one answers. I swallow down the snaking fear inside of me, keenly aware of my vulnerabilities. The blade grows heavy in my hand as the weight of everyone's gaze falls upon it and me.

"No deal," JJ says.

Naomi's eyes seek her sisters in earnest, but by her look of misery, I can only imagine Nova's eyes remain downcast. I steal myself against the current of my emotions, forcing them to the side to focus on the situation at hand.

A howl cuts through the night air, soon followed by another. Then another.

"More company," the vampyré says dryly, "and here I thought this was a private party. Very well then," he continues with a sigh, "Nova, kill them. *Golems*"—the shrubbery surrounding the clearing gives an angry shake—"*kill.*"

In a tidal wave, they swarm us—*golems,* grotesque creatures composed of old earth and rot. They stand some three feet tall and are shaped to form some beastly semblance of a man. In their possession are crude iron-wrought knifes and daggers.

We surge into action. Fighting to flee. Naomi flashes toward me, seizing one of my guns and immediately firing into the hoard to accompany Wyatt. I spin around as she steps past me, gauging the scene as my heart goes into overdrive. The vampyré is nowhere to be seen, but Nova—sweet and funny Nova—is barreling toward JJ. JJ who doesn't have a single thing to protect himself with other than his fists. With a strangled roar, Nova breaks free from her restraints, her eyes bleeding red and canines lengthening to deadly points. A bullet hits her shoulder, but it does little to stop her.

"No!" The scream pitches from my body just as a golem launches itself at me, along with three others. The blade cuts through them easily enough, but my fists do more damage with the help of the dormant Borealis Matter inside me suddenly flaring to life.

There is a firestorm occurring around me. Shots are sounding off at every moment, more than seem logical. My ears ring with shock, but there is nothing to be done about it. The fight drives me into a tunnel vision. All I can focus on are the little savages assaulting me. Their knives glance off my duster as I spirit around them. They haven't a clue to go for my legs with no conscious thought tumbling through their empty heads. It's lucky for me that they aren't creative with their method of killing.

They're senseless creatures, driven to obey the command of their master by dark magic. If they had any sense to them and attacked us with direction or coordination, we would be in much worse trouble. As it is, their bloodlust is enough to keep us on our toes.

"Wolves at six o'clock!" Naomi shouts. My foot plows through the chest of a golem when her alert sounds. I almost topple over as I attempt to spin myself around—the golem still lodged around my foot. With a vicious swing of my leg, it slides off and catapults into a few of the other creatures. The impact takes them out, and they crumble to the ground in heaps of black earth.

This is why we'll win. Because we work together as a unit, taking up each other's slack and watching each other's back. The methodical order by which we eliminate the golems balances me. It keeps the darkness away with its whispers of malice and menace.

I take a short moment to scan the forest. The wolves are difficult to spot, despite the brief flashes of light from their rapid fire. They hide amongst the trees, using the thick trunks for coverage against the threat of return fire. I swing my gun in their direction, letting off a flurry of shots toward the southeast.

"Motherfu—" I rip the golem from my back onto the ground with such force it bursts immediately upon impact. My chest heaves as I step in a tight circle. The golems still surround me. It seems like no matter how many I take out, more and more take their place. The whispering darkness in my head sounds louder.

"Fall back!" Wyatt shouts.

Wyatt manages to grab one of the assault rifles when his handheld is finished, taking out half a dozen golems with his usual precision. JJ is—I stop midstep, almost falling to my knees at the sight of JJ struggling to pull himself into the van with one arm. His feet fail him as his spare hand spreads itself over the growing dark spot across his abdomen.

"JJ!"

Naomi fumbles backward, reduced to using her body as a weapon to defend against the attack. The contractions of my heart feel like an assault all their own. I can't seem to get a grasp on my breath, and the spike of adrenaline at the sight of JJ does nothing to help. I fire the last of my rounds into the mass of unearthly creatures, but it's clear what holds their interest now: Wyatt, Naomi, and most importantly, JJ's blood. And more trouble is coming. Large dark figures start to bloom from all around. Wolves.

"Callie, let's go!" Naomi shouts, swinging her fist and knocking back a golem.

But I can't. I realize it the instant Wyatt starts firing into the hoard. There is at least a dozen golem still after us, and all of them standing between them and me. The darkness threatens to take control, my desire to destroy the golems almost blinding me to my senses. *I have to be strong.*

Though the gunfire from the trees ceases momentarily, I know they are closing in. The wolves. My heartbeat sounds loudly in my ear as I watch Wyatt begin to use the assault rifle as a club.

"Go!" I yell back, working at undoing my belt and dragon skin armor. "Take care of him!" Naomi scrambles into the side of the van, a flash of understanding crossing her face as I chuck the clothing off me. I run the blade over my forearm, letting it sink deeply into my flesh to draw fresh blood. "I'll find her. Just go!"

The hoard stills as one, each taking their time to turn and face me. Their glass-like eyes almost seem to gleam with hunger. I take a tentative step back, ignoring the pain in my arm and the heavy stream of blood. If it's blood they want. It's blood they will get. I just hope Nova and the vampyré aren't still lurking. The truck rumbles to life, stealing some of the golems' attention. *At least they're out*, I think, *now time to fly*.

I turn and race into the forest, heading straight for the wolves. It's a daring move. A stupid move, really. They could cut me down with their bullets easily, but they could have done so before and hadn't. I have to believe they won't now.

The golems give chase, just as I knew they would. Their hog-like grunting and hollering sounding nearby along with the beating of their stump-like legs against the ground. I can see them more clearly now, the wolves hidden amongst the trees. They press closely to the trunks, guns positioned at the ready in their hands.

"Fire!" The command comes from farther away. It spurs me on faster, along with the lurch of fear curled deep in my belly. The firestorm begins once again, bullets raining down every side of me in sharp *cracks* that make my ears scream. But they don't fire at me. I fight the urge not to cry in relief, knowing all too well my fight is far from done. I swerve to the west, back from where we first came, ducking around trees and letting the commotion behind me drown in the sound of my heavy breathing. I can feel my energy depleting and glance at my injured arm. That's when I'm hit. A body slamming so strongly into my side I bash into the nearest tree and smash my head. *Hard*.

I slump to the ground, the wind knocked out of me completely, as my vision blurs around the edges. A hand pushes against my shoulder, sending me back against the tree trunk. My struggle is weak, pathetic really, but I do my best. It's a stupid move, draining me of my remaining energy and propelling me into unconsciousness.

DANCE WITH THE DARK SIDE

- Chapter 8 -

Failure is always a bitter pill to swallow—even more so knowing it's your fault. And I failed. Failed Nova and her sisters. Failed my brother. Failed my family and the Wardens of Starlight. It makes me feel ill. I need more than a Hail Mary pass to turn the tide in my favor. I need a miracle. If those even exist. With my luck, the world has most likely run out of them.

Last night's end is still fuzzy in my mind, and from the way my head aches, I assume I have a slight concussion. The cut on my arm is healed, no stitches required, though a long pink scar remains. The results of the Borealis Matter, no doubt, I think to myself. How much longer can I count on it to boost me? When exactly will the mystical power fade from my bones? Will it ever? Even now I feel some intrinsic connection to the bracers around my wrists, a certainty that we are now... one. With any luck, the Borealis Matter will continue to work its strange magic and heal the remainder of my head injury. I cannot afford the disadvantage. Not when miracles are scarce.

I assume it's morning, which means JJ, Naomi, and Wyatt will be nearing Calgary. *God, I hope JJ is all right.* A stab of worry drives through my heart at the memory of his blood-soaked abdomen. *He's okay. He has to be.* There are protocols for battle-time injuries. While one drives, the other stabilizes the wound. *Will it have been enough*? My feet take me back and forth across the cell I've been placed in. *JJ is strong*, I tell myself sternly. He *will* survive, and so will I.

Vogart's Blade and my butterfly blade are absent from my person when I awoke, leaving me with only my bracers to assist me and another item on my list to take back from the wolves. *As if I don't have enough on my plate.* I know I have only a few days—a week tops—to finish this job. The others will return, and the Council won't hesitate to coordinate a counterattack. *If that happens...* I shiver at the thought. If the Council comes before I can complete the job, more pressing and permanent consequences of failure will hang over me.

I glance about the room, my eyes landing on the cell bars that keep me contained. Unfortunately, attempting to bend them using the bracers and the Borealis inside of me isn't an option. I can't afford to waste the Borealis Matter. Besides, they can't leave me in here forever, can they? Surely someone is watching my agitated movements from the camera at the far end of the room? Will they send someone down to interrogate me? Will they try and torture information out of me? I release a heavy sigh, stopping my pacing to sit on the cot in the corner of the cell where I had woken. They'll probably send *him* down to interrogate me and use the soulmark against me.

A new worry blossoms in my chest. I must stay strong. Keep my muddled head in the game.

A door opens and closes somewhere nearby. My heart beats a fraction faster. Footsteps yield a soft dull thudding as they make their way in my direction, and I look to the room's only door expectantly. Seconds seem like minutes as I wait for it to open, and then, it does.

I sit up straighter, tamping down my worry with ease. It's him, just as I predicted. Our gazes lock immediately, dark brown to dark brown. He pulls two chairs into the room behind him, setting them across from each other with but a few feet between them. He leaves the room once more to retrieve a tray filled with a small meal and approaches the cell with it in hand.

"Hungry?" A steaming cup of tea and a small plate with some kind of pastry sits upon it.

"Not particularly," I tell him, though we both know it's a lie. I give the food and drink a skeptical once-over to further my point. No doubt laced with some witchy mojo meant to make me more malleable. I haven't forgotten about the wolves' alliance with the witches.

He raises a thick eyebrow. "When was the last time you ate?"

"Doesn't matter," I respond curtly after his eyes wander briefly down my body. I'm not built like some kind of Barbie doll. I have hips and long legs, muscular arms and taut abs that I've worked hard for in the gym. I've a fighter's body... almost like his. Except where Keenan's facial features are strong, even a bit harsh, mine have a softer touch to them.

"Eat," he counters, the muscles of his forearm straining slightly as his grip tightens on the tray. It's my turn to raise an eyebrow at the roughened command.

"No."

He turns and sets down the tray on a thin metal table behind him. "I hope you're not thinking of starving yourself," he comments while crossing his arms over his broad chest.

"I'm thinking more along the lines of fasting. Or one of those diets where you don't eat or drink anything your captors bring you. You know, just in case they're trying to poison you."

"Sounds a lot like starving yourself," he tells me dryly.

"I can see how the concept would go over your head," I tell him sweetly. He grunts in response, taking something out of his pocket and going to the cell door. It opens a moment later, his large frame filling the space.

"We need to talk." He jerks his head toward the chairs and leaves me space enough to pass by him. "Hands behind your back," he tells me once I've seated myself. I do as he asks, barely restraining my smirk as he secures a pair of handcuffs just above the bracers.

"Did you want to continue our discussion on my eating habits?"

Keenan is good at keeping his discontent hidden behind a blank facade. Without a sound, he sits across from me, legs spread wide as he rests his elbows on his thighs. He barely needs to lean forward to disrupt my personal space, but that's the point. I stretch my legs out in the open space between his legs, crossing them at the ankles.

"We have both your knives, but couldn't get your bracelets off. Why is that?"

"Is that right?" I let my amusement show, a soft smile brimming on my lips. "I hadn't noticed."

His scowl informs me of his disapproval. "Why couldn't we get the bracelets off?" he asks again. My smile grows wider. The bracers can only be taken off by the wearer. Though, it isn't completely unheard of for the wearer's hands to be removed as well to do the job. He doesn't need to know that though.

"I'm afraid I can't say." Keenan leans closer, close enough that I can see a few faint scars running along the top of his scalp through his closely cropped black hair. "Trade secret."

He gives a slight nod, eyes darting to my lips. I let my smile fall faster than a greyhound out its gate. "Last night those carvings lit up with some kind of green light. What was it?"

"Hmmm...." I let silence reign between us, taking my fill of the sterile wall above his head. "If I correctly remember, that's *also* a trade secret."

Keenan leans back in his chair, folding his arms back over his chest. "You seem to have a lot of those."

"What? Trade secrets?" He nods, and though his eyes go half-mast, they retain their piercing quality.

"If you won't answer questions about your bracelets, then we can talk about something else."

"Oh, you're definitely not getting an answer about the 'bracelets.' Tell me, if I had drunk or eaten any of that food you brought down, would it have made me tell you?"

Keenan pauses. "Yes." *Knew it,* I think vindictively.

"By human alteration or witchcraft?"
Keenan straightens his posture, rolling his neck from side to side. A distinct crack sounds from the motion, and then he is staring at me once more, eyes more alert than before. "Witchcraft." Of course, it would be witchcraft. Thank God I didn't take any of it. "My turn," he continues, unperturbed that he has relayed this information to me. "Where's your soulmark?"

The question catches me off guard, and I pull myself upward to mimic his posturing. My crossed legs tuck themselves under the chair as I eye him more thoughtfully. He doesn't flinch beneath my studious regard, and I make sure to take my time this go around. Even sitting he is a large man, taking up more space than seems humanly possible. It would be intimidating to a lesser person, but it suits him. The muscles and tattoos and ever-present glower. It *fits* him.

I take a deep breath, letting it release in a steady stream of air. "I don't see how that's any of your business."

Keenan snorts, and I dare think a hint of a smirk plays around the corner of his mouth. His own soulmark is on display, hidden somewhere amongst the myriad of tattoos covering his forearm.

"Well," he drawls, "you know where mine is. I thought it only fair to know where yours is."

"Life isn't fair," I tell him flatly. Keenan leans forward once more, taking his time to draw his gaze up my body. Though I keep an unaffected air, my heartbeat is not inclined to do the same. It races along as his eyes linger over my waist, as if somehow drawn to the mark hidden there. When his eyes return, they have softened. It's not what I expect.

"You don't have to be afraid of me—"

"I'm not afraid of you," I interrupt quickly. He quirks a wry grin.

"Your scent says otherwise, that and the sound of your heart." I force myself to calm, thinking of silent nights huddled beneath layers of fur-lined blankets and attempting to count a million dazzling stars. My calm returns. Mostly. "Impressive," he murmurs, shifting back only slightly.

"I'm not afraid of you."

"And you don't have to be," he continues smoothly. "You're my soulmark. I'll always protect you."

I swallow at that, feeling my heart give a traitorous leap at his words. *Starry nights, Calliope*, I scold myself, *think of starry nights.*

"Well," I begin, finally resolving my composure, "it's in your best interest to be afraid of me. You stole from my people, and we won't stop until we take back what's ours. What does a pack of wolves want with the Amethyst of the Aztecs anyway? What good will it do you?" I uncross my legs and set my feet shoulder width apart.

"We're keeping it safe," he assures me calmly.

I scoff. "That's our job."

"Didn't do a very good job of it, did you?" I purse my lips at the slight, though there is hardly a thing to say against it. "There's another pack who wanted the ring—"

"The something-wolfs?" I ask tartly.

Keenan grunts his affirmation. "The Wselfwulf's. They've made some deal with a vampire—"

"*Vampyré*," I correct.

"Are you going to let me finish?" he asks, tone deceptively light.

"Are you going to tell me something I don't know?"

Keenan scowls, but I shrug in return.

"They're working together, aren't they?"

"Yes," he answers, "they were trying to get the ring for the vamp. He goes by the name Vrana." Again, I shrug. He is only confirming Naomi and my disjointed theory. Keenan's eyes narrow upon me at the flippant action.

"I already told you, my people will retrieve the ring. It doesn't matter who has it. They won't stop until they do, and neither will I."

Keenan looks wary, letting his shoulders roll back. "You know, I didn't think I'd ever find my soulmark. Not all lycans do," he tells me with a sigh. "But here you are. Handcuffed in my alpha's cellar while I question you. I don't even know your name." He gives a short bark-like laugh. "Hell, I'm pretty sure you hate me."

The last comment stings more than it should. As offhanded as it may be, it hits a mark I thought well hidden. Hating the supernatural is the common thread among all Wardens of Starlight. Our purpose, to eliminate the supernatural and protect the people of Earth, binding us together. Except my track record of summoning the feeling wasn't so stellar. My lack of it had landed innocents dead. I let my eyes fall shut for a short moment. *Hate,* I wish it was that easy.

"It's Calliope," I say, surprising myself as I offer the information freely. His eyes widen, lips parting slightly to mime the words. I bite my lip to keep from saying anything else. *Stupid girl,* I scold myself internally.

"That's a beautiful name, Calliope. I'm Keenan," he finally says, leaving us both to color at the compliment.

"Don't," I tell him, feeling a wave of distrust and dismay flood my body.

Both of his eyebrows raise. "Don't what?"

"Don't talk like that," I force out, feeling my cheeks heat even further. "It's unnecessary and highly unprofessional."

His eyebrows hike higher. "Unnecessary? Unprofessional?"

"Yes," I sputter, feeling more flustered than necessary. My gaze dodges to the left as I give the handcuffs a frustrated tug. He's probably trying to soften me up with compliments, but I'm not a fool to that game anymore after Wyatt.

The heat of Keenan's gaze is unexpectedly suffocating. "A beautiful name for a beautiful woman," he whispers in a husky timbre. Another well-placed hit. I smother my blush and turn a furious glare his way. He has a sort of smile on his perfectly chiseled face. The kind that softens the appearance of a man his size. It comes close to breaking my resolve, a fact only I am privy too.

With my resolve weakening, I do the only logical thing I can think of. I activate the bracers with a harsh twist. Snarling, I rip my arms outward, the handcuffs snapping easily. Feet planted firmly on the ground, I give a mighty push and send myself and the chair back several feet.

Keenan stands slowly, body alert and very much attuned to my own. Though my previous movement reeks of hostility, I rise from my chair with a cool disposition. The air seems to seize around us, constricting with constrained energy.

"Calliope—"

I give him a devastating smile. The one I like to save for special occasions such as these. "Call me, Callie."

Keenan's eyes narrow. The muscles bound to his body, holding tight before he charges. I move just as fast. The Borealis spurring me on.

I spin around as he nears, snatching the wooden chair as I go to swing it around and smash it against him. He lets out a coarse burst of air, saddling sideways upon impact. The chair doesn't break, but the crack and crunch it makes inform me one more hit will do the job. So be it. I propel myself in a wider circle—chair still in hand—and arch it upward to hit his back. But Keenan is prepared.

He ducks my second attempt and catches me around my middle. The chair clatters to the floor, my hands finding new purpose in groping his face, thumbs aiming for his umber eyes.

"Damnit!" he curses, releasing me. Keenan dodges backward and levels me with a glare. "I don't want to hurt you, Callie."

"Can't say I feel the same," I pant, launching myself at him again. Adrenalin flares inside of me, and not a beat behind it is my darkness egging me on. *If I can subdue him for just a moment, I can make a move for the door.* He blocks my right hook and scores with his fist, driving it into my side and effectively pushing me back. I move with the hit, fists in front of my face as I skip backward.

A scowl threatens at my brow while I weave from side to side, fists launching themselves at Keenan's torso and face in rapid succession. He's pulling his hits, and now he's refusing to do little more than hold a defensive position while I assail him.

"Fight back," I growl. *Fight back so I can end this.* But he doesn't.

A spell of nerves begins to gnaw at my focus—at my drive and energy. His defense is too tight. There is no managing a solid enough hit to break his stance. I let out another growl, this one full of pent-up frustration. I have failed so far, but not in this. The thought drives away the nerves and the darkness, as I forcefully draw on the Borealis Matter. The bracers shine more brightly as I throw out jabs and crosses.

A side kick pulls a grimace from his face. *Good.* I slip close to deliver a left hook, but it's the move he's been waiting for. Keenan redirects my fist, and with his other, then punches me in the chest. The hit is pulled, but I'm still left reeling and gasping as I teeter backward.

"I don't want to hurt you," he tells me, a pained expression on his face, one that isn't caused by my attacks.

"*I* want to hurt *you*," I snap back viciously, all too ready to launch myself back at him, the drive to put him down trumping all others.

"Why?" he asks breathlessly.

The question pulls me to an abrupt stop. With horrible realization, my mindless campaign falls out from under me. When did it turn from momentarily stunning him to putting him down into the ground in order to gain my release? I'd become senseless. Driven by the force inside me to inflict pain and death, and nothing else. *The darkness.* I take two steps back with a shaky gasp, eyes widening in revulsion at myself. Keenan approaches with cautious steps.

"Don't," I say in a ragged whisper. Dangerous thoughts fill my head. Some of them seemingly not my own. How did I not notice it coming to a head? If I can't differentiate between strategy and senseless fighting—senseless killing—then I'm no better than the monsters my people faced daily.

"It's okay, Calliope," he tells me gently in that gruff voice of his. "I'm not going to hurt you. No one is going to hurt you." My eyes shift to him and take in his proximity. When had he gotten so close? I shift back more, bumping into the cold bars of my cell.

"Don't." My teeth grind painfully together at the gripping panic flaying me. *Not again.* I can't lose myself again. He reaches out a hand tentatively, and I can't help but note how large and calloused it is. It nears my cheek with clear intent, but I break before I can feel his touch. "I said *don't.*"

I lash out. My fist slams into the center of his face with superhuman strength.

"Fuck!" He stumbles back, both hands going to cradle his nose as his eyes water. "Shit, Callie."

I stand in shock, fist still held at the ready, but feet planted firmly in place. My eyes dart to the door at the opposite end of the room. My escape. Yet, if I leave now, I might not be able to gain access to the house again. And I don't know if my blades or the ring are here. Keenan straightens, his eyes guarded as he takes in my stance. I let my arm fall and take a step forward.

"I told you...," I say, contrite.

"I wasn't going to hurt you," he tells me harshly, his hand still pinching tentatively at his nose.

I roll my eyes. "Let me see."

"No." He wears a scowl meant to dissuade me, and the entire population, from coming nearer, but I give no credibility to it.

"Stop being a baby and let me see. I think I broke it." He shifts out of my reach. "I'm trying to be nice," I snap. *I've also decided to stay,* I think to myself bitterly, *and it has nothing to do with the brute in front of me.*

"No thanks."

My hand darts out and grabs his wrist before he can stop me. His eyes widen in alarm as mine flash with triumph. When I pull his hand away, I don't take much account of the way my hand slips down a few inches, that is, until I feel it.

It's like being doused with ice water, bringing about a chill that wracks my body, only to be chased down by feverish flames. It is mind-numbing this feeling. This sensation. It dulls the senses and forces upon me wave after wave of intoxicating rapture.

The door to the cellar crashes open, and we leap apart, though our eyes are unable to release each other.

"Well, well, well," an oddly familiar arrogant voice coos. My gaze turns to him hesitantly, eyeing the newcomer with veiled interest. Had this man been one of the wolves robbing the Banks Facility? "Isn't this going to be fun."

Keenan's shoulders stiffen, his back going needle straight. He turns a vicious glare on the intruder, some twenty-something, raven-haired man with a devilish grin. It has little effect.

"It was nothing," Keenan manages to say past gritted teeth. I swallow at the harsh words, but make no move to speak up. The other man takes a step forward, mouth opening to address us once more when Keenan makes a beeline for the door. I watch with a grim expression on my face as Keenan's shoulder smashes into the man as he makes his escape.

"Don't take it too personally, sweetheart," the raven-haired man mocks, rubbing lightly at his chest as he observes me in my state of mild distress. *Too late for that*, I think, wondering what kind of wolf I've been left to deal with this time. "Be a doll and get back into your cell, will you? Someone will be down later with lunch, while I attend to Mr. Grouch."

Though his words are spoken jovially, the underlining steel to them isn't something I'm willing to test. Nor are the two men who stand only a few feet behind him. I walk stiffly back into the cell. Closing the door with a heavy hand as I stare down the grinning wolf.

"Good girl," he mocks, before walking out and closing the cellar door firmly behind him.

GIRL TALK

- Chapter 9 -

Hours pass slowly as I drift in and out of fretful sleep. Though my body longs for rest, my mind is a flurry of activity, planning and plotting what to do next. A rapping sounds against the cellar room door, three quick knocks, one after the other, and effectively pulling me from my reverie. A blonde head pokes out from behind the door a second later.

"Knock, knock," she announces in a cheery voice, stepping fully inside. Her hands go behind her back as she approaches my cell. Head twisting with feigned curiosity as she examines the room. Not that there is much too examine now that the chairs and debris have been cleared.

I give her a long once-over during her perusal of the room. Long blonde hair. Blue eyes. Not exactly tall, but with the heels, she gains a few extra inches. *Barbie doll,* I think faintly. It's a far cry from the last person I saw. Some lanky teenage boy carrying a tray with an impressively stacked sandwich and a glass of water on it. The new food tray replaced the old, my refusal still standing strong. But this woman brought nothing with her, except for that curious look on her face.

"You know," she drawls, eyes sparkling mischievously, "the last time I was down here, I thought it was some kind of sex dungeon."

Huh. I give a rather pathetic raise of my shoulders in response. My energy has long since left me since this morning, and refusing the food has left me feeling more drained than I want to be. "Interesting theory," I finally say as her expectant gaze lingers on.

"It's not," she assures me, leaning up against the bars of the cell, "but, rest assured, sex has been had down here." The blonde attempts to wiggle her brows then shoots me a wink instead. "The pack prefers to use this place as a holding cell of sorts—oh, I'm Quinn, by the way." She outstretches her hand to me, easily slipping it through the bars. "I'm a 'normy,' if you were curious about that. It's what I'm calling all nonsupernatural persons. And yes, I am working on a better name."

"How about human?" I offer halfheartedly.

She rolls her eyes, hand still extended and waiting expectantly. "That's so passé," Quinn informs me. "Are you going to shake my hand or keep sitting there brooding?"

"I'm concussed," I tell her dryly, "so no. I'm not going to get up and shake your hand." It drops back down to her side, but she remains leaning against the bars, giving me an unimpressed look. "And I'm not brooding. I'm *plotting.*"

"Oh!" Her eyes sparkle with true interest. "I love a good plot. You know, before finding out that all of this was real—lycans, witches, and vampires—I was a *very* distinguished thief." A soft humming stirs from her throat as she gains a far-off look in her eyes. "I could orchestrate some pretty grand schemes back in the day. 'The day' being just a couple weeks ago. You and yours should really think about upgrading your security system against *non*paranormal beings."

Her words hit their mark, but it's the somewhat smug expression dripping from her eyes that makes my blood pressure rise. "You planned that? *You*?"

"Well, not just by myself. I have a partner in crime now—literally." She lets out a soft, breathy laugh. "Ryatt helped coordinate specifics since I'm used to doing more solo ventures."

"You," I breathe. "I remember you." And I do. She was the human hidden amongst the wolves on the night of the first wolf attack.

"Yeah," she responds, followed by a light scoff, "and I remember you. You tackled and pinned me to the ground. Then had some weird panic attack. Then"—her eyes go slightly wide—"you stabbed my boyfriend in the foot. He was not pleased about that, and you ruined a very nice pair of boots. Don't worry, it healed quickly enough, and he got a new pair of boots."

"I did not have a panic attack," I snap back. I'm surprised at the amount of venom coating my words, and from the looks of it, so is she. A flash of momentary distress flickers over her features before it smooths back down into a perfect mask of indifference.

"Fine," Quinn responds, tone bearing frost, "you didn't. *Whatever*."

"Is there a reason you're down here?" I finally ask, forcing my sour attitude down.

She flicks her hair over her shoulder. "I just thought you might like to know that we have your weapons here. And until we can figure out what to do with you, they'll be staying in our possession."

How unsurprising. "Like calls to like," I tell her dully.

"And what's that supposed to mean?" she asks after a moment's hesitation. I put on a bemused, yet patronizing look and draw myself up from the bed.

"You've heard the phrase, 'birds of a feather flock together,' right?" I ask as I approach Quinn's leaning form. She nods, lips thinning ever so slightly as mine stretch into a wide smile. "Good. Then you'll understand why it's not so hard for me to believe that a *thief*, and her rousing band of wolf thieves, would decide to keep pieces of property that don't belong to them."

Quinn flashes me a false smile. "Gee, thanks for explaining that to me."

"You're welcome," I quip, walking back over to the cot and sitting down. There's a dull, yet persistent, throbbing at the base of my skull. It somehow radiates down into the rest of my body, making my new bruises slightly more painful. Fighting had proven to be a bad decision for my mild concussion. "Anything else?"

"It could be worse, you know."

"Worse than having priceless artifacts stolen from your community? Worse than risking everything to save a friend only to fail? Worse than being stuck in this glorified dog cage?" I scoot back on the cot, resting my back and head against the cool cement wall. My eyes trained straight ahead.

"Your stuff could be with the vampire." I turn my head to read the look on her face. The cool mask she wears seems to have dropped, replaced instead with something a bit more honest.

Human, I think. What is this human girl doing here? And helping a pack of wolves, no less? The man she spoke of earlier, Ryatt, must be a wolf in this pack. And if this woman is allowed to know their supernatural secret, then she must be his soulmark. I pivot my gaze, swallowing past the odd lump in my throat.

"It's *vampyré*, technically speaking," I correct her gently, "and you're right. It would be much worse if the vampyré got hold of our stuff."

Quinn lets out a little sigh and folds down to take a seat on the floor. "Vampyré sounds terribly chic in comparison," she voices thoughtfully.

"They're definitely terrible," I remark. We make eye contact. A strange understanding passes between us.

"I know," she says, a small frown pulling at her brow as her gaze darts to the floor. "The vampyré who was out there yesterday night—he's the one we're trying to keep all your stuff from—his name is Jakub Vrana. I used to work for him, and I know just how terrible he can be."

"Do you make a habit of working for supernatural creatures, or is it just a weird coincidence?"

A laugh tumbles from her mouth as she shakes her head. "The latter," she confides, stretching her legs out with a happy sigh. "I didn't actually know I was working for a vampyré until I met Ryatt, which is a whole other story that I will not get into unless tequila is involved."

"So, you took the ring to keep it away from this Mr. Vrana?"

Quinn stays quiet for a while, mulling over my answer. At one point, her gaze shifts to the camera in the far corner of the room, looking contrite.

"Yes," she finally says. "He's been after it for some time now, but we can't seem to ferret out why."

I raise my shoulders an inch then let them fall. "True daylight rings are something like the Holy Grail to vampyrés. They have all this power and strength, which only grows with age, but they're bound to the night. It's their greatest limitation, and a daylight ring circumvents that limitation." I hate to think about what Vogart's Blade might mean to the collection of vampyré on this earth, but it's one I cannot avoid. If the legends are true, it could turn back only the newly turned, which might not mean much to centuries-old vampyrés. Unfortunately, the blade is still a weapon to be coveted, and if knowledge of its true origins is learned, we'd have another problem on our hands.

"Gotcha."

"Anything else of significance happen last night that I should know about? Did any of your pack happen to grab a thigh-length jacket from the forest floor?" I ask the questions lightly and manage a cool veneer, though I'm desperate to know more news.

"I don't know about the jacket, but I can check for you," she offers. "The only other significant thing that happened last night was Mr. Vrana and his associate getting away."

The lingering worry I harbor over Nova washes away with Quinn's news. She is still alive. There is still hope. I settle back against the wall a bit deeper and let out a long, steady sigh. Good. This is good.

"Vampyrés are known for their speed," I comment. "It's not too surprising they got away, especially considering they were prepared for our arrival."

Quinn's eyes narrow. "He did seem unusually prepared, but the associate of his is a new addition."

"Interesting."

"It is," she agrees. "After hearing Ryatt's version of last night's events, it sounds like Vrana was more than prepared, for both you and your friends, along with the pack. Whatever those creatures were, they stirred up enough mayhem to distract the pack and your people from chasing after Vrana and his associate. It was a well-planned exit."

"It's unwise to underestimate a vampyré," I say, avoiding the topic she edges around.

"Trust me. I know." A dark look flashes behind her eyes before they focus on me with clear intent. "Vrana is working with a rival pack to secure the ring, but even they wouldn't have known you'd be coming last night. We certainly didn't expect to see you. Not after that small group of your people ran the other night during a different fight at the territory line. So how could Vrana have possibly known you would come back? He's not omniscient."

I focus on my breathing instead of Quinn's questions and implications. It comes at short intervals and makes the throbbing in my head seem more pronounced, especially as I try to think of an answer to give Quinn. Is it worth it to tell her the truth? What will it accomplish if I do? I certainly didn't trust this pack of wolves with the truth about Vogart's Blade.

"Well?"

"The new associate, she's my... friend," I choke out, a storm of emotion clogged in my throat. "My best friend. She was with the group that was out here the other night, doing surveillance on the wolves and the witches. Your Mr. Vrana took her."

"Oh." The small utterance passes as a condolence, and again our eyes meet. "He certainly likes to make a habit of killing people as a means to show off his power," she says bitterly.

"We did come for the ring," I tell her truthfully, "but we also came for her. We thought Vrana turned her just to leave her at the mercy of the wolves."

"What exactly were you going to do if you caught your friend? Aren't new vampyrés supposed to be crazy?"

"Not so much crazy, as they're driven by bloodlust," I remark, dodging the question.

"Sounds crazy to me!" she chirps. "Anyway, aren't you and your friends like, professional supernatural haters?"

"Professional supernatural haters?" I repeat dubiously. "That is—who said that?"

She waves a hand dismissively at my indignation. "It doesn't matter. It's totally obvious to anyone with eyes that you don't like supernaturals. Which begs the question as to what you planned to do with your newly turned vampyré friend."

"Turn her back." The words feel like bombs as they drop from my mouth. The weight of their significance heightened when said aloud to one of my captors. Quinn looks startled from their impact. "And we're not professional haters," I correct before she can chime in. "We're the Wardens of Starlight. We're blessed with the power of the Aurora Borealis to protect the people of the world from dark supernatural creatures."

"But vampyrés are dark supernatural creatures," she ventures softly.

I give a grim nod. "I know. But there was—there is—a small chance that if we get her back to our base, we can reverse the effects. The longer she stays turned though, the smaller our chance gets." The words are painful to say, but that happens sometimes when dealing with the truth. Chances of helping Nova grow smaller and smaller as the minutes tic by, but I'm determined to hold out hope.

"Reverse vampyrism? Like with a potion?"

I don't offer any confirmation, though I hear the trace of curiosity in her voice. "All magic—curses, spells, and charms—have a counteract of some kind. A way to reverse what has been done. A back door. A loophole," I explain. "Even the strongest of spells and curses do."

Quinn remains quiet for a moment, mulling over my words. I feel the seconds pass by like minutes, my mounting anxiety growing as the silence stretches on.

"I don't think everything has a reverse," she says pensively, her sharp crystal blue eyes cutting into mine. "What about soulmarks?"

Well, I didn't expect that to come out of her mouth. Nor the look of earnestness she wears. "The soulmark is a bit different," I concede, "but not in the way you're thinking. The 'curse' of the soulmark is being split in the first place. It's the coming together that is the counteract."

Quinn frowns. "But why did it have to be that way in the first place?"

"I don't know. Maybe it was some vengeful god or spiteful spirit who triggered the soulmark. There are too many legends and too much lore from a whole variety of different supernaturals to know." I give a fleeting shrug. "Maybe it's because finding your true soul mate was always meant to come with a price."

"Do you really think that?" I give another rise of my shoulders in answer. "What about Keenan? You know, the big guy you broke a chair against?"

I flush unwittingly. "What about him?"

Her eyebrows shoot to her hairline as she levels me with a look of exasperation. "Seriously?" I cross my arms over my chest and direct my gaze to the side. "You know, he might be gruff and moody, and he hardly ever breaks a smile, but he's pretty considerate, all things considered. And loyal. And when he does smile, it has a very swoon-worthy effect."

I let out a small huff. "If you like him so much, then why don't you date him."

"Don't get me wrong, Keenan's great. A total hunk, but he's not my type. I've always leaned more toward the rebellious bad boys, ya know? That reckless behavior gets me all riled up."

"Why are you telling me this?" I ask through barely gritted teeth, heart hammering in my chest.

Quinn lets one eyebrow arch delicately this time, her shoulders rolling back as that smug look ventures back onto her features. "We all know, Callie. That look of pure orgasmic bliss on your face when you touched the soulmark on his arm kind of gives the game away. Don't you think?"

A full flush covers my neck and cheeks at her brazen tone. "I did not have a look of... a look of...." I screw my eyes up momentarily as I sputter on. "There was no look, all right?"

Quinn gives me a pitying glance before pointedly looking at the camera across the room. "Are you sure you want to stick with that answer? Or should we review the footage?"

The color intensifies on my face. I can feel it. "That won't be necessary," I tell her tersely.

She stands, the motion made slightly wobbly by her tremendous heels. Her hands are quick to wipe away the small margin of dust and dirt that has collected on her clothing before she returns her full attention to me. "Did I mention you'll be having dinner tonight with him?"

"Excuse me?" The news startles the color from my cheeks.

Her head bobs along solemnly, even though a grin begins to play at the corner of her lips. Quinn walks toward the cellar door. "Yep! Someone will be down to escort you to a bathroom so you can clean up a bit, and then you'll be taken to the dining room. Don't worry, it will just be you and him."

"I don't think—"

Quinn's voice steamrolls over my protests. "All right? Great! They'll be down in an hour or so. Oh, and you should really try and eat something. It will help with your concussion. Plus, Zoe is cooking, and she's brilliant in the kitchen. Okay, see you later!" With a dainty wiggle of her fingers, she peels out of the room before I can say anything further, the heavy slam of the door getting the last say in the matter.

LET'S MAKE A DEAL

- Chapter 10 -

The person they send down is—and I admit this quite begrudgingly—charming. Atticus looks like the boy next door all grown up and filled out with muscle. There's a disarming effect to his smile, one that makes it slightly difficult to keep a stoic atmosphere about my person. He wears it the entire time he escorts me to the guest room and bathroom, as well as to the dining room.

"What the...?" My voice trails off in mild disgust as I survey the simpering glow of the candelabra and spread of food meant for someone with a far more voracious appetite than me. This is the dining room? It looks to hold a party of ten rather than a meal for two. My feet are glued to the floor as I continue to appraise the room.

"This looks like Irina's work," Atticus laments, hand scratching at the back of his neck as he passes me a what-can-I-tell-ya type grin. "She's very enthusiastic about new soulmarks."

"She can take her enthusiasm and shove it up her ass," I mutter, taking my seat like a petulant child.

"So...." I begin, stretching out my legs beneath the table. I'd been lent a clean set of clothes. Simple black pants and a quarter-length black shirt. Nothing fancy, but highly preferable to my dirt and bloodstained clothes. "Where is he?"

"Right here," a voice interjects from the other side of the room. My head whips to the side to see Keenan standing in the midst of the doorway, his bulking frame taking up the majority of it. He's changed too, but not into anything impressive. Unless that is, one considers how flattering the cut of the shirt looks against his sculpted torso. Or the way his dark pants hug his thighs. Keenan eyes the table speculatively, heaving a sigh as he enters fully into the room. "Interesting setup," he comments, eyes shifting to me.

"Have fun you two," Atticus says. "No knife fights please."

I roll my eyes, but give the knife snuggled up to my plate a somewhat lustful glance. I can't afford to waste my energy on another fight, even if my headache from earlier has washed away with the scalding hot shower I took. The last of what remained of the concussion will heal overnight, of this I'm certain, but only if I replenish my body with food.

"You look... clean," he says, taking the seat next to me at the corner of the table. I scoot my legs back at the action, pulling further into my seat to make my sentiments about the current arrangement clear.

"You look unscathed," I reply.

He gives me a wry grin. "Lycan healing and witchcraft."

I turn my attention over to the plates of food displayed on the table. A pot roast with baby carrots and onions. Creamy mashed potatoes. Green beans with what looks to be bits of bacon. A basket full of rolls and a large saucer filled with gravy. "Zoelle cooked," Keenan explains. "She owns a—"

I give a sharp shake of my head, cutting off his sentence. "I don't care." His hands pause midreach for the serving fork and knife placed next to the meat.

"I've been told it isn't laced with anything," he says carefully, continuing the process of filling his plate. "And even if it were, I'd be consuming whatever you did."

The food does look good, I think. It smells amazing too. "What about our drinks?" I gesture weakly to the filled glasses of water set before us. "The food might not be laced, but my drink could be." Keenan sighs and stops what he's doing to take my glass and drink a gulp of the water.

"Satisfied?" he asks.

I sniff delicately. "Enough, I suppose." I let Keenan finish filling his plate before placing small scoops onto my own. My stomach might have won the battle, but my pride is in it for the petty war. I can feel his eyes weigh down upon me as I help myself to the food. They linger over my forearms that boast numerous tattoos, each undoubtedly looking for my elusive soulmark.

"I didn't ask them to do all of this," he says once I've finished and poke at my food with a fork. I give him a blank stare in return. "The dim lighting. The candle thing. The fancy food. We were just supposed to talk."

I spy a bit of color fuse his cheeks as he explains himself and hold back a smirk. "Just supposed to talk? The dinner wasn't supposed to be included?"

"No." He shakes his head, fork stabbing into a carrot. "I mean, it was. You haven't eaten all day, but I didn't mean for it to be so… elaborate."

"But you did want us to talk over dinner? Privately?" He gives a short nod, the guilty flush building on his face. "Like a *date*?" The fork drops from his fingers, landing with a clatter on the porcelain plate. "Careful, wouldn't want to ruin all this finery." I'm surprised at how teasing the words come out and reel back in my seat. Keenan doesn't notice, at least I don't think he does. His eyes are too focused on his dinner plate and cutlery.

"I'm sure I'd be forgiven if I did," he finally says, eyes returning to me as he subtly straightens. "This wasn't meant to be a date," he confides. "It was meant to be a negotiation. My alpha thought it would be best for me to handle the matter, seeing as we're soulmarks."

I scowl angrily at the reminder and stab into the mashed potatoes. It's not nearly as gratifying as I hoped it would be, but the forkful I jam into my mouth is. A tiny whimper escapes at the buttery concoction. *Damn.* When I dare to meet his gaze, I find him watching my movements with unveiled interest.

No. Not interest. There's too much intensity behind it. For a long moment, I'm reminded vividly of the way Wyatt used to look at me. The lust-filled glances. The wanting looks. But this is different. There is more to his gaze than just unbridled lust. There's a deeper want searing through it. It's the difference, I realize, between the way a man looks at you and the way a boy would.

"Good?" His rumbling vibrato rolls over my skin like a summer's breeze.

"It's... adequate," I mumble, scolding myself once again for slipping. My earlier honest conversation with Quinn, combined with my refreshing shower, has left me feeling a little too generous and open. *Too vulnerable.*

"I always thought the Wardens and their infamous warriors were just some scary bedtime story my mother would tell me to make me behave."

"A scary bedtime story?"

He nods, chewing his food quickly before responding. "There isn't too much to be scared of when you're a lycan, but I suppose the same could be said for all supernatural creatures. We're stronger and faster than humans. We don't succumb to illnesses easily. Of course, the threat of exposure haunts us, but other than that and the occasional sworn enemy, it's your kind that's meant to scare us straight."

"And do I scare you?"

I should have anticipated the attentive regard I receive for my question, but it still draws the hair on the back of my neck to attention. Our eyes clash in a battle of wills. Neither of us willing to break.

"No," he finally says. The word comes out harsher than I expect. My eyes dive toward my plate of food, already almost half gone due to my small portion sizes.

"Well," I begin, "maybe you should be. The Wardens are everything your mother told you about and more. So much more," I trail off in a whisper.

The room grows to a stout silence as we continue to eat, neither of us willing to end the hushed interim. Too soon my food is gone, my stomach aching for a few helpings more—

"Eat," Keenan grunts, eyeing me over a forkful of pot roast.

"I'm full." The look he spares me expresses his thoughts on the matter. I let out an impatient sigh. "Are we going to negotiate anytime soon, or were you waiting for us to talk over a shared dessert?" I mean for it to sound more sarcastic, but the passive hostility falls flat. It makes it sound more... wistful. Keenan stops once more, the look he passes me this time more considerate, pensive. He sets down his fork and knife and places his hands in his lap.

"We can talk now," he answers, face and tone solemn. "The safest place for the ring is here, Callie. Our pack is aligned with a powerful coven, and because of a magical barrier they've erected, no supernatural being with malicious intent can cross into our territory. Meaning Vrana and the Wselfwulf's can't get to us. Granted, the high amount of concentrated magic they're using to keep up the barrier does have the unwanted effect of drawing other supernatural creatures' attention." He frowns at the last bit, and so do I, my reserves drawing up.

"That hardly seems like a good reason to keep it. If anything, it will only make more trouble for you. Case in point, the Wardens and these other supernatural creatures," I argue.

"Tell me more about the blade we took off you," he requests.

"Excuse me?"

He shifts in his seat, one foot stretching out and bumping into mine. He doesn't pull it back. Nor do I. "The blade. It's old. That much is easy to tell. Why would you want to fight with it?" I temper my heartbeat and let my gaze flicker over the food once more. The strangest temptation runs through me to speak the truth, but I easily snuff it out.

"I thought we were negotiating the return of the ring, not making idle chitchat about my choice of weaponry. And for the record, I stand by my previous point and would further like to note that the Wardens are a *global* force. We could hide the ring anywhere in the world."

"I'm surprised the thing is still usable, to be honest," he continues, ignoring my commentary. "I saw you using it on those creatures and thought maybe it was some magical dagger meant to inflict a heavier wound. But then I saw you cut yourself with it."

I rein in my annoyance at his persistence and take a deep breath, forcing a stiff smile on my lips. "It's an old family heirloom. My favorite, actually. I can show you how I like to use it if you're interested?"

Keenan holds back a smile. "I think I'll pass on that offer," he says, the right side of his lips defiantly curling upward. He ducks his head quickly to hide it and clears his throat before looking back to me. I'm surprised at how the simple action draws a strange flutter to my stomach. "The ring then."

"Yes, the ring."

He pauses, clearly searching for the words to begin what I'm assuming to be a scripted negotiation. "Having spoken with my alpha earlier, I'm confident that the ring can be delivered back to your people," he says, "as long as you agree to a few conditions."

I sigh and lean back in my chair. "Go on then," I say. This is bound to be interesting.

"The ring will be sent back with a small guard of wolves and Eldritch Witches to the Banks Facility. Terms will be—"

"Absolutely *not*," I snarl.

"Why?" he asks calmly.

"A small guard? The Wardens won't stand for it. The Banks has been hit twice with wolf attacks in recent weeks, and you want to bring combat witches into the mix? They'd destroy every last one of you then use your blood as a message to any others who would dare try something similar. We don't forgive and forget," I tell him savagely, feeling my hostility grow.

Keenan looks fit to spit, his hands balling into fists as a quiet rage settles across his features. It's a glimpse of the hardened warrior I know he must be, one unwilling to submit to a person they deem inconsequential.

"Fine. Then the ring will be sent back with a few of ours to a select group of your people, after which, the envoy will return unharmed." My righteous anger dies down at the modified terms, but his hardened features still set me on edge. "Of course," he murmurs, "during this transaction, you would be required to stay behind as an act of good faith. As the pack's ward, of sorts. After all, you did say your kind kills mine. I'm not sure how much we can actually trust your people with not killing us."

I bite my tongue to quell my retort. Of course, they expect me to stay behind... but is it really as an act of good faith? Or does Keenan have more selfish reasons coming into play? My stomach gives an upsetting grumble, distracting me from my immediate thought.

"There's plenty of food," Keenan continues in that soft murmur, his eyes compelling me to sate my obvious hunger. I avert my gaze as I snag another roll, tearing it into a few bite-size pieces before indulging. There is a strange stirring in my blood as his gaze remains on me, one I'm not wholly comfortable with.

"Did your alpha come up with this plan B or you?" I ask.

"I did," he responds coolly.

I make a humming noise, popping another bit of bread into my mouth and chewing thoughtfully. "He trusts your negotiating skills that much?"

"He trusts *me*."

My eyebrow knocks upward in speculation. "What are you, the third? You don't seem like the beta type. Maybe the fourth? You have to be somewhat high ranking in order to make a deal with the enemy without your alpha's supervision."

"I'm the fifth." Another noncommittal noise sounds from my throat as I avert my gaze to my plate. Out of my peripheral vision, I can see Keenan tense very subtly. *Men and their egos.* "And though we might be 'enemies' as you put it, we have a common interest in keeping the ring out of the hands of the vampires."

"Vampyré," I correct absentmindedly, "and how long exactly did you think your pack would keep me as their '*ward*,' hmm? My people will expect me to return. Along with everything I came here with, which includes my duster and my weapons. You can't really expect me to stay here forever," I finish a bit dramatically.

Keenan sighs a bit ruefully, a tender smile crossing his lips. "It was worth a shot, I suppose." He lets the weight of his full regard rest upon me, the same heavy look to his eyes as before. The one filled with want. *With need.* I swallow, losing the strict words at the tip of my tongue. I can hear my shallow breathing as the seconds tick onward. The sound of my heartbeat an echo in my ears.

"You...." I shake my head, attempting to clear my thoughts. This couldn't be. *We* couldn't be. "I'm promised to someone," I tell him hoarsely. "He'll come for me." *Because he thinks I'm his property,* I think bitterly.

Keenan doesn't respond right away. A strange energy builds around him as he moves one hand to toy with his dinner knife. His fingers move it methodically between his fingers in a figure-eight while his regard narrows.

"Promised to whom exactly?" he asks softly. I open my mouth to speak, but a rather unnerving smirk paints itself on his face. "The one dying in the witches' house?"

My heart contracts. "What did you just say?" I whisper aghast. "What are you talking about?"

The point of the knife drives into the table with a soft thud. "The one with his stomach ripped to shreds," he informs me calmly, eyes tracing every movement I make.

Oh God. JJ. Not him. My eyes flutter closed. Why hadn't he made it into the truck? How could they have left him behind? A wave of nausea rises from the pit of my stomach. And they are having the witches hold him prisoner? *Fucking wolves.* My eyes flash open and meet Keenan's watch with a mighty glare.

"Take me to see him. Now," I demand.

Keenan pulls the knife from the wood and slams it flat on to the table. The whole thing reverberates with the collision. "I think a new deal is in order," he says, voice still achingly calm. "The man, ring, and blades can all be returned to your people once he's healed, but you stay, Calliope. You stay and you complete the sealing."

My jaw drops open at the ludicrous proposal. *Complete the sealing and create an unbreakable bond between this wolf and myself?* I can't. My family would disown me. A future with Keenan is unthinkable. It's completely unheard of, and yet my heart gives a wild beat at the thought.

"You can't be serious," I argue, but Keenan makes no move to correct himself. A flood of emotions run through me. Anxiety, fear, anger... curiosity.

I know they all must run across my features in harried succession, but I can't seem to pull myself together. All the while, Keenan remains undisturbed. My hands clench into fists, fingernails digging into the soft flesh of my palms as I rake over his proposal. Stay here and complete the sealing to ensure that JJ and the artifacts are returned safely? I don't know if I can do it, but I know what JJ would do.

He wouldn't hesitate. He never has when it came to me.

He would take the deal and someway find his way back to our family, but he would make sure I was out safely first. I wish I had his strength and fortitude. If it was any other in my position, a *true* Stellar Warrior, they would remain steadfast and reject the deal. The Wardens of Starlight don't compromise with the enemy. Yet here I am, willing to do just that in order to save one life. *JJ would do the same for me*, I think grimly steeling my resolve.

"I'll accept with the following conditions. First, before you release the man, I want to see him so I can make sure he's unharmed by your witches. That he's fit to travel."

Keenan nods stiffly. "The second?"

"The blades stay with me," I tell him with a shaky breath. "They belong to me. I'm their protector."

"Agreed," Keenan says immediately after I've finished, a flash of triumph flaring behind his eyes with a sprinkling of gold. "We'll complete the sealing tonight," he tells me, standing abruptly, "after I relay the news to my alpha."

"Wait! What?" I cry, standing as well, but he is already halfway out the door. It slams shut behind him. The telltale sound of a lock sliding forcefully into place after it.

SEALED

- Chapter 11 -

I'm escorted to some study. An honest to God study. It's done up in rich cherrywood, accented by leather couches and chairs, and a large desk. I navigate the room in what can only be described as an agitated manner.

What am I doing? Have I gone insane?

Only a complete idiot accepts the deal I just did. And why is there something so dastardly akin to hope rising in my chest? I have plans. Plans that are going up in flames faster than I ever thought possible. No Nova, no relics, and now JJ and this ultimatum. This isn't how it is supposed to go. I'm meant to return victorious and prove everyone wrong. Show them I'm capable and reliable. That my head is in the game.

Then everything will fall back to its rightful place. I would return to my station as a Stellar Warrior and follow every order faithfully till the day I die. Nova would be reunited with her sisters. JJ would rise high among the ranks and restore honor to our family name.

But what if none of those things occurred as a result of my victory?

Wyatt's words come back to haunt me. Do I really think if I'm victorious the Council would hail my return? Chances are the Council would still punish me, whether through traditional means or by enforcing their own sense of justice. Like finally forcing me into a preordained life. Forcing me to marry Wyatt and live out the rest of my days as his little wife. Sitting behind some desk and doling out new protocols as a member of the Council, my greatest hope of achievement to pass some new law or settle a dispute.

I'm not made to be a judge. I'm an executioner through and through, and therein lie the problem. That dark ache inside of me has too much hold over me. How can I ever be trusted to wield such powerful weapons when I'm no better than some mindless harpy when it comes down to action?

Can I ever fit into the cookie-cutter role they want to place me in? Would I ever be happy?

Can I ever be happy with my soulmark?

I trip over my own feet as the thought stumbles through my mind. I cast a furtive look about the room, double-checking I am alone and no one sees my blunder. What am I thinking? I can't possibly be thinking of Keenan as a viable option.

He's not awful, well, too awful. For a wolf. Stoic, yes. A bit grim, most certainly. But also… collected. Put together. Like he's in control of himself and the beast that I know resides inside of him. I'm aware these are dangerous thoughts. Especially as I was brought up learning lycans have no absolute control over the beast inside of them. The fateful curse upon them does more than restrain the wolf. It drives them *mad.*

But maybe that isn't exactly true.

I shake myself at the thoughts. Notions like that got me kicked out of the Stellar Warriors. Doubting my teachings. Going with my gut and letting my emotions cloud my better judgment. Just like my father said.

I stop my pacing as I pass a window, gazing out into the darkened world. Will the Stellar Warriors come for me? Or just the relics? I'm not quite sure.

I issue a long sigh. None of it matters. JJ is what matters. Getting the relics back matters. Whatever might happen to me is just… collateral damage. It's not personal. I nibble at my bottom lip. I will take responsibility for my actions. No more moping. No more being self-centered. I'll make matters right. There is no—

The door slams open, the force of the action making me jump. I whip around, unprepared to face this particular emotion: anger. And he is most certainly angry by the glower on his face. It softens only marginally when he spots me near the window. Then he's off toward the other end of the room where the decanters full of liquor and crystal glasses are stashed.

"And here I thought I'd be on the receiving end of a warmer reception," I mutter to myself. Keenan shoots me a stern look over his shoulder, the amber liquid splashing hazardously into a tumbler. Enhanced hearing. How annoying.

"Sorry," he grumbles after downing his glass and setting it back onto the rolling cart.

"You got what you wanted," I comment. "I thought you'd be… smugger about it."

He takes a few steps toward me, folding his arms over his chest and letting his feet stand shoulder width apart, as if he's about to deliver important news. I straighten in response, eyeing him dubiously. "I didn't imagine it happening this way," he admits, softening considerably once his confession is aired. "I didn't think it would ever happen, actually, but at the very least I thought I would have had the chance to know you before we..."

I raise a brow. "You know me," I tell him. Keenan looks faintly awestruck at my confident words, and even I feel a small bout of astonishment. Forging onward, I battle down the minor flush that creeps onto my cheeks. "Fighting is intimate," I say carefully. "You can learn a lot about a person you've fought if you pay enough attention. Are they an honorable fighter? Do they adhere to some subset of rules? Or are they the type to shake your hand just before stabbing you in the back?"

Keenan nods along slowly. His gaze turning into one of appraisal. One warrior to another. "Agreed," he finally murmurs, taking another step forward, "but you have to admit, our circumstance does come across as a bit... dramatic." He grimaces at the word, and a laugh bubbles up from my chest.

"Yes," I agree wholeheartedly, surprised by how quickly my anxiety evaporates at his words. "I would definitely categorize fighting to the death as dramatic."

Keenan's coming smile turns a bit wry. "For the record, I was fighting to subdue you. Not kill you."

"You were choking me."

"To force you to lose consciousness," he rebuts easily.

I lick my lips a tad nervously as an unsteady silence balances between us. My earlier ambivalence returning. "Maybe we can reconsider our deal. Instead, we can agree that you'll let me go along with the others to avoid all the unnecessary drama," I offer. The frown resurfaces, prickling at his brow as a sigh falls heavily from his lips. "I'm sorry, Calliope. I can't. There's too much to lose at the moment. At least if we're sealed, there's more bargaining power for future attacks or coalitions," he tells me.

I turn back toward the window, gazing at my solemn expression in the reflection of the glass. *Of course*, I think, *I'm a pawn in another's game once more.* Another piece of property, to another man. To a stranger. A wolf. I hear Keenan walk away, and the gentle rattling of the liquor cart sounds as Keenan prepares another drink. I attempt to compose myself in the interim. I shouldn't take it so personally, yet I am. Why?

The crystal tumbler crashes against the drink cart, seizing my attention. I catch Keenan's stricken look over my shoulder and frown.

"I'm sorry," he tells me earnestly.

Reluctantly, I turn back toward him, wrapping my arms comfortingly around my waist as I put on a stoic mask. "Don't be."

"Not...." He shakes his head in frustration and walks determinedly toward me. "What I just said, it upset you, and I'm sorry." My eyes go wide. *Enhanced sense of smell.* Stupid lycan abilities.

"I wasn't upset," I argue.

"I'm not very good at talking to people," he continues, as if I haven't spoken at all. "I try to think more logically and strategically than most, and sometimes it makes me come off as rude or detached. So, I'm sorry."

I shrug a shoulder. "It's fine."

Keenan's lips thin minutely. "It isn't. I'm pleased I found you, Calliope, and that it's you who I share this mark with. You're a formidable woman. Especially if you're fighting is anything to go by," he tells me warmly. I swallow at the compliment, the familiar stirring in my blood occurring once more. It makes my skin feel hypersensitive and my heart give a somersault.

"Oh."

"And beautiful," he tells me.

"*Oh.*"

"How am I doing?" he asks, voice dropping slightly into something huskier. I find myself caught in his gaze; lips gently parted as my chest begins to rise and fall a bit more steadily. The stirring grows. It makes my palms warm, and my fingers flex as our eyes continue in their deadlock. And I can tell that same stirring is winding its way through Keenan. His eyes, which are already a deep caramel, seem to darken further. Split second fractures of gold piercing through the iris are the only hint that the beast inside him is at attention.

Keenan exhales, visibly shaking himself from whatever spell we've both fallen under, an embarrassed flush climbing his cheeks. "There's one more thing," he admits, the anger from earlier trespassing back into his voice. "The food tonight was tampered with."

My eyes widen at the information, all feelings of warmth disappearing as I take a step back. "With what exactly?" I ask curtly.

"Zoelle is a witch," Keenan tells me, softening his posture, "but she has a rather peculiar talent when it comes to cooking."

"Which is?"

"She can impart emotions into her cooking," he laments. The frown on my face deepens. "If she's feeling anxious, then whoever eats her food will feel anxious. If she's feeling happy, then whoever eats her food will feel happy. It's why her little bakery does so well. She can also impart intentions into her food."

"Intentions?" The word falls flat, my reserve of calm leaving me.

Keenan nods and lets out another sigh. "Zoelle could be feeling anything while she cooks, which is why having the intention of what she wants her patrons to feel at the forefront of her mind is so important. If she does, she can impart that into her cooking instead. I'm not sure of the exact mechanics of it all. I don't like magic enough to learn about it," he finishes with a grunt of disapproval.

"Keenan," I ask tightly, "what did she do to our food?"

"She made us 'open-minded' and 'receptive,'" he confesses.

I chew over the supposed "intentions" and hate to admit that I am not as outraged as I feel I ought to be. *Stupid witches and their stupid magic*, I think bitterly.

"I guess that isn't completely and utterly terrible," I admit begrudgingly.

Keenan scratches the back of his neck, head bowing slightly to look at me through half-lidded eyes. "About the 'receptive' part. Quinn, the blonde you met earlier? She's the one who mentioned that particular intention, which means it might mean something more."

I find myself swallowing. "More? As in... what exactly?" My words come out breathier than I intend them to, and so I bite my lip in retaliation, hoping to stem the come-hither quality of my voice. Keenan's eyes lock onto the action, nostrils flaring as he steps not toward me but to the side. I'm acutely aware of the change in his body language. Though held loosely, it is wound in anticipation. Ready to pounce at a moment's notice. And his eyes... his eyes slowly burn into me.

"I would hazard a guess to say something more akin to desire," he murmurs, continuing his path and slowly circling closer. I follow his movement with rapt attention, beginning to shuffle in a tight circle so as not to let him at my back. "Which might make the sealing more intense."

"Then maybe we should wait until the magic wears off," I offer, "and complete the sealing tomorrow."

Keenan shakes his head. The only hint of displeasure showing in the corded muscles of his neck.

"There's no time. As we speak, the pack is preparing for more attacks. Since crossing the border yesterday to investigate your disturbance, there's been a rather dramatic increase in the spotting of unusual and foreign entities in the forest."

"You mean more supernatural creatures?"

He nods solemnly, inching closer when my gaze flits to the window thoughtfully. "Whatever is out there wants the power we possess, and since witnessing our entering and leaving the magical border without incident—"

"It's made them curious. More daring," I finish, locking gazes with him once more.

"It's a veritable shitstorm out there, which is why we do this tonight while we have the opportunity." The temperature in the room rises, or maybe it's just the way Keenan looks at me that brings my blood to a boil. "Where is it?" Keenan's eyes sweep over my body meaningfully as he closes the space between us.

I'm hit with a rather intoxicating dose of adrenalin as I let my hand fall to the mark that lies low on my hip. Keenan's eyes glue themselves to said hand, and a sudden reckless desire thunders through me to show him exactly where the soulmark lies. My fingers cross the distance to the fastening of my black pants and a low growl rumbles forth from Keenan.

It's the magic driving me, I reassure myself as the button slips from its closure and the zipper inches downward. With both hands, I adjust my clothing to reveal the dark mark upon my skin. It rests intimately against another tattoo, seemingly apart of it. Which is the point. Keenan's growl cuts off abruptly as he shifts into my personal space, his hands snatching my wrists a tad too tightly and pulling them away from my clothing.

"I think," he tells me in a smooth baritone, hands releasing me to refasten my pants, "that it would be best to use my soulmark for the sealing." His Adam's apple bobs as his eyes travel north to meet my own.

"Agreed," I reply. My earlier constraint wades into the deeper recesses of my mind, falling away as his lips inch toward mine, my focus completely captured by his slow and measured movements.

The weight of one hand rests heavily on my hip, while the other comes to cradle my jaw, tilting my head upward. His cognac breath perfumes the air between us. "May I?"

My bottom lip finds its way between my teeth again. *Why bother asking*? I think somewhat sorely as my bruised pride pops up. *Because he's different*, I defend to myself, *because he cares when he doesn't have to*. I nod as best I can, the action caked in uncertainty. What harm is one kiss?

When his lips press to mine, I am pleased by their warmth and fullness. They expertly free my bottom lip, only to take it prisoner between his own. A thrill of excitement runs down my spine at his diligent attention. The meticulous working of his lips and tongue turning out delicate gasps and moans from my throat, ones I never knew I could make.

His hand slips to the dip in my lower back, urging me closer with the lightest of pressure. I accede, pressing my body into the hard panels of his chest and abdominals. Keenan hums his approval, kissing me deeper and leaving me absolutely *breathless*. How can a kiss be so hypnotizing? As if with a mind of its own, one of my hands begins to drift up his obliques, the other anchoring itself near the crease of his elbow, fingers digging into the slope of his bicep.

"Ready?" he breathes the question against my lips as my hand glides along his forearm. I nod mutely. Keenan need only say a few words as I touch his soulmark, and the sealing will be complete. It's simple, really, and certainly no reason for my nerves to be such a jittery mess as my fingertips near his soulmark. *I'm doing this for JJ,* I repeat over again to myself.

The instant my skin touches upon the edge of the mark, I am drawn into a void of nothing and then... everything. A thousand brilliant stars surround us. A vibrant cord of light winding around us as Keenan speaks, "Let it be known that thee are found and my soul awakened." Our eyes meet and my heart gives a sudden leap. "The stars incline us, and so, *we are sealed.*"

A whimper escapes me when his fingers thread through my hair and pull me into another kiss. My own hands clamp onto him as a burst of sudden need catapults through me, like some kind of shooting star. Its blazing tail, coiling tightly around us. *The books at the Banks Facility never detailed* this *part of the sealing, or any of these feelings for that matter,* I think wildly.

Keenan issues a groan as I melt into his possessive hold. A flip suddenly switches within him as he begins to dominate the kiss truly. He drives me backward until my back hits the cold window. With a gasp, I arch away from the cool glass, my hands momentarily releasing their grip on his body and severing our intimate connection. A whine issues from my lips, but is stifled by the pressure of Keenan's own. He disengages from me slowly, his lips leaving me last as he straightens.

"Are you all right?"

The words get stuck in my throat as I catch the look of reverence and admiration beaming down at me. His watchful amber-spiked gaze trails attentively over my expression, as if he's memorizing this exact moment.

"I—" *shouldn't have enjoyed that* "—should go to bed."

Keenan takes a deep breath, and for one terrible moment, I think he is about to lean in toward me again to steal another kiss, but he does quite the opposite. With a heavy exhale, he takes a large step back, allotting me more than enough room to make my escape.

"Of course," he rumbles, all calm and cool disposition. It throws me off guard, this new confidence. The look in his eyes reads of calculated patience. Patience for what though? "I'll escort you to your room."

"That won't be necessary," I tell him.

Keenan purses his lips. "Someone will escort you, regardless," he responds. I nod a bit stiffly and move past him with a measured cadence toward the door. I would take what I could get. Keenan doesn't further pursue the matter, standing idly by as I go. Thank God. My thoughts tumble into turmoil as I'm seized by my new reality. One in which I am forever bound to this man—this wolf. *There will be no returning from this*, I think hollowly, *but at least JJ will be all right.* If I can't save myself, at least I can save him.

BROTHER WHERE ART THOU?

- Chapter 12 -

There is a hole in my heart I never knew about. A tiny, minuscule thing that's now half full. How had I never noticed it before? It's all I can think about now. Well, that and the current dismal state of my life. I've just done something irreversible and equally unforgivable. A real warrior would have never acceded to Keenan's demands. A real warrior would have waited the situation out patiently, for surely the full force of the Stellar Warriors would rain down upon this pack in only a few days' time. So why didn't I wait?

Because you want an escape.

The thought worms its way into my mind, bringing with it a sharp twist to my stomach. I can't bear the treasonous reasoning, even if it's but a passing whisper in my mind. I push it away. There is no going back now. The only thing I can hope to do now is make sure JJ is sent off with the ring and try and do right by Nova. If I can find her.

Keenan dropped by in the morning to my new "holding cell"—a room on the second floor guarded by two wolves—informing me we'd visit the injured male later in the day. His delivery was brief, yet stained with overtures of jealousy in his voice, a sentiment I further encouraged with a sardonic response.

Now I wander the neatly manicured subdivision, a pair of wolves huddled together behind me, trailing my movements. I don't mind being followed. I expected as much to happen. What does rub me wrong is the way everyone peeks out of their homes to catch a glimpse of me. Like I'm some exotic animal.

"Callie!" I turn at hearing my voice shouted from across the street. It's Keenan, exiting a small home and pocketing a set of keys. He jogs across the street to meet me, giving a brief nod to the two wolves behind me.

"Hi."

"How are you?" he asks, eyes combing over me. I raise a shoulder deftly, focusing more on taming the sudden erratic beating of my heart than a real response.

"It's only been a few hours since you last saw me," I finally say when he continues to wait patiently for an answer.

"It's been roughly six hours since I last saw you, which I'd consider being more than a few," he tells me. I look at him with mild shock. "You've been counting the hours?" I ask, somewhat incredulously.
Keenan gives me an impish grin. "I might have," he admits. "You've been on my mind a lot today."

The comment makes me catch my breath before I stuff my hands in my pockets, shifting my gaze up the road. "It's just the soulmark," I inform him without emotion. "It drives the need and want to complete the process of joining our souls. We've only sealed the soulmark. Hence, why I'm on your mind more."

"That's one way to look at it."

"It's the only way to look at it," I refute, glaring at him to emphasize my stance on the matter. *There will be no marking or binding,* I think stoutly, *my end of the bargain has been met.*

Keenan sighs and takes a step back, pointing toward a truck parked across the street. "Are you ready to go?" I nod my head eagerly, half a step ahead of him before he can say anything more.

We drive in relative silence toward the witches' headquarters. Just Keenan and me. No auxiliary wolves to watch over me. Briefly, I wonder if this is because of the wolf's territorial nature, or because Keenan believes he can handle me on his own. Either way, I'm pleased to have less company on this venture. Especially since my hand keeps creeping closer to Keenan's, and the chance of anyone noticing my transgression leaves me feeling mortified. Just because the soulmark is sealed doesn't necessarily mean the marking or binding must happen. It's just a very probable outcome. After all, the whole point of the soulmark is to identify the other half of one's soul. The sealing, marking, and binding are the steps that bring the halves together as one. If only the process didn't drive my senses into overdrive and rid me of all rational thought.

My gut clenches, whether in dismay or anticipation I'm unsure. My head tells me the former. My soulmark tells me the latter.

It's odd to catch myself drifting toward Keenan, no matter how involuntary the action. The Wardens of Starlight aren't exactly known for being overly affectionate. Or affectionate at all, but as far as I've gathered, the wolves are. They're close-knit in every aspect of life. And they liked it that way.

"We're here," he announces, pulling up outside a large house on a tree-lined street.

"This is their headquarters?" I ask doubtfully.

Keenan nods as he unbuckles, tossing a rather bored look toward the home. "The Elder Triad lives there. The leaders of the Trinity Coven."

I approach the house a step behind Keenan, keeping a wary eye out for anything out of the ordinary. I don't like being cooped up in a house full of wolves, and now I'm about to enter a house full of powerful witches—I can't imagine things being much worse. At least I have my bracers on. The iron cuffs never felt so comforting heading into witch territory.

"They won't bite," he tells me with an amused look.

"Of course they won't," I grumble back. "That's what vampyrés do. Witches cast spells and curses, you know, like your friend Zoelle." Keenan's amusement fades with a grimace.

"Sorry about that," he laments, ringing the doorbell. "Zoelle didn't mean any harm to come from it. I think she just wanted us to be able to communicate without getting into another altercation."

"Quinn didn't."

Keenan frowns and looks as if he is ready to scold me, or at least justify her involvement when the door jerks open.

"Hello!"

What the...?

"Hi Luna," Keenan offers kindly. "May we come in?"

"Of course!" the petite woman practically squeals. Keenan enters, snagging my hand to tug me in after him, but I continue to stand stock-still. My eyes stay trained on the... on the....

"What are you?" I ask once the door is closed. Her hair just barely reaches her shoulders and is an icy white. Her eyes are a startling violet. Even her skin seems unnatural. The longer I stare, the more I think I see an odd shimmering quality to it, as if something is slithering beneath the surface.

Luna stands more proudly. "I'm a fairy!" she chirps.

My jaw drops as I take a step toward her, eyes wide as I inspect her more closely. A warm hand wraps around my upper arm, but I easily tug out of Keenan's hold.

"You're a fairy?" I ask dubiously.

She nods her head enthusiastically. "Yes, though you wouldn't know it from looking at me. Gran and Aunt Mo put a glamor on me to hide my wings and flowers."

I toss an incredulous look to Keenan, but he watches us interact dispassionately. I take a step back away from her, my head slowly rotating from side to side. "Fairies don't look like you," I inform her, feeling oddly flustered. Luna looks startled and then confused, her wide eyes turning to Keenan expectantly.

"She is," he affirms with a grunt.

"No," I reason stubbornly, "fairies are small and green with pointy teeth. Not—" I wave my hands in Luna's direction. "—*this*." Ethereal and gorgeous.

"But," Luna looks hopelessly between Keenan and me, "I am a fairy. I'm from Hollow Woods!"

Keenan's hand comes to rest on my upper arm again, this time tugging me back toward the staircase. "It's all right, Luna; I'm sure Callie is confused."

"I'm not—" I begin to growl in frustration before Luna cuts me off.

"I'm a fairy," she insists with a stomp of her foot. "You're talking about *imps*. They're green and small. They have lots of pointy teeth." She dazzles us with a wide smile. "See," she says eagerly, "not pointy!"

This can't be right. It can't be. Everything I've learned at the Banks described fairies so differently. No bigger than three feet tall. Boney green bodies. A mouthful of needle-like teeth. No wings or *flowers*.

I glance frantically at Keenan. "I—"

"You know what I call imps?" Luna casts a suspicious glance around us before whispering,

"*Hellspawn.*" Hellspawn? "The ones you fought last week. Don't you remember, Keenan?"

"We really have to be going now, Luna," Keenan says, his grip tightening a fraction on my upper arm. "Please tell whichever Elder is around that we'll be upstairs with your guest."

"Oh." Luna seems to deflate before us, her gaze wandering up sullenly to the stairs. "I'm not allowed to go up there and see him," she tells us with a pout before wandering away.

"What the hell, Keenan?" I seethe on the stairs landing, wrenching my arm from his hold. "First your pack makes nice with a coven of witches, and now fairies? They're not even from this world," I hiss indignantly. "And from the sound of it, your pack is dealing with a lot more than just curious passersby."

"Now isn't the time, Callie," he tells me firmly, jawline set to hold his stern facial expression.

"You tried to tell me the ring was safe here," I continue to argue, feeling my anger rise. "It obviously isn't with all of these attacks. And if the ring isn't safe, then JJ can't possibly be safe. I want him and the ring out of here before nightfall."

Keenan's jaw ticks. He steps up onto the landing step with me, towering over me once more. "I've already told you, your lover and the ring will be returned as soon as he's healed. The witches have been taking care of him, so I'm sure he'll be in a state fit to travel soon."

"My lover?" I choke out. Keenan's eyes darken a fraction, but his intense regard doesn't waver. "He's my *brother*," I tell him bluntly, pushing past him up the stairs. I feel a small pang of guilt in my heart and realize a short second later that it doesn't come from me, but Keenan. I fight the urge to turn around and face him and argue till I'm red in the face. It isn't the time or place.

"It's the third door on the right. The one at the end of the hall." I follow his instruction, knocking gently on the door before opening it without delay.

"JJ," I breathe. He lies prone on the bed, shirtless and with a sterile white bandage around his waist. No one else occupies the room, but a number of miscellaneous bottles and bowls are scattered across a large dresser near the bed. I close the door behind me as softly as possible, not wanting to wake him from his slumber.

A sheen of tears clouds my vision momentarily, and I hastily work to blink them away. *He's alive.* That's all that matters. A lonesome tear escapes and falls down my cheek. I quickly dash it away, afraid that with it more will follow.

"Cal?" his hoarse voice whispers.

"JJ." I'm kneeling by his bedside before I can blink, my hand reaching out to take hold of his. "You're okay."

He grunts, blinking away the sleep as he works his way up higher on the pillows. "I've been better," he tells me gruffly, sitting up straighter. "How did you find me? How did you get here?"

I swallow past my swell of emotion as the memories come rushing forward. "The full force of the swarm was too much. I cut myself to draw the golems attention and led them to the wolves hiding out in the woods. I heard the van peel out, but I thought you were in it, JJ. Why weren't you in that van?"

"I rolled under it. I don't think Naomi or Wyatt saw. I think they thought what you thought, that I made it into the van."

"But you didn't," I whisper horrified.

He shakes his head grimly. "Some of the golems took chase after the van, but they didn't get very far once they realized I was still there."

"So how did you survive?"

"The wolves," he says bitterly. "You?"

My mouth goes a bit dry. "The wolves."

"I don't like this, Cal," he whispers, eyeing the door suspiciously. "We've got to find a way out of here. They've got me on forced bed rest, but whatever the witches have given me has sped up my healing process tenfold. I could be good to go by tomorrow. We just need to make a plan."

"There's already a plan in place, JJ," I tell him softly, not daring to meet his eyes. "I made a deal with the wolves. Once you're able to travel, you and the ring will be sent back to the Banks Facility."

JJ's face screws up in confusion. "What? How did you—"

I shake my head sharply, effectively cutting him off. "I stay. I stay with the blade." JJ opens his mouth to speak, but I give his hand a sharp squeeze and shake my head more slowly, giving a sidelong glance toward the bedroom door. He nods with understanding, regarding me with solemn eyes.

"So, they just get to keep you? For how long?" I shrug and keep my face composed in a neutral expression, turning my gaze back to his. "You didn't have to make this kind of deal, Callie."

I give JJ a sad smile, mustering an ounce of warmth to it. "Come on, JJ. You can't always save the day. Besides, this was all my idea in the first place. It's my responsibility to set things right."

"You know we'll come back for you. The full force of the Wardens. Do they know that?"

"I know they'll come back for the blade at the very least," I tell him with a weak laugh. This time JJ is the one to squeeze my hand, and with a surprising amount of strength.

"*I'll* come back for you, Cal. Always."

I shake my head sadly. "Don't make more of a mess of this than it has to be. Follow orders, JJ, and do right by our family. We both know there's no real coming back from this for me. It doesn't have to be that way for you too."

JJ looks pained at the words but doesn't argue. He pulls his hand from my grasp, resting it gently on his abdomen with a rasping sigh. I curl my arm inward and duck my chin down to rest it on my forearm.

"You'll stay with me?" he asks tiredly.

"For as long as I can," I assure him. He frowns back at me.

"Where are they keeping you?"

My fingers toy idly with the end of the blanket. "The alpha's residence." JJ's eyes widen. "It's fine. My accommodations have been recently upgraded from prison cell to heavily guarded guest room. Anyway, I don't know why you're making that face at me. You do know you're staying at the coven's leader's home, right?"

"The old ladies?" he asks dubiously.

"There's a fairy here too, JJ," I tell him, real excitement tingeing my voice. "And she's not at all how you'd imagine. She's beautiful. Completely unearthly. Snow white hair. Purple eyes. She says the witches glamoured her wings and flowers away."

JJ slowly shakes his head, and my idle play comes to an end. "That's not what a fairy is, Cal. They're—"

"I know! Green, gross, and gnarly teeth. But she says she's a fairy and whatever we described is an imp."

"But that's not what the books say," he continues, a bit condescendingly.

"Well," I give another shrug and straighten my back, "maybe the books are wrong."

JJ scalds me with his glare, so much so I have to look away in shame. "The books have been around for centuries, Cal. We've learned everything from them. When have they ever been wrong?"

His comment is a sharp reminder of my past wrongs. "They haven't," I whisper dejectedly.

"Don't let them fool you, Callie. They can play nice all they want, but never forget what they are. They can't be trusted."

I sink down to sit fully on the floor. "I know," I mutter, feeling a pang of guilt once more, this one all my own.

LESSONS LEARNED

- Chapter 13 -

Keenan gathers me from JJ's room when the witches come to apply more of their medicines. I make a note of their faces. One has cocoa skin and hair pulled back into a neat chignon, her eyes green and piercing, cat-like almost. The other has her white hair plaited and draped over her shoulder. Her alabaster skin is covered in scars, but they don't mar the kindness in her eyes. They are "the aunts," Keenan tells me as we make our way down the stairs. Even as we leave, I can hear them making a fuss over JJ: shaking out his blankets, opening the lone window at the far end of his room, the tinkling of glasses and bowls whose contents will no doubt be smeared across his skin. He answers them in short responses, ones I strain to hear as we reach the landing step. Then a round of laughter sounds from the room. Including JJ's.

"He's fine," Keenan tells me quietly, placing a hand on my lower back and urging me gently forward. "They know what they're doing."

I allow Keenan to guide me toward the front door, but I can't help but glance around for the not-fairy. She's nowhere to be seen.

"She's in the forest."

Keenan holds the door open for me. "Good for her," I mutter. His sigh of frustration is almost inaudible as I steam past him toward the truck. The remainder of my time with JJ hadn't gone as planned. I hoped to receive some kind of praise or acknowledgment for my plan but had been dealt a monotonous lecture on the importance of our cause.

As if I need reminding of the people we have sworn to protect, or that we are in the midst of terrible and powerful creatures. I know, for heaven's sake. After an hour of hearing himself speak, JJ finally took note of my putout demeanor and wrapped up his lecture. He clasped my hand and told me he would always be my big brother. That he would always look out for me and make sure I got home safe and sound.

Then I lied to his face and told him I'd be waiting. *Waiting*! The soulmark felt like some ugly brand against my skin as I hid the truth from him.

"Do you want to talk about it?" Keenan asks once we've gotten into the truck and fastened our seat belts.

"Not particularly," I respond, resting my head against the passenger side window and gazing at the witches' house.

Keenan's hand envelops my own, capturing my full attention with ease. "Are you sure?" The question is low and soft. It takes me unaware when combined with the solemn set of his brow and the concern pulsing through our bond weakly. My chest constricts as I nod dumbly and pull my hand from his.

"Let's not pretend like you didn't hear every—"

Keenan shakes his head swiftly. "I was downstairs with Luna. I may have heard bits and pieces at the start, but I did my best not to listen. Thankfully, Luna can be quite the handful, so I was distracted easily enough with her ramblings."

"Oh," I murmur, averting my gaze to the dashboard.

"You're upset," he says simply. My disagreement is on the tip of my tongue when Keenan reaches out and cups my chin. He turns my face back toward his then releases me. "You are," he continues, baring his forearm and pressing his fingers to the soulmark. "I can feel it."

"It's nothing," I tell him dispassionately, schooling my features into one of indifference. "We just talked."

"Clearly about something unpleasant."

I shrug. "It was nothing I haven't heard before. Can we go now?"

Keenan sits back in his seat and pulls out the keys. When the engine rumbles to life, he passes me an unreadable look. "Big plans tonight?" he asks gruffly. For a moment, I am struck stupid by his blasé comment until I recognize the wry note of sarcasm in it. A gurgle of laughter pushes past my lips at his remark, one I try desperately to cover with a scoff. The smirk that plays on the corner of his lips tells me I haven't succeeded, but at least the heaviness inside my chest is lessened. I even let our fingers brush against each other on the way back.

+++

Dinner is a lackluster affair. A plate of food is brought to my room, per my request, but I merely poke at the white fish and rice. I can't seem to get the conversation with JJ out of my head. Nor the niggling notion that I've made an awful mistake in sealing the soulmark and not telling him. What will happen if the Wardens do come for me and I am separated from Keenan? Slowly go mad? Sink into a depression I can never fully recover from? Be forced to marry Wyatt and forsake the soulmark? There is far too much nervous energy careening through my body for me to have much of an appetite. I need to fight to clear my head. Or at least get my hands back on my butterfly knife. My hands feel incomplete without it.

A knock sounds at my door. "Come in," I call, pushing aside my plate

Keenan's head pokes around the corner of the door, his eyes quickly darting to my half-eaten plate of food before turning their focus on me. "Busy?"

I fight down the urge to grin and quell the stir of excitement in my stomach at his presence. It's just the soulmark. He steps more fully into the room when I don't immediately reply.

"I'm obviously not," I finally respond.

"I was wondering if we could pick your brain for a bit?" he asks casually. I raise a brow.

"Who's 'we'?"

"A few of the top-ranking wolves and myself."

My eyes narrow on his neutral expression. "About what?"

"Other supernatural creatures."

I capture a lock of hair and twirl it loosely around my finger as I weigh the pros and cons. If I go along, I can potentially learn more about Nova's whereabouts and even more about the magical barrier. It also meant sharing trade knowledge with the enemy, something I'm hesitant to do.

"All right," I agree unenthusiastically as I stand, brushing imaginary crumbs from my lap. If it means learning more about Nova or the dangers JJ could encounter on his way back to the Banks Facility, it's best to go.

We walk to the study we were in yesterday. In it are six men and two females. From the bunch, only two faces are familiar to me. Atticus gives me a smile and nod as I enter with Keenan. He makes room for us to stand around the large desk, very clearly nudging aside the other familiar face. One with dark hair and a devious smirk. His eyes scream mischief as they follow our entrance.

"About time," he tells us jovially. This is the man who kissed Quinn, I realize, the night of the first robbery. The boyfriend, Ryatt. "Shall we all go around and say our names and favorite hobby?" I scowl at his imprudence and cast my gaze around the gathered wolves.

"I'm inclined to agree with Ryatt," a man with olive skin and dark hair that reaches almost to his shoulders says. He has piercing green eyes, even more so than the witch I met briefly earlier with JJ. From his words and stance alone, I know him to be the alpha. "I'm Xander," he continues coolly, not minding at all the minor glare I send in his direction. "You've met Atticus, my beta." Atticus bumps me with his elbow and sends me a wink. "Beside him is my younger brother, Ryatt. Our third." Ryatt inclines his head, the wicked smirk still plastered across his face.

"Kevin," a surly looking redhead offers. "I'm the fourth." He bears a fresh black eye and keeps tossing scowls to the raven-haired beauty next to him. The woman's hands are stuffed in the pockets of the long vest she wears, but I'm sure they're coated in bruises.

"Irina," she says with an overly sweet smile directed my way. Her eyes take a leisurely path in their assessment of me. I don't bother to straighten under her regard and wait for the next man to announce himself.

The lean blond smiles softly at me, head ducking as he gives me his name. "I'm Micah."

"Keenan's protégé," Ryatt pipes in. The lean man sends a short glare Ryatt's way, but his eyes don't make it past the other's collarbone. He must rank much lower in the pack if he can't meet Ryatt's eyes, which begs the question as to why he's here in the first place. Keenan is only ranked fifth, after all.

"Hi, Calliope," a dainty woman with golden brown skin waves shyly at me from across the desk. I give her a small, strained smile in return. "I'm Zoelle."

My smile drops. "So, you're the one who likes to mess with peoples' emotions?"

She rolls her eyes toward the alpha, a scowl emerging over her features. "I just wanted to help facilitate a calm and open-minded environment. You were hitting each other earlier!" Zoelle's voice is flush with agitation, as well as her cheeks. "It was Quinn who kept harassing me to do the other one."

"Was that supposed to be an apology?" I ask dryly.

She huffs. "I can't help putting emotions into my dishes. Okay? It's just a part of my magic. At least I didn't make you angry or sad." She crosses her arms defensively and seals her lips shut.

"Don't worry, Calliope. You're not the first person to fall prey to Zoelle's particular magic. Think of it as a test all new members of the pack have to pass," Ryatt says.

"I'm not part of your *pack*." I spit the word out with as much venom as I can muster. All of the wolves' shoulders sink in response, the somewhat lighthearted mood dropping out of sight.

"She's right," Xander comments, meeting my glower unflinchingly. "Not until Keenan's marked her. For now, Calliope is a ward of the pack. Her position here will help to maintain a ceasefire of sorts with her people." Everyone reacts a bit differently, but the tension does ease out of the air at the alpha's confidence.

"Let's just get this over with," I say begrudgingly. "Tell me about the crystal you have. The one that attracts the other supernatural creatures."

"It's called the Wielding Crystal of Dan Furth," Zoelle says. "It's an important artifact to my people and very powerful."

"How powerful?"

She chews on her lip, eyes skirting over to Xander briefly before answering. "It acts as a booster of sorts. Radiating a supernatural energy that stimulates the growth of the products of the land. Like plants or already in place magical spells."

"How exactly does it stimulate their growth?" I bite out.

"By enhancing their efficiency, potency, and power. Tenfold."

I suck in a sharp breath, eyes going wide momentarily before I curb my reaction. "That's... *a lot* of power for a bunch of witches and wolves to have."

"It is," Xander says seriously, spreading out a topographic map of the region onto the desk. "The crystal's primary use is to keep a vengeful and rival pack out of our territory. They've proven that they'll do whatever it takes to bring us misery, including siding with a very dangerous vampire."

"Vampyré," Keenan corrects absentmindedly. A short burst of pleasure unknots the nervous energy in my stomach at the casual comment, and I find my focus easier to keep.

"Don't forget siding with other witches or sorcerers," I add a tad snidely.

Xander arches a brow, jaw ticking. "What do you mean?"

"The golems," I continue, trying to find the area where we were attacked. "They're *magically* animated beings made up of the earth; like rocks, mud, and sediments. Their sole purpose is to serve their master's will. And even though their purpose that night was to follow the will of the vampyré, they were created by a witch or sorcerer—a powerful witch or sorcerer considering their numbers."

The wolves look at me in obvious interest. *There's one trade secret down the drain,* I think. Oddly, I don't feel too uncomfortable in sharing the information. I'm more surprised and irritated they don't know anything about golems considering they're allied with witches. Do these wolves really know so little about their own supernatural community?

"Interesting," Xander murmurs, finger pointing out on the map where we're located. He draws an oblong shape with his finger to encircle the town and surrounding forest area. "We experience the majority of attacks from the western line. In the beginning, all we had to worry about were the Wselfwulf's, now...."

"The crystal is drawing the attention of other supernatural creatures. The power calls to them," I finish. "It doesn't help that there's a not-fairy in the picture."

"A not-fairy?" Zoelle voices, eyebrows rising to her hairline. "What do you mean?" The eyes of the room fall to me again.

"We have hundreds of books on the origins and lore of supernatural creatures, as well as a collection of their strengths and weaknesses. And those books don't say anything about fairies looking or behaving like *that*," I tell her, mandating my voice and tone into something nonnegotiable. That woman—Luna—couldn't be a fairy. It went against everything I learned in my training and growing up.

"But she says she's a fairy," Zoelle responds, the eyes of the pack returning to her. "Shouldn't she know what she is?"

I shrug and examine the map, keeping an unaffected air. They asked for my expertise. They would get it. "Whatever she is, she isn't from this world," I continue coolly. "She carries her own source of power, one that may or may not be amplified by that crystal. There's a good chance it isn't just the crystal the other supernatural creatures are after, but her as well." It's a good guess at least. Otherworldly creatures typically house their own bundle of power inside of them unlike anything on Earth. Well, they do if my teachings are true. Assuming the crystal amplifies Luna's power isn't such a leap.

The group breaks into a swell of chatter, one that simmers down with a raise of Atticus's hand. "That might be true, but that doesn't change what we need from you: information. We need to know how to protect our people, and we count Luna as one of our own. She's innocent in all of this—"

"Annoyingly so," Irina mutters loudly enough under her breath for everyone to hear.

"—so whatever information you can tell us about these creatures. How to defeat them, their strengths and weaknesses, anything to push them back and give our people a rest. The Wselfwulf Pack isn't just calling on the supernatural to join their bogus cause," Atticus tells me. "Since they can't cross the border—no supernatural can without receiving an express blessing from the Elder Triade—they've begun to bring high tech devices into play. Drones, in particular. They're trying to take out the crystal, or the witches who stand guard over it."

"So, technology, wolves, witches, sorcerers, vampyrés, and golems," I list off with a sigh, crossing my arms over my chest. "I'm impressed. What the hell did you do to piss off so many of your kind?"

"For your information, the vampyré problem is a recent development due to our witchy counterparts. The Wselfwulf animosity goes back several years when the pack initially split. They never really got over the slight," Irina says with a haughty air.

"And lycans do love to hold their grudges." Only the witch nods in affirmation to my comment. "What other creatures have you encountered?"

"We've had a few shape-shifters who didn't know any better. Along with two creatures that looked similar. Both green, with large black eyes and mouths full of daggers," Atticus explains. "One group comes straight out of the trees and has no visible ears. The others come crawling out of cracks in the ground, like some horror movie. Those cracks keep cropping up closer to our border. We're getting anxious that one of these days the latter will figure out how to open up a crack on our side of the borderline."

I stare at the map on the desk, my thoughts reeling at a hundred miles per second. I know the first creature, but the second… the second is what I know to be a fairy. Giving that answer will undoubtedly confuse the group and recircle the conversation back to fairies and not-fairies. A conversation I do not want to have.

"The first creature you mentioned sound like goblins. They're otherworldly woodland creatures, ergo why they appear to come out of trees. They can sift through them. The second are imps, by Luna's definition. Where have they appeared?"

Keenan leans over me, his finger pointing out several spots on the map along a hillside. I barely register the pattern he makes as his finger trails downward toward the town—toward the crystal—when his body presses up against my side. He runs hotter than the average human, and his body heat penetrates through my clothes. It's… distracting.

"…and here," he states in a low voice. My fingers itch to tuck my hair behind my ear as his breath passes through the strands, my concentration smarting as his scent hits my nose. Pine and frankincense. A hint of sweat.

I clear my throat subtly. "And the vampyré?" My heartbeat is already slightly elevated due to Keenan's nearness, a fact I can't deny to the wolves in front of me, but I can use it to my advantage. I'm eager to know if Nova or Vrana are setting their own pattern, but it's not something I want to let them onto. I shift my weight and let my body bump into Keenan's lightly.

"We've spotted him here and here. The first time at night. The second sighting during a bad storm," he says, voice still pitched low. "The cloud coverage was enough for him to be out along with the thick canopy of the tree line."

"Both spots are within a few klicks of your perimeter," I mention, disguising my disappointment with my commentary. Two sightings positioned so far apart don't leave me enough clues to suss out their possible whereabouts. "He's never been spotted farther out?"

"We don't venture far past our boundary line," Keenan tells me, his voice taking on a semi-irritable tone. I turn my face to look at him, surprised to see a flash of ire directed the alpha's way.

"Keenan," the alpha's voice dips with a warning, enough so that each wolf around the table straightens. I too find myself straightening and gazing at the imposing man at the end of the desk. Xander's hands are placed on the table in two fists, knuckles edging on white.

"Why the hell aren't you out there? Maybe if you showed some force or action all of these supernatural creatures would take a hint. Including the vampyré." The wolves remain silent at my critique.

"Because," Xander says, the hint of a growl in his voice, "this isn't a game. Men and women are risking their lives out there—"

"And they will continue to do so until you *beat* your enemy. Once and for all."

Xander clenches his jaw. "I can't risk it."

"You *won't* risk it," I correct him sharply, unafraid to needle the alpha with the harsh truth, "and because of your unwillingness to grow a pair, you'll probably lose everything regardless. Stop pussyfooting around and stand your ground. Get them off your land. I thought you were wolves, not scared dogs." My reprimand is not appreciated. The wolves stiffen in response, their alpha doubly so. *Whatever*, I think viciously, *I never said my advice would be nice.* Besides, seeing the alpha get so wound up feels like pure vindication for this entire situation.

"And if I do, I could lose everything. It's a catch-22," he snaps back viciously, slamming his fists on the table. "These are real people with real lives. Real jobs. Real families. I'm asking them to take time away from all of that to help guard our borders. To protect our allies while they provide extra protection to the crystal. I won't ask them to risk their lives in a needless attack that could cost them their lives."

I take a deep breath, rest my hands on the desk, and lean toward him. "I think you're forgetting something." Xander regards me with icy rage, and though it draws the hair on the back of my neck to attention, I keep my cool composure. "This town and the *innocents* who live here. Don't you get it? You haven't just aligned yourself with a coven, but this *town* as well. Honestly, I couldn't give a damn if you lost every single wolf and witch in your campaign, but the *real* people of this town? They don't deserve to be caught in the middle of this mess, and make no mistake, they are. If this war is personal between you and that other pack, what do you think they'll do next? They've gone full 21st century on you now with drones. They've joined forces with other supernaturals. If they can't get to you, who do you think they'll go for next? Your neighbors. Your colleagues. Your friends. So man up," I continue passionately. "Every war has casualties, Xander."

Xander snarls and launches himself away from the table in a few angry strides. It brings far more satisfaction than it should knowing I've gotten under his skin, but it lessens when Zoelle watches on anxiously before rushing over to him. She places a comforting hand upon his back, and he leans into the touch, head bowing toward hers. I avert my gaze, the moment turned terribly intimate. Even the wolves around the table shift uncomfortably.

"Down, girl," Atticus rumbles quietly from my side.

"What have you been doing so far to manage the attacks?" I ask with a ragged sigh and turning back to Keenan. My nose nearly bumps into his chest, and I startle back, nose twitching in agitation at the near slight. "Excuse you," I mumble.

He offers me a quick smirk before he replies. "We've been attacking from a defensive position."

"Keenan is our resident military man," Ryatt interjects. "He's got a good head for strategy and tactics, and advises us on our movements."

"Is that so?" I ask mockingly. Keenan gives a short grunt of acknowledgment in response. "If he's so good, then why are you still taking a defensive position? You're *wolves,* up your game. Go after these guys and take them down."

"I've advocated for a different method," he responds.

I snort. "Hopefully one that isn't so passive."

Keenan leans into me. His body presses flush against mine once more as he bends his mouth to my ear. "I wouldn't call it passive at all." A shiver falls down my spine at his words, but I refuse to peel back even an inch and give him ground. He pulls away slowly, but the impression of him lingers as he inches back.

"Oh honestly." Irina makes a gagging noise and looks sullenly toward the alpha who is still in deep conversation with the witch. "Get a room you two."

"They have rooms," Ryatt counters. "They're just separate."

Irina turns a quizzical brow toward us. "How dull," she replies.

I roll my eyes at the unsolicited opinion and glance at Keenan. "What exactly are your thoughts on new tactics and dealing with all of the supernatural creatures creeping about?" *And how might they affect my quest to track down Nova?*

"We've stuck faithfully to a defensive position," he answers, voice stronger than before as he addresses the room, "which is why a feigned retreat would suit our needs perfectly."

I pass Keenan a somewhat impressed look. "Have your frontal force fake a retreat," I murmur, mulling over the idea. "Draw out your opponents in the pursuit then launch a second assault with an even stronger force that's held in reserve. It's not a bad plan. I guess." Keenan rolls his eyes at my blasé tone. "But you'll need to do some reconnaissance to find where your enemy is holding out in the first place. You know, venture out past your territory."

"I'm aware," he grunts. "We've got our own set of drones arriving tomorrow."

The regard of the wolves is slightly unsettling. Their piercing gazes drill into me as I speak with Keenan. It makes me feel self-conscious of the advice I give. Am I saying too much? Am I overstepping my position? Probably both. *Why do I even care*?

"That's great and all," I say, after a long moment's silence, making sure to cast a speculative look toward Xander, "but you're not going to get to use Mr. Military over here unless the leader of the pack gets his head out of his *ass*."

The wolves seem startled at my use of language, at least Kevin and Micah do. Atticus, Irina, and Ryatt wear matching grins. Xander turns a scathing glare my way, and the room quickly reverts back to its earlier tension, the alpha's displeasure once more rolling through the room by the wolves' rigid postures. Keenan's hand spans itself across my middle back, startling me momentarily. The steady connection provides an odd amount of comfort, a settling of my frazzled energy. I don't know whether to attribute it to the soulmark, or the fact that I am unused to such casual contact.

"Listen," I plead, "you're about to have way more trouble than a bunch of vindictive wolves and pesky gremlin knockoffs. The Wardens will come." Xander and Zoelle make their way back toward the desk, the group adjusting to their presence once more. Atticus moves to stand by his alpha's side, but the reassuring presence of the beta does little to lessen Xander's glower. "We sent out three, then sent out four. Now you have two of us under your roof and our relic still in your possession. They're going to come full force, and that magical border of yours? It's not going to keep them out. We're not supernatural."

"Xander..." Zoelle's grip tightens around the arm she holds in her grasp, "maybe we should do what they're suggesting."

A pained expression crosses the alpha's face. A visible tremor courses through his body that seems to echo over each wolf. "You're sure they're coming?" he asks through gritted teeth.

I nod dumbly at the look of helplessness beseeching me through his eyes. "They will come. They won't stop until they have what's theirs. If all is returned, then at least you won't have the vampyré to deal with anymore."

"Well, it looks like our little supernatural poacher is proving her worth, brother," Ryatt comments, eyeing me slyly out of the corner of his eyes.

"First off, I'm not little," I snap. "I'm just as strong as any of you. Second, I'm not a poacher. I'm a Warden. My job is to protect the people of Earth from—"

"Us?" he offers blithely.

I bristle, as does Keenan behind me. "*Yes.*"

The room quiets. Ryatt's smirk turns cruel. Past him, the alpha and beta look to me in disappointment. The toxic vice of guilt clenches around my gut, but just what do I have to feel guilty for? My life's purpose is to protect the people of the earth from the supernatural. They can't be trusted. I know this. They're monsters. Beasts disguised as men who think only to the needs of their dark desires… and….

These are real people with real lives.

Real jobs.

Real families.

Xander's earlier words storm my defenses. My carefully crafted beliefs and teachings suddenly smothered away by his passionate reasoning.

"No need to get so testy, darling," Ryatt coos mockingly. Before I can help myself, my fist snaps forward and lands on the side of his nose with a satisfying *crunch.* "Fuck!" Ryatt stumbles backward, hands gingerly pressed over the offended olfactory organ. With wild eyes stained with amber, he snarls and darts forward.

"Let's go," Keenan grunts, his arm coming around my middle and jerking me away.

"Don't call me darling!" I shout at the raging wolf. Blood seeps out of the small cut on the bridge of his nose, as well as from it. The sight brings a righteous flare of joy, even more so when Atticus bars him from coming after us with a curt command.

"What the hell was that?" Keenan speaks harshly in my ear as he tosses me out into the hallway.

"He doesn't know when to shut his mouth," I reply, breath coming in short bursts as I curb my adrenaline. "He's fine," I continue snidely. "He'll heal in an hour."

Keenan ushers me away from the study, past my room, and down the eccentric grand staircase. "That's not the point," he finally says, voice strained.

I step away from his guiding touch and stop. "Then what is the point? And where the hell are you taking me?"

Keenan gives me a somewhat pained look, stopping as well and turning to face me. "Just... follow me, all right?"

"No," I say stubbornly, crossing my arms over my chest. "Why should I?"

"Just trust me." Keenan extends his hand to me, the pleading look on his face seems completely out of character for a man of his size and stature. A lump forms in my throat as I stare at the large, calloused hand. "Please."

Hit Like A Girl

- Chapter 14 -

"You want to fight?" I stare in a stupor at Keenan as he diligently wraps my knuckles in protective material. He nods, eyes peeking at me through thick, dark lashes that I somehow have only just noticed. The corner of his lips quirks upward, leaving the faintest impression of a dimple in his stumble-stained cheek.

"Yes," he tells me. "I was like you once. Ready for every hit that could come my way. Even more ready to dole out a punch or two myself as a preventative first strike. I was a pretty unruly kid."

"I'm not a kid," I reply testily, yanking my hand out of his hold. He takes it back patiently and finishes wrapping it.

"You're right, you're not, which is why going around hitting people when they get on your nerves isn't okay," he gently scolds me. I avert my gaze to the forest behind him, the endless trees and scent of earth a calm backdrop to the outdoor workout place. "My dad left us when I was ten, but the lycan gene passed onto me through my mother's side, so that made things slightly easier. She put me in mixed martial art classes, and since I was never a straight-A student, once I graduated high school, I enrolled in the army. It gave a lot of stability to my life."

"The army?"

"The army and fighting. It helped me control the anger inside of me. An anger that was naturally heightened and unstable due to the lycan gene." His eyes flit from my reaction to the hand he still holds carefully within his own.

"I'm not angry," I argue, once more slipping my hand from his hold to rest at my side. *Liar.*

Keenan observes me with a mild look of disbelief on his face. "You don't have to lie to me. Anyway, if you do feel the need to get out your anger," he hedges at my growing scowl, "I'd prefer it if I was your punching bag."

The comment draws the blood from my face with Wyatt immediately coming to mind. It hadn't been too long ago when he was the one asking that, but for entirely different motives. Keenan gives me a cautious smile, one that does something strange to my heart and draws a tingling sensation from the soulmark.

"I'm not angry," I tell him again, the words feeling like lead as they exit my mouth. I lick my lips nervously as I draw back toward the rack of free weights, my heart thumping madly in my chest. "I just... have this—" My eyes squeeze briefly shut. "—darkness inside of me. I know that sounds like an excuse, but when I start fighting, sometimes it's as if all I see is red. I can't *not* go after that kill shot. I can't *not* take down my enemy. There's always this rush of power that comes with it. It's what makes it so hard to ignore because I need that power. Sometimes it's what tips the scale in my favor and leaves me the one standing at the end of a fight."

The weight of my confession lies heavy between us as I wait for Keenan's verdict. *Why am I even telling him this?* "Does this feeling only get aroused when you're fighting? Not before or after?"

"It's only during the fight," I confirm cautiously, finding myself breathing easier by the look on Keenan's face. He doesn't look at me as if I'm some sick fanatic. Or some dog that needs to be put down. His gaze is solemn yet knowing, as if he understands this dark feeling inside of me.

"It's not unusual to feel that way, Callie. There are plenty of people in the world who do. All things considered, I don't think it's too surprising that you feel that way, this conflict of emotions. You've been conditioned—"

I blink owlishly at his assessment. "I haven't been *conditioned*."

"—to kill. The way you fight speaks of your years of experience. You're an excellent fighter, Callie, but that's all your life has revolved around. Am I right?"

"You just said you grew up fighting," I respond defensively, watching him with wary distrust.

"I did, but fighting was an outlet for me. Later in life, it became something more meaningful to me because I was saving people's lives—"

"I save people's lives!"

Keenan takes a step toward me, his body language posed as nonthreatening. "I know that," he reassures me. "What I'm trying to say is that the fight for you was always about the kill. The importance of making that kill, because it meant saving lives. But maybe somewhere along the way it lost that importance and changed into something more like sport. And that's where that darkness stems from. I'm not going to condemn you for enjoying the kill. I know the satisfaction that comes with taking out the bad guy, but it's still taking a life. We have to respect that or else we're no better than the *real* bad guys."

I spin round to hide the filter of emotions as they stream across my face. My hands grasp onto the weight rack now in front of me as if it's a life jacket. For it's the only thing managing to keep me upright after Keenan's rather keen evaluation of my person. But is he right? Yes. No....

Maybe.

"I only want to be honest with you, Callie. This thing between us, the soulmark? It isn't going to be easy. But I figure the least we can do is be honest with each other," he tells me, voice raw with sincerity.

"So, you decided to psychoanalyze me?" I give a piteous laugh, dragging a shaking hand along my jaw as I rein in my baser emotions.

"That anger you have? The darkness? It's a problem, and if we're going to be together—"

"Who the hell said we were going to be together?" I ask, turning around to face him, mouth agape at his gall. His crestfallen expression seals my lips shut, and I set my sights on the concrete floor.

"You know what will happen if we're separated." Keenan lets his response drift off into the rocketing silence between us. I nod my head reluctantly. "Being together doesn't have to mean being together in that way. We can just be friends," he tells me. "Hell, I've already told you I'd be glad to be your punching bag. If that's what the soulmark amounts to, so be it."

I take my time to think over his words and settle my flood of emotions. "And what about my little 'problem'?" I finally ask.

"We'll work it out, all right? First, we'll try and pinpoint when you began to feel this way. Once we do, we might be able to better understand and resolve any feelings or misgivings you're holding onto. After that, I can teach you some techniques to calm and center yourself during a fight. Whether it be repeating a phrase or envisioning something to draw your focus to, we'll figure it out, " he tells me calmly.

"Have you done this before with somebody?" My eyes run over him appraisingly. "This has a weird *Karate Kid* vibe to it."

"I have. With myself. Troubled kid, remember? It might not work for you, but it's worth a try. But today we're not going to do any of that. Today we fight to get all that energy out of you. You seem like you've healed up from the worst of your injuries." Keenan takes a step closer and raps his knuckles against my braces. "But maybe without these?"

"These stay on," I tell him pleasantly, masquerading the knowledge of the darkness's origin with an overly sweet smile.

"Fight me without them," he rumbles, the challenge clear in his twinkling eyes. "When was the last time you fought without them?" I heave a sigh and walk around him, pressing my thumb against the top lip of the bracer. It lets off a series of clicks before unlocking from my wrist. I do the same to the other, turning back to him after placing them carefully on one of the workout benches.

"No one is going to take them, right?" The accusation stands clear in my tone, but Keenan wears that familiar serious face when he nods back. "I'm trusting you." *I really am*, I realize. Hope and fear tangle together inside of me uncomfortably, which I guess is what I get for trusting a wolf.

"Ready?" I follow him wordlessly to the makeshift-fighting ring, noting briefly the flash of happiness in his eyes.

"Ready."

+++

Sparring with Keenan is much different than sparring with a fellow Stellar Warrior, or any Warden of Starlight, for that matter. He's well practiced in different styles and shows me as such during our warm-up. It's during the warm-up I realize how heavily I relied on my bracers. I feel sluggish compared to him. The familiar weight of the bracers is gone from my hits and leaves me overcompensating.

It's not pretty.

Distracted by the missing element, I ignore the obvious tells from Keenan's body language and eat mat time and time again. It's only after a few rounds in the ring and a whole lot of curses that I am able to more evenly match Keenan.

But I'm still eating mat. Hard.

"Ugh." The groan I issue is full of frustration. Normally I enjoy panting and howling and clawing beneath a handsome man. Just not when the panting is from sheer lack of breath. The howling issuing in response to pain from a near crippling kneebar. The clawing done as a last-ditch effort against Keenan's back to gain release. "*Ugh.*"

"Better," Keenan notes, extending his arm to me, not at all breathless. *Ass.* My hand locks gingerly around his wrist, careful not to touch the soulmark that lies only a few inches below it. Once I'm on my feet, he glides over to our water bottles, tossing me mine with a flick of his wrist.

"Mm-hmm," I mutter sarcastically, taking a swing. "I lasted a total of three minutes that time." Keenan looks entirely too pleased with himself at that. "Don't look so smug," I gripe, tossing aside my water bottle. "If I had my bracers, you'd have face planted a dozen times too." He shrugs and takes another slug of the water, the grin on his face achingly wide.

I also typically enjoy being under a well-versed man. Just not when said man is bringing me pain and not pleasure.

"You need to learn to fight without the handicap. No enhancers. Just you. Make it personal again. Make it mean something. The darkness is just a state of mind; you can get past it."

I issue a heavy sigh, making my way back into the middle of the ring. "I thought today was just about getting out all of my energy?"
Keenan gives me a short shrug. "It never hurts to start a bit early," he admits. I scoff, eyes wandering to the side at the small audience our practice has brought; e.g., Keenan handing me my ass repeatedly for the better part of a half hour. Atticus even has popcorn.

"You can do it, Callie!" Quinn shouts from Atticus's side, fist pumping in the air. "I got money on you, girl!"

I catch Keenan's eye roll just before he pairs up against me, fists raised and on the balls of his feet. I let my eyes linger a tad too long over the droplets of sweat making their way through the thick thatch of hair covering his pectorals and down—

His fist sails an inch past my face, skimming my ear as I weave to the side. My left hook darts out in retaliation, finding a home on Keenan's chin. He remains unfazed, going in for my body at a pace I can hardly keep up with it. I spot a familiar gleam in his eye—the one that means he's about to take me down—and grind my teeth in vexation. Twisting does me little help with his legs clipping my own.

I don't fight the fall, not with the way Keenan continues to pursue me. Tucking my shoulder in, I hit the mat with a dull thud and roll. My idea to spring back up is foiled when his heavy body is suddenly atop me, a muscular arm stealing around my neck as his elbow jabs into my ribs.

In a whoosh, the air rushes from my lungs, my hand tapping at the arm wrapped around my neck in defeat.

"Not better," he says as he eases off me.

"Fuck you too," I mutter under my breath much to the amusement of... everybody. Quinn raises both eyebrows at me, an expectant look on her face. This time I stand without his help, rubbing my rib as well as the side of my boob.

"Who's winning?" Ryatt asks, bounding over to Quinn and sitting by her side.

"Keenan," the small crowd replies.

"Why is she touching herself like that? Is this the kind of fight we have to be paying to view?" Ryatt continues to ask.

Keenan eyes can't help but drift to the workings of my hands. Like him, I've stripped down to the bare essentials, which meant I'm standing in a borrowed sports bra and workout shorts. My lack of clothing doesn't bother me, but Keenan's regard, no matter how slight, brings an unwelcome warmth to my skin.

"Are you all right?" he asks.

I roll my eyes, turning slightly away from the group as I continue to work the spot. "What, with you beating me up or narrating my problems to the world?" Keenan cringes and casts me a sympathetic look. I hold back my smirk and place a solemn frown on my face instead, an idea blossoming in my head. "I could do with a little less of the latter. The former I can handle. I'm a good fighter despite my showing," I tell him quietly. Keenan nods and steps forward as I raise my fists with lackluster. It's poor form, I know, but it's all the better to lure him into a false sense of security. I turn my back even more to the crowd and let out a soft sigh.

"I'm sorry, Callie." I nod my head to indicate my readiness, and Keenan, the absolute sucker, absently nods back. "We can stop if you want for a while. Have these guys clear out."

"I thought you said I could trust you, Keenan." I hit him with the saddest puppy dog eyes I can manage, my hands dropping to my side as I face him. My soft-spoken words stop Keenan in his tracks, a look of abject horror coming across his face as my words sink in.

I capitalize on the moment, pivoting into a powerful roundhouse kick. It hits, and Keenan stumbles back. The gathering of wolves lets out excited crows as I plow forward. Just as Keenan did before, I crowd into him, relentless as ever, and drop to the ground to deliver a punch to the back of his knee.

On a regular person, this combination would have taken my opponent to the ground. But not Keenan. The giant man wobbles slightly then rights himself. The next thing I know, I'm on my back. The crowd groaning with me as we land. But I refuse to be cowed into submission this time, even if the weight of Keenan's body is too much for me to knock off.

"Cheating, huh?" he asks, the closest to breathless I have heard from him all evening.

"You're the one who nodded back," I counter, "and it wasn't cheating per se."

Keenan lets the weight of his flushed body dig into mine a bit more. "It was definitely cheating."

I lock eyes with Keenan and wrap a leg around his hip, arching so that my body presses into his sensuously. His eyes visibly darken as he inhales sharply through his nose.

"Sometimes you have to play dirty to win," I whisper into his ear, letting my body writhe beneath his.

Cracks of gold emerge in his eyes as he visibly gulps, unwilling to take his eyes off me as I boldly hold his gaze, even if I color at the catcalls we receive from the crowd.

"Calliope," he growls, hips shifting forward ever so slightly even as his hold on me lessens. "Stop." I don't, earning an extra loud holler from Quinn as I hook my other leg around Keenan's waist.

"Now why would I do that?" I ask breathlessly, not at all bothering to hide the sudden grip of lust as I rock my hips against his. His growing arousal presses intimately against my core. It leaves me overly attuned to the fact that he need only angle forward a tad more to hit my sweet spot.

"Holy shit," I hear Atticus exclaim, echoed by several of the other males. "Should we... intervene?"

Quinn scoffs, and out of the corner of my eye, I see her steal the popcorn bowl. "Absolutely not," she says loudly. "Show 'em what you got, girl! Those hips don't lie!"

With my legs locked securely around his waist, Keenan has a rather difficult time extracting himself from me. Though he dutifully tries. The action frees up my hands, and so I defiantly drag my nails down his chest and over the slick abdominal muscles he possesses. Keenan grits his teeth at the action, but not from pain. His length hardening further to press more insistently against the V of my thighs, earning him a soft moan.

The minor sound is all it takes to break the large man. He swoops downward, hands diving into my hair and dragging me up to meet him in a searing kiss. One I don't fight.

Now this is the type of "beneath a man" I can get behind—well, under, to be exact. The world fades away as his lips claim mine in a bruising kiss, the shouts and encouragement from the wolves dying out in my ears as his guttural moan intones around me. I purr back encouragingly, and almost falter when his hips grind back down into my own.

"What the hell is going on here?" Xander roars. *That's my cue.* Keenan stiffens above me, pulling back to stare at me wide eyed just as I deliver a knock-out punch right between the ribs.

"*Omph*!" Keenan glares as my next punch aims dangerously close to his groin. And then we are flipping over so that I am on top. "Cal—" My forearm and elbow in his throat cut off his exasperated plea.

"I said what's going on?" Xander shouts again. Keenan's arms are splayed comically to the side to show he is no longer touching me inappropriately.

"Do you tap out?" I pant, continuing to throw my weight into his throat. My hips sink down into the still very present hard-on he possesses, but nobody else but me can see. Keenan holds my eyes with a fierce glare and slaps his hand on the ground.

Quinn's squeal of excitement is pitched particularly high, but I laugh and smile regardless, peeling slowly off Keenan so that he can adjust himself. Xander strides over to us, his face a mixture of displeasure and amusement. I shrug my shoulders at the man and stand.

"Just showing your fifth how it's done," I casually remark as I snag my water and toss Keenan his. He remains on the ground, staring up at the sky.

"She cheated," he explains with a half-hearted sigh.

"You should have seen it, Xander!" Quinn calls. "It was pay-per-view level shit." I keep my back to the wolves as they yammer on excitedly, taking off my knuckle and hand wraps.

"We'll make pack of you yet, Callie," Ryatt shouts, earning a few hearty cheers. The comment has the unusual effect of souring my mood, discontent riding through me as his words brand themselves across my mind.

"Thanks for the fight," I murmur, slipping out of the ring and vanishing away into the house.

+++

Baths are great for many things. They offer great solace when one wants to be left alone. Provide "shelter" to people during natural disasters. They can even make a fine gin. Tonight, I solicit its services to soak away my aches and pains, and have been, for the past forty minutes. My toes nudge the hot water back on, filling the tub up precariously high to rewarm the water.

Why did I let Ryatt's words get to me? Why?

My eyes slip close as I contemplate my indisputable answer: I'm afraid. Afraid that I'm letting go of my dream to be a Stellar Warrior. Afraid that I have accepted Keenan's deal too easily and let down my family and friends. Afraid that I've taken the easy way out of my problems with the Wardens and will be branded a traitor and coward. Afraid that I don't mind as much as I let on.

What am I going to do?

Today had been a huge flop. I'd learned next to nothing about Nova's whereabouts. JJ will be leaving soon. And I'm getting a little too comfortable around the wolves. The stresses are piling up like building blocks, teetering tenuously as I continue to add to their load. And then there is the soulmark.

Absentmindedly, my palm covers the fateful brand.

I don't know why I'm letting myself get so worked up about my future. In reality, it's already been narrowed down into two paths. Accept the soulmark and the pack or somehow return to my people and eventually go mad. To do either would be an act of betrayal. One that I might not survive. To put it simply, I'm screwed.

The water splashes as I rub my hands across my face, disturbing any chance of tears spilling. A strand of hair falls from the loose topknot I wear. The end instantly becomes soaked and sticks to the side of my neck. With a nudge of my toe, I turn the running water off.

"Callie?" Keenan's soft voice breaks me from my reverie.

The door to my bathroom squeaks open, a veil of steam momentarily obscuring Keenan from view.

When it clears, I note his eyes are steadfastly downcast. He steps in, clearing his throat a mite awkwardly as he shuts the door behind him. "You've been in here awhile."

"Yep," I reply, making sure to pop my P. "It's all right, you can look. I've got a ton of crap in here, so the water is murky. Your eyesight isn't *that* good."

Keenan hesitates a moment before his eyes find my face. "You left pretty abruptly."

"I'm aware."

"Why?"

I sigh, averting my gaze to the green-tinted water made courtesy of a bath bomb. "I just didn't want to be gawked at anymore." I steal a look at his disbelieving expression, confirming what I already know: he doesn't believe me. I wouldn't either. I might be a decent liar and able to keep my cool under duress, but there's just some things you can't hide. Especially not when a pack of wolves is studying your every move.

"I brought you something." He presents a basket, which looks comically small in his hand. I'm surprised I didn't notice it before and peer at it curiously.

"What is it?"

"They're special bath oils. The witches—"

"Pass."

We stare at each other in a silent standoff at my abrupt reply. I have no desire to ease my aches and pains using magic. I convey my determination to Keenan silently, and with an exhale, he walks toward me. Taking a knee by the side of the tub, he places the basket next to one of its clawed feet.

"It's here if you need it." My chest tightens unusually. "And I know I've said it before, but I'll say it again, Callie. I'm here for you if you need me. You can trust me."

I swallow down the wild and desperate desire to hold his words close. To bask in their warmth, security, and sincerity. *It's just the soulmark*, I remind myself. I pull my knees to my chest and hug them close, my chin resting neatly upon them.

"You must really like the sound of your own voice," I respond blandly, the words forced. It's a fact I'm all too aware of as my floundering emotions surface too close to the edge. When did it become difficult to force disdain? When did he move from enemy to....

I shut my eyes to the torment of my thoughts and reach blindly for the washcloth hanging along the edge of the tub. When my hand bumps into another, I flinch in response, eyes startling open only to watch with bated breath as Keenan slips it in the water before running it across the length of my back.

"I've never heard that one before," he responds gruffly. "People tend to mock me for my silence if anything."

"I would have thought they'd take a jab at your sparkling personality," I rasp, mildly stunned by his gentle treatment. His eyes stay steadfast upon his work, never venturing toward my look of wonder or the nervous sheen of my stare.

Keenan runs the washcloth from shoulder to shoulder, then in small circles on my back. "Despite all the shit you tossed in here," he says, "I can still smell your distress. It's faint, but it's there. I know we don't really know each other, but you can talk to me. I'm a good listener if nothing else."

I scoff, brow pulling into an effortless scowl as I direct my regard toward the wall in front of me. Keenan doesn't pause once in his ministrations, nor his attempts to get me to confide in him.

"I'm your soulmark, Callie. You've got me to watch your back for the rest of your life. No questions asked. I know it's not the most appealing thing to you," he tells me. "You've made it plenty clear on your views of the supernatural, but I hope you can see past that. See the man in me and not just the wolf. I might not always have the right words to say, or any for that matter, but I'm dependable. Reliable. I take pride in my work and make an honest living down at Nate's Family Auto Shop in town. And when something is mine, I take care of it."

I shrink out of his touch with a roughened gasp, eyes flying toward his earnest expression. Words feel stuck in my throat. Thwarted by what's left of my pride. He had said it himself, hadn't he? I turn my gaze back to the wall, breath falling in steady puffs. I have my beliefs. I've been taught the horrors wrought by Keenan and his kind—of all the supernatural. Yet a reckoning of doubt shouts at me to believe otherwise. Keenan is... he is....

"I'll leave you to finish up," he says softly, draping the washcloth back along the edge of the tub and preparing to stand. *Say something, say anything, Callie*, I think desperately to myself, but no words surface. Keenan begins to rise, and I feel the trickle of disappointment lance through our soulmark. It breaks my resolve. There is too much disappointment rounding out my horizon. Tonight, I could be spared from it if just for a little while longer.

My hand shoots out and grabs hold of his wrist, gripping onto it like a lifeline. He stills, his eyes digging into the side of my face as I stare into the water. My grip loosens enough to slip down further into his open hand, fingers curling tentatively around his calloused palms.

Keenan sinks back down slowly onto his hunches, before maneuvering himself into a more comfortable seated position. His fingers remaining locked on mine until the water grows cold around me. And even then, I realize with chagrin, I don't want him to let go.

DOWN THE RABBIT HOLE

- Chapter 15 -

There's something to be said about the importance of human contact. Of human connection. How the simple pressure of skin upon skin eases doubts and provides reassurance that you're not alone in the world. Or the deep comfort it provides as some roughened grasp holds you together. How it effortlessly proves you are alive.

I didn't realize how much I craved it until I came here. Nor how quickly a few casual touches would turn into something more meaningful. I've become enraptured by spotting it amongst the pack. Everyone touches one another. A hand upon the arm. A warm embrace. A bump or a nudge in jest. The absentminded caress of one to another. They are always touching, these wolves. Always connected. Always in contact.

The Wardens of Starlight didn't teach me that. And for all the support they provided me throughout my life, cheering me on from the sidelines or securing me scholarships, they never were quite adept with human connection. The Wardens of Starlight connect with the cause, and it's in *that* they are connected to one another. We don't hug. We rarely shake hands. Nova was the only exception. She didn't seem to mind casually touching, but only with me. You'd think they'd act differently, more affectionately, considering the dangerous nature of our job and our rather short lifespans as a result.

I adjust the bracers on my wrists, thoughts slipping to last night. When the water had finally run cold, Keenan helped me from the bathtub. Eyes averted like a gentleman. After securing me in a towel, he placed a kiss on my head and left. The bracers were left on my bed for me to find.

It's early in the morning when I wake. Early enough that I don't expect to run into anyone as I make my way downstairs to head to the indoor workout room. The weather is awful outside, with rain and wind beating against the house in a fury. When I near the gym, I stop short, hearing Keenan arguing with Xander.

"She might be your soulmark, brother, but she's dangerous. I'm not letting off on the guards with the bracers back in her possession. Especially since her brother is set to leave in an hour. She might go after him," Xander tells him. "Speaking of, I thought I remembered telling you I wanted to see the bracers. I don't remember mentioning you giving them back to her."

"You did see them: outside yesterday, specifically. And you're right, you didn't mention giving them back to her, which is why I did," Keenan responds smoothly.

"They make her stronger somehow," Xander gripes. "I don't want her lashing out at one of the wolves."

"She's not going to." There's a brief pause. "And Ryatt brought it upon himself yesterday. He's not upset about it; we talked." I inch closer to the door.

Xander's next words are slightly muffled, but Keenan's are crystal clear. "Callie is smart. She's not going to try and sabotage the pack out of malice. She's not like that."

"I didn't realize spending two days with her let you know her well enough to say that," Xander challenges somewhat caustically.

Keenan lets out a soft warning growl. "She has honor and lives by a code. She's a warrior. And yeah, maybe her whole life she's been told to hate us, but that doesn't mean she does. At least I hope she doesn't. I don't think she does."

Xander remains silent for a moment before responding. "I don't think she hates us, brother, but she sure as hell doesn't like the position she's in. I hate to think she'll be unhappy here, but I have to do what's best for the pack. Which means—"

"I know what it means," Keenan replies resentfully. I straighten at the strict sound. "That doesn't mean I have to like it."

"No," Xander says with a sigh, "it doesn't."

The floor creaks underneath me as I lean my ear closer to the door. A furtive silence follows, and I mentally scold myself. *No use in hiding now*, I think. Without a second of hesitation, I walk through the door and come face-to-face with the two wolves.

"Morning," I say, striving for casual as I walk past them to the far corner of the room. Hushed words are spoken as I stretch, but I don't take offense. This morning my heart feels a little lighter. The burdens I carry, not so insurmountable as last night.

"Good morning." I twist and spare Keenan a small smile at his greeting. "I wasn't expecting you to get up so early."

"You have military time. I have warden time." Keenan nods at my explanation, face unreadable as he watches me continue my warm-up.

"What were you planning on doing today?"

"Weights, I guess. I'll probably go at the punching bag a bit too. Don't worry, I'll try not to knock it off," I tell him sweetly, flashing my bracers at him.

"Can I join you?" The question makes my heart skip a beat.

"Sure," I reply. "We can even spar again if you want and work on some of those techniques you taught me yesterday."

My throat feels uncomfortably dry as I wait for his response. He's watching me closely. Too closely for comfort, surely. I try not to let the underlying heat in his gaze shake me, but my throat gives a traitorous bob as I lock eyes with him. He has clearly already worked out, his workout shirt half soaked in sweat, body glistening.

"I'll get the hand wraps," he finally says. I stare at his retreating form, trying and failing to ignore the way the soulmark prickles my skin. I rub at it absently, but it grows stronger the more I seem to acknowledge it. *That isn't good.* A fluttering erupts in my stomach as Keenan returns.

"Here!" I remark overenthusiastically. "Let me." I reach for the wraps, but Keenan looks at me in confusion, keeping them tightly in his hand.

"It will be easier if I do it," he reasons, pulling away from my searching hands.

I paste a false smile on my face. "I've done it a thousand times before on my own. I assure you I'm more than capable of doing it."

A frown threatens his face. "You don't have to do it on your own anymore," he tells me with meaning.

My hands still, eyes darting nervously to his. I'm suddenly doubly aware of the shift in the air between us. Last night changed things. Another layer of intimacy has been added to our unconventional relationship. One I can't deny. Keenan stirs forward an inch, never breaking eye contact as his hands reach out tentatively for my own.

Goodness, he really is quite... large. *Masculine.*

Muscular and tall are an intimidating combination, especially when the face is disinclined to wear a smile. But there is something about his serious attitude that is appealing. No one would ever doubt Keenan's ability to do anything he set his mind to, and I am terrified to find myself thinking that I'd like to be something he set his mind to.

It's just the soulmark, I tell myself with markedly quicker breath.

Keenan leans in as his hands take mine, his face unreadable except for the smallest hint of wonder. I swallow as I feel the wings of the butterflies drive into a frenzy in my stomach. When had the fluttering turned to butterflies?

"I know," I finally whisper back. Something unreadable passes behind his eyes. Something that makes me suck in a sharp breath as his gaze narrows on my lips. For a moment, the world stills. Then, I am surging forward on the tips of my toes to press my lips firmly against his.

Keenan locks up as my lips move skittishly over his own. I'm not usually so clumsy, but I can barely think with the sound of my heart pounding so loudly in my ear. Then I feel it: shock. It seems to rattle through the soulmark followed by... more shock. With a gasp, I pull back, wide eyed and feeling foolish.

"Oh my God," I say, completely mortified by my actions. "I'm so sorry. I thought—no! I wasn't thinking at all. Just forget I said anything or did anything. All right?"

I attempt to secure my hand back from his custody, but Keenan holds tight.

"Don't be sorry," he rumbles, easily pulling me back into his personal space. "I'm just surprised."

My head shakes fiercely from side to side. "I shouldn't have done that. I thought you were leaning in. So then *I* leaned in. I'm so stupid." I squeeze my eyes shut to avoid his piercing gaze, when his hand squeezes mine.

"You are not stupid. You're… magnificent." My eyes shoot open to stare at him, the moment only lasting for a second, long enough to see his head dive in toward mine.

Keenan's hand slips behind my head, as his other leads mine to the center of his chest. Relief brings a pleasant sigh from my lips against his. Any previous doubt quickly swept aside as his tongue teases and taunts me. I find myself leaning into him, and his arm steals around me in response. The kiss is languid but thorough. Enough to steal my breath and make my soulmark burn.

Kissing Keenan feels natural—right, I think. But it's with this unforeseen realization that I pull back. Beneath my hand, Keenan's muscles tense, as though he is ready to pounce once more at a moment's notice. *And I wouldn't mind at all*, I think faintly.

"Did I do something wrong?" he asks, voice pitched low. I shake my head. "I didn't bite you, did I?" Again, I shake my head. "What is it then?"

I can't verbalize a response. *Because I don't have one*. Because he didn't do anything wrong and kissing him is so damn right. The answer resonates deeply inside of me. Another unignorable fact between us.

"Nothing," I rasp, holding still as I continue to stare at him. Keenan stares back, his eyes searching for something more than my words can provide. My heart is fit to burst as I stand in his arms, attempting to decode my fight-or-flight response. He must sense my inner conflict for he leans forward and captures my mouth to answer my unspoken questioning.

His mouth opens just slightly. Enough to cradle my bottom lip between his own, giving him ample opportunity to drag his tongue across it. The taste snaps us both into action, and I am pulled flush against him. I tug at his lip with my teeth, taken in by the hot-branding want coursing so suddenly through my veins. Keenan makes a sound that seems to echo between my thighs. *Oh lord.* This is so wrong. How can he possibly be making me feel so good?

The feeling resonates through the soulmark, and I am once more reminded that my life is now dictated by it more than anyone or anything else. Maybe that isn't such a bad thing if it means more of this. This warmth and comfort, and the sensory overload of him. As his lips continue to work on my own, leaving me deliciously close to breathless, Keenan's hands tighten down upon me. As if he never wants to let me go.

I feel myself tremble against him, and suddenly I'm kissing him with a vengeance. Hands grappling his arms and shoulders. Legs securing themselves around his waist. Lips furiously battling with his. Keenan matches my enthusiasm, kissing me as if this is the last time our lips will meet. Like he is ravenous.

I'm not sure if I want to be devoured, or devour him.

A heat stirs strongly below my waist, one I am unable to ignore. I maneuver my lips away with a whine, tilting my forehead to rest against his. I need... more.

"Mark me," I whisper harshly against his lips. Keenan freezes. His fingers dig painfully into my waist as he frantically tries to read my expression. I'm shocked by my declaration but find myself more shocked at the fact that I have no regret in saying them. The soulmark is already sealed between us. It was only a matter of time before the marking and binding happened. Or so I rationalize to myself.

"Are you sure?" His voice comes in a ragged whisper.

The soulmark quivers against my skin, and I give a slight inclination of my head, my heart stuck in my throat as he swoops back down to kiss me.

His hand weaves into my hair, skewing my ponytail effortlessly as he guides my head to kiss me deeper. I moan against the onslaught and let him lean me up against a wall, my legs locking more tightly around Keenan's waist. His hands move faster than I can keep track of. They glide over me expertly, exploring every dip and curve to leave me panting. When his fingers slip teasingly beneath the waistband of my workout shorts, I let out a harsh gasp.

"The—" *soulmark.*

Keenan steals the breath from my body in a harsh gasp as we catapult into a cosmic chasm of feeling and sensation. I submit to the magnitude of the simple touch with a keening noise, head tossing back as my hips drive forward into his touch. Keenan lets out a noise of his own. It sounds with primal need through his throat.

He allows his hands to wander up my torso, his normally hot touch suddenly scorching. Calloused fingers leave burn marks in their wake as they savor my flesh. My nails dig into his shoulders as he adjusts his stance and creates more space between us. My abdominals tighten in response, and I'm flooded with gratitude over my more muscular build. With some effort, I still manage to grind my hips against his hardened length.

We both hiss in response, Keenan's hands catching my waist and slowing my movements to a torturous pace. When I begin to pant from the exertion, he gives a stinging slap to my thigh, his head falling to my shoulder as another growl tears from his throat.

"I have to draw blood for the marking, Callie," he whispers harshly.

I nip at his earlobe in response, breath coming in hot pants over his clean-shaven jaw. It's all he needs to precede. Keenan closes the distance between us, crushing me to the wall with his body and rolling his hardness against me in such sweet splendor that I near my edge.

His lips work their way across my shoulder and to my neck. "And now I lay my mark for all to see," he growls against my skin. "By blood, be one."

My cry echoes throughout the room as stars burst behind my eyes, slipping over the edge with only few strong strokes of his attentions. Never before have I felt so alive or connected to something. Not even with the Borealis Matter, but even it will fade from me eventually.

The bond I have with Keenan won't. It will never grow weak. Only stronger.

Keenan's hands fall to my thighs, gripping me almost painfully. His tongue bathes and soothes the bite mark on my neck. Each stroke becoming softer and more languid than the last, his lips caressing the length of my neck as I settle into his embrace.

"Knock, knock, lovebirds."

My eyes startle open, but find nothing but Keenan's imposing frame rigid, completely blocking my view. He sends what I can only assume is a murderous expression at whoever has dared to interrupt. The animalistic show of possession, though startling, doesn't bother me as much as it should.

"What?" Keenan asks in a clipped voice, one much tamer than the growl he just released.

"No morning greeting?" The man, whose voice I now recognize as Ryatt's, lets out a chuckle. "That's not very—"

"What?"

"We've spotted one of them."

Keenan stiffens, though the movement is hardly detectable. If I hadn't been so securely pressed against him, I might not have been able to notice.

"Who?" I breathe.

"One of the vampyrés. The girl." I suck in a harsh breath and maneuver myself out of Keenan's hold with surprising speed. "Which poses to be a problem considering your brother is set to leave quite soon with a certain package." The ring. Nova.

"We have to go. Now."

Ryatt makes a tsking sound with his tongue, taking a step forward cautiously, his eyes still trained on Keenan's body language. "If by 'we' you mean members of the pack and not yourself, then yes."

My heart gives a painful lurch in my chest, a protest ready on my lips when Keenan takes a calculated half step in front of me, partially blocking me from Ryatt's view, again.

"She is pack."

Ryatt can't help but spare me a quick once-over, eyes lingering over my neck. A smug smirk tugs at the corner of his lips.

"Indeed she is, brother," he concedes with a slight inclination of his head. *Indeed I am.* I can feel the difference... I can feel the pack. They are the strong and steady undercurrent to the soulmark, but it still pales in comparison to the fierce river that is the tether between Keenan and me. I can feel him. Feel his rolling jealousy and possessiveness. Feel the constant pouring of affection directed at me. I wonder if I'm feeling breathless due to it or the news.

"Where is she?" I ask.

The wolves pass each other an unreadable look, before Ryatt's lazy gaze turns back toward me. "The southwest borderline. Near to where we found you and your gang."

I ignore the slight and process the information. "Take me there," I tell them. "Send JJ now, and I'll distract her."

"She's a newborn vampyré, Callie," Keenan replies. "She's too strong. Too fast. We'll hold off on your brother's release, set up a wide parameter around the vampyré's location—"

"No," I persist earnestly, my hand shooting out to grab hold of Keenan's arm. The room goes oddly quiet around my next words. "Don't do that. Send JJ away. Now. But let me deal with the vampyré, please. I... I know her. She's my friend. She's the reason we came back in the first place."

I turn pleading eyes on Keenan, pouring all my want and hope through the bond until his face softens. He sighs and turns to the third.

"Well then," Ryatt breathes, "far be it from me to deny a lady's deepest desire. I'll let the big man know, and then we can go."

+++

We navigate the woods on a mix of ATVs and motorized dirt bikes. I ride on the back of an ATV with Keenan, eyes scanning the rapidly disappearing forest line in front and behind of us. The weather gives no reprieve, the rain coming in heavy sheets from the sky, while the wind tosses through the trees with a vengeance. The brigade of vehicles slant to the left as one, slowly spreading out farther and farther from one another to cover more ground.

"Breaker 1-9, do you copy, Callie?" Keenan's voice crackles to life in my ear.

"Affirmative. Over."

Our ATV slows to a stop so that I can hop off, the other off-roaders spearing out into the dreary day. I pass my helmet off to Keenan, squinting into the rain as I stare at my blurred reflection in his visor. Our hand's brush, and the connection between us brightens like a solar flare. "I'll be okay," I say softly, knowing my words are too muted amongst the rain, but that our proximity grants him the ease to understand. For a second, a surge of fear plunges through the bond before being snuffed away. Keenan gives me a curt nod, his sentiments quite clear regarding my plan, and peels off.

I dodge backward to avoid the muddy backsplash, barely able to do so. My brilliant plan is to act as bait and draw her out. To cut a small slice in my skin and hope the scent of my blood reaches Nova before the rain can wash it away. If she came, I would keep her occupied for as long as possible, giving JJ and the ring the time they needed to make it out safely.

My trusty butterfly blade is tucked into a holster on my side, but Vogart's blade is decidedly missing. I haven't been granted access to the artifact, despite my passionate argument. Which means the second, and very much *undisclosed*, part of my plan, can't happen. There will be no attempting to change Nova back today, but I can at least tell her of the blade and give her hope.

Of course, this grand plan of mine works only if all my teachings are wrong. That Nova still possesses her right mind and won't kill me the instant she smells my blood. If not... well, that's why the wolves are creating a perimeter, and I have my bracers and butterfly blade.

With a twist of my wrists, the bracers illuminate, the power of the Borealis called to life from inside of me. I let out an exhale and shake my head. I can't allow myself to be taken under by the rather intoxicating sensation. If I'm to face Nova, I need to be completely levelheaded.

"Warden in position, over," I speak clearly for the mic to pick up as I give a slow walk around the small clearing.

"Pack in position, over."

My hand slips to my waist and removes the butterfly knife. From habit alone, I let it flip open and around my fingers with expert ease. It feels oddly warm in my hand, no doubt from the Borealis Matter it now hosts inside of it. When I finish my tricks, I hold the handles tightly within my grasp and press the flat side of the blade against my forearm. I wish desperately for my dragon skin armor, but there is nothing I can do about that. The wolves have not been able to find it, for whatever reason.

"Please find me, Nova," I whisper, stealing myself for the quick pain of the blade. My hand jerks back, but the blade doesn't touch my skin. I jump at the cold touch on my forearm, but can't rip my arm from the vampyré's hold.

REVELATIONS

- Chapter 16 -

"What are you doing out here?" She all but snarls at me, eyes flitting across the forest.

"What am I…?" My brow scrunches in confusion. "I came out here for *you*. To save you."

Nova scoffs and releases me, taking a few large steps back. She eyes the forest line nervously, shaking her head. "There's nothing you can do to save me," she spits, but sorrow lines her words.

I take a moment to look at her. Nova crosses her arms at my inspection, but it doesn't stop me from my cataloging. She's soaked through. Her long hair hanging in thick wet strands that cling to her neck and shoulders. She still wears her standard issue Warden-wear. Its stains dampened and hidden due to the inclement weather. She looks... worn, but there is no difference in her appearance otherwise—except for the cooler tone of her tawny skin and the hunger in her eye. "You have to go. Get out of here."

"Nova…." I lick my lips nervously and shift forward. "I have the Vogart."

Nova stills, eyes widening and filling with hope. Her bottom lip trembles. "You do?" I nod my head fervently, and Nova stands before me an instant later. "Where? Is it on you? Do you have it now?" Her hands fly over my body in a panicked search, and there is nothing I can do to stop her. Even if I wanted to "Where is it?" she asks, her eyes bleeding red with sudden hunger.

"It's not on me," I confess, holding my breath as I wait for her next move, aware of my vulnerability.

"I…." Her voice shivers with emotion as her eyes flicker back to brown. "I'm sorry," she whispers hoarsely.

"It's all right. It's all right," I soothe, reaching out tentatively to touch her arm. I'm surprised she doesn't flinch back. Instead, Nova stands perfectly still, like a marble statue, as she gazes at me in despair. "They have it, but I can get it. I can use it on you."

Her perfect veneer splinters as her eyes go glossy. "I don't think I can last that long," she grieves, eyes closing shut as if in pain. "He keeps making me come out here. Night after night. Trying to draw out the wolves or the witches or you. That's why you can't be here. I'll have to tell him—tell him everything—and if I don't…." Nova wheezes, eyes a brilliant scarlet once more as they open to stare at me. "He'll punish me. He already punishes me. He won't let me feed, Callie. He's starving me. He's ordered me not to feed, and I can't fight it. I can't fight the sire bond." Nova's hands knot themselves into her hair as she lets out a pained moan and begins to pace.

"It will be all right," I try to say, but she only moans louder. I take a few steps back and tighten my grip on the blade.

"No, it won't! It can't be! Look at me." She turns her tearstained face toward me. "I'm a monster. Just put me out of my misery, Callie. I can't stand this hunger. I can't stand the thought of hurting someone.

Please," she begs, dropping to her knees. "Please kill me."

I stare at Nova in horror. I can't possibly.... There is no way I can bring myself to do that. Not to her. Not when her sisters are counting on me. Not when I so desperately want to right this wrong.

"You're not a monster," I tell her harshly, surprised by the candor in my voice. "You've kept yourself in control this whole time around me, and we both know you didn't have to. You could have taken me out easily."

Nova stares at me, bottom lip still trembling but unmoving otherwise. "I'm so hungry," she cries softly, shoulders sinking. "And I can smell them, you know? The wolves surrounding us. And they smell good, Callie, so much better than just your average human. It doesn't matter that it's raining. I can smell them even from here. Even like this. My senses are in hyperdrive. I bet they have guns, don't they?" A hoarse laugh issues from her lips. "To take me out? Just let them, Callie. Let them do it. And tell my sisters—"

"No!" I interrupt viciously. "Don't say another word." Emotions clog my throat, the rain feeling suddenly colder as it seeps its way to my bones. I press my fingertips against the earpiece. "Keenan, do you copy? Over."

"Roger that. What do you need? Over."

"Swear to me you won't let anyone harm her." The line stays static for too long. Long enough that Nova and I both turn uneasy eyes toward the forest line around us. My heart clenches painfully at the look of raw hope on Nova's face. One I'm sure is mirrored on my own.

"Roger that. Callie, don't do anything—"

"Over and out." I snap into the receiver before pulling it off and pocketing it. I reholster the blade next, hands shaking with nervous energy.

Nova stares at me wide eyed. "What are you doing?"

What am I doing?

I swallow. "Tell me honestly. How much of you is left? How much control do you have?"

"I... I'm still *me*, Callie. But this hunger is unrivaled. It's unignorable. I'm a predator now, more than I've ever been in my life. The hunger is just a part of my nature now. I can't help it," she tells me, "but I think I can control it. I have so far. I just don't know how much longer I can if I don't feed. He won't even let me eat a fucking rabbit."

"Then feed on me."

Nova stares at me aghast, shaking her head from side to side. "I won't."

"You said it yourself; you won't be in control much longer if you don't feed," I argue, stepping closer to her kneeling form.

"He told me I couldn't."

"Couldn't what?"

"He said...." She frowns as she tries to recall his exact words, trying to hide the desperate hunger form her expression. "He said 'I may not feed unless I give him what he wants.'"

"And what does he want?"

"The ring. One of the wolves or witches. You." Her breath hitches on the last word, a different kind of longing and loss drawing into her gaze. I drop down to my knees in front of her.

"I thought you said he wanted you to draw us out."

"He does," she says, sniffling and wiping the rain and tears from her face.

"Well, you did it. We're beyond the border. So feed. Feed on me. I trust you. You won't kill me." I slip my hand into hers, amazed when she squeezes my hand back painfully tight.

"Callie... I don't think I would ever forgive myself if I hurt you."

"You won't," I assure her, griping her back with equal ferocity.

Her eyes flit across my face, searching for reassurance. When she finds it, she takes a deep breath, licking her lips. Nova leans forward, hand rising to my face to caress my jawline and tentatively run her fingertips over my lips. My breath hitches, as does hers.

"When you told me he was your soulmark, I was crushed. Could you tell? Did you know?" She lets out a weak laugh, fingers still tracing my cupid's bow. "And I'll admit, I thought that if we had to take out any wolves during our recon, I would go for him. That way, even if you were forced to be with Wyatt one day, maybe you could find comfort in me. I knew if you found your way to him that there would be no hope for us." Her eyes drop to my neck. "I don't suppose there's any chance you haven't sealed the mark, is there?"

My mouth feels suddenly dry, even with the smattering of raindrops slipping past my parted lips. "Nova...." The tone of my voice gives me away, but she only shakes her head softly. A small, wistful smile gathering on her lips.

"It's all right. It was a fool's hope." Her eyes alight back to mine, the scarlet that stares back at me leaving me speechless. "Just one kiss, before...." Her lips press swiftly against mine, the action freezing me almost completely.

Her lips are unnaturally cool against my own. But they are soft. Softer than I would have ever imagined as they move tenderly against my own. The kiss is brief, yet I find myself short of breath when she pulls away.

"You know," she murmurs, "I don't need to breathe anymore, but somehow you still manage to take my breath away. Funny how you can still do that even now without trying."

"Nova," I whisper back, not knowing what to say.

"Shh. No more talking. I'll only take as much as I need. I promise." Then without another second's hesitation, she dives toward my neck. I catch the barest glimpse of her fangs and then—

"*Ahh*." The startled cry shoots out of my mouth before I can help it. The pain, though not the worst I have felt, is unequivocally the strangest I've felt before. Especially knowing my blood is being drunk straight from my body. The hot wash of it spills over my shoulders past the seal of her mouth, and Nova gives a hearty moan, biting harder. "Careful," I mutter as I grit my teeth against the pull of her mouth.

She makes no reply, only holds me more securely as she lessens the drag of her gulps. I feel a fever break on my forehead, a strange heat unfurling inside me as she continues to feed.

"Oh." My eyes flutter closed as a wave of desire rides through me unexpectedly. *What is this*? How can I possibly be feeling this way? A gasp tears from my mouth as a particularly deep pull is initiated by Nova, accompanied by a guttural moan from the woman. It's as if it pulls straight at my core. "Stop," I rasp.

It takes her a moment, but she does. She licks at the wound, sending a caustic shiver up my spine as I feel the puncture marks close. Nova's breathing sounds heavy in my ear, a heavy metallic tinge to her breath. Her head turns ever so slightly and accidentally brushes her bloodstained cheek against my own.

"Thank you," she says, still breathing heavily. I give a dim nod, closing my eyes to the pain that radiates from my neck and the lingering pleasure in my loins. "Callie, I—" A sharp crack echoes through the forest, and I am suddenly on my back with Nova above me. Red veins run from the bottom of her eyes, fangs fully extended as she lets out an angry hiss toward the west.

"Get off her!" Keenan shouts. Another shot is fired, and Nova grunts in pain.

"Nova, get off me! Get off me! He'll kill you!" The next shot rings out, but Nova rolls us to the side faster than I can comprehend. My head spins at the action. "Nova," I pant, pushing at her with effort. Even with the strength of the bracers, it has too little effect. "Run."

She looks down at me fretfully, her scarlet eyes reverting to brown. I can hear Keenan's heavy footfall and give one last push.

"I love you," she whispers hoarsely. "I won't let him hurt you." She goes to touch my face one last time but thinks better of it, sprinting off in a flash of speed.

"Are you all right?" Keenan comes sliding down next to me, mud splashing onto both of us at the action. He wraps me up in his arms to sit me up.

"I'm okay," I croak, wincing at the motion. I raise a hand to stop the rain from pelting in my face, suddenly feeling extremely cold and weak.

"She bit you," he snarls, eyeing the mark on my neck with anguish, "and you liked it."

I suck in a harsh breath. If I had more blood circulating in my system, I'm sure I would have been blushing. "I couldn't help it. Vampyré fangs release a toxin that make their meals more malleable. Besides, I told her to. Vrana's starving her. She was going crazy."

Keenan's features harden as he lifts me up. The roar of engines sounds in the background, but my focus is entirely taken by the man holding me. "She's a vampyré, Callie," he scolds me harshly. "She would have killed you."

I swallow painfully, but stare him determinedly in the eye. "And you're a lycan. You're just as capable of killing someone. She might be driven by a hunger for blood, but you have a wolf inside you that's just as untamed and wild as that hunger." My answer shuts him up effectively, and me, if I'm being honest.

"We're going home," he grunts.

+++

I'm immediately given a slew of potions to drink from Zoelle when we return. Her face is crestfallen at seeing my bloodied shoulder and pallor but sets firmly a second later, ordering me into the kitchen, where I am fussed about until I'm fit to scream. I give my account to both Keenan and Zoelle, then Xander once I have finished with them. It feels like ages until I'm allowed to go back to my assigned room, Keenan hovering closely behind me.

"Wait," he says once the bedroom door closes behind us. "Let's talk before you take your shower."

"Keenan," his name comes out in a whine. "I'm tired and cold. I just want to get out of these clothes and under some hot water. Can't this wait?" I don't bother to turn around to face him. I can feel his body heat on my back, mere inches away.

"All right," he utters. I walk away from him and lock myself in the bathroom. I don't need visitors this time around.

When I'm under the fall of hot water, I feel as if I can finally breathe. Whatever tonics and potions Zoelle forced down my throat are slowly working their magic. Thank God. Nova had taken too much by just an ounce or so, enough for me to feel it.

I turn my back to the stream of water, letting it pound against the back of my neck and shoulder. The Wardens would have my head if they learned of my actions today. Allowing Keenan to mark me? Check. Allowing a fledgling vampyré to feed on me? Check. What else will I find myself doing before the end of the day? Announcing my allegiance to the Adolphus Pack?

Or have I done that already by allowing Keenan to mark me?

I exhale long and slow. Everything I've known is being turned upside down. Lycans aren't mindless beasts set to kill at the slightest insult. Vampyrés can control their hunger. And Wardens sometimes do act like poachers. Maybe that is the darkness inside of me? Maybe I have become too desensitized and no better than a lowly poacher. The thought gives me a stomachache, but if Nova can rein in her thirst, then I can rein in my darkness. Perhaps the key to doing so is to reteach myself about the creatures I fought, find out for myself what they are made of instead of relying on my teachings.

I dread to get out of the shower, but know my time is reaching its limit. Locked or not, Keenan will be coming to get me sooner rather than later. When I emerge from the steam-filled bathroom, Keenan is waiting patiently by the window. Arms folded across his chest, face expressionless though adorned with a downward tilt of his mouth. His body language communicates his frustration, but it's the bond between us that speaks to me of his fear. And his anger.

"Hey."

"Why don't you take a seat? Zoelle said you should rest as much as possible to recover from the blood loss."

I raise a brow and sit on the edge of the bed. "What did you want to talk about?" My hair is bundled atop my head in a messy bun, but droplets of water drip down my neck. I wipe them away.

"Why did you let her do that?"

"I told you," I say, not bothering to hide the aggravation from my tone. "He was starving her. She's one of my best friends, and I made a promise to her sisters that I would find a way to help her. If drinking my blood helped her to find some sanity, or help her stand strong against Vrana, then who was I to deny her?"

"She could have killed you," he argues.

"She didn't," I counter swiftly. Keenan turns his regard toward the rain outside, his disappointment washing through the bond. "I know why you're really upset," I finally manage to say, "so do you want me to say it, or you?" Keenan doesn't say a word. "It didn't mean anything, Keenan. It was just a chemical reaction—"

"It didn't look like a chemical reaction," he grouches.

"It was, all right?" He remains silent for a time before turning his stormy gaze my way. "And the kiss, it didn't mean anything. At least not to me. I never knew Nova felt the way she does about me."

"I don't want other people touching you. Men or women." There's that possessiveness again. In his speech and in his eyes. "We're the ones who are meant to be together."

I force myself to steer my gaze to the floor. His words aren't wholly unappealing. And that might be a problem. For I find the thought of being with someone else wholly unappealing. I glance back to Keenan, finding his stormy regard still aimed my way. It's nothing like the way Wyatt would have gazed at me in this sort of situation. Wyatt would have looked like a child denied his favorite toy. Keenan looks at me as if he would tear the world apart just to be at my side.

Wyatt.... The thought of him makes me cringe, but I can't help but compare the two. Keenan reacts with a deeper slanting of his mouth.

"I'll leave you to rest," he says simply and heads toward the bedroom door. I realize my mistake almost too late.

"Wait!" I cry. "You don't understand. I was thinking about Wyatt, not you." Keenan's scowl deepens, and I find myself cringing at my own words.

"That's not what I meant either. Well, it is, but it isn't. I was thinking about Wyatt, but nothing particularly nice. That's why I cringed. Not because I wasn't thinking about you." I take a deep breath. "I'm not making any sense, am I?"

Keenan stops, though he still looks put out. He opens his mouth to respond when a few quick raps sound at the door. Without waiting for permission to enter, Irina opens it and steps inside.

"Keenan, Xander needs you."

Keenan's mouth trims to a short, firm line, and he gives me a meaningful look.

"You know he doesn't like to be kept waiting," she continues dryly, sparing me a glance as she tucks a strand of perfectly straight black hair behind her ear. She was not among the pack sent out to try and fetch Nova and looks disgustingly stunning in simple, everyday clothes. Jeans, a 3/4 length black shirt, with not but a ring to garnish the ensemble. My eye catches the dark impression of a sideways 8 on the inside of her wrist, an infinity symbol. She doesn't seem like the type to sport tattoos, could it possibly be her soulmark?

She catches my regard and arches a brow haughtily. "Nice ink," I comment dully, eyes darting between Keenan's slow movements and Irina's disposition.

"*Humph.*"

I roll my eyes at the rather-childlike reaction, but in doing so catch the glint of her ring once more. The deep purple is brought out by the nest of gold that holds it. Irina notices my stare and tilts the ring out of view, her body straightening somewhat defensively. I pass a brief look of confusion to Keenan but note he too is oddly tense. Even through the bond, I feel his sudden spike in fear. Why?

My heart jumps a beat.

"Can I see your ring?" The color falls from Irina's cheeks.

"I have to be going as well, I'm afraid. It's not just Keenan that Xander wishes to speak with," she explains, turning her back on me. I cover the distance between us in a few quick strides and grab hold of her upper arm. "Release me this instant!" she shouts in alarm, trying to shake me from my hold.

"Let me see that ring," I snarl, yanking her hand out so I can see it. "Oh my God." I release her as if I've been burned, stumbling back a few steps as I stare in horror at the two of them. "You lied to me."

Keenan takes a wayward step in my direction, eyes wide, full-fledged panic adorning his face. "Calliope—"

"You lied to me!" My breath comes in heavy pants as my own panic sets in. "I trusted you. And JJ...." I bend at the waist, hands on my knees as I try to process the information. "Did you even let him go? Or was that a lie too? He's still at the witches, isn't he?"

"No!" he shouts over me. I see his approach and move backward with jerky steps. "No, I swear. He's gone, but the ring...."

"You lied to me." Tears flood the side of my face. There is no point in hiding them. My disappointment and sorrow score the bond between us. It aches all the way to my bones. "What the hell is going on?"

"Keenan had nothing to do with it," Irina tells me. "Xander had very strict orders in place that the man be sent with a false ring. No one was allowed to let on or say anything. Or write anything. There was no way around the order."

"I trusted you." I whisper the words more to myself than the others. "I trusted you, and you betrayed me. You manipulated me—"

"No, I swear—"

"Get out!" I scream. The wolves look horrified at my reaction, but they don't fight me. Irina tugs at Keenan's hand.

"Keenan, let her be. Give her time." Keenan is reluctant to go but does with lead feet. I want to yell and scream at the door. I want to tear the entire room apart, but my hollowed-out heart leads me to the bed, where I collapse in a fit of tears.

WALK ON THE WILD SIDE

- Chapter 17 -

I resume my "fast" almost immediately after Keenan and Irina leave. At least, that's what I tell the people who try to bring me food later in the day. Not even Zoelle's gentle chiding from outside the bedroom door can stir me from my spot against the foot of the bed. I pay for that particular insolence later. Her magical medicine wears off more quickly without food in my stomach.

No one pushes the matter. We all know the truth, and that is I'm too sick over the pack's deception to have any appetite. How could I be such a damn fool? Haven't I learned anything? It's like the wendigo fiasco all over again, except this hurt so much more. I have been maneuvered and manipulated effortlessly. I let the soulmark blind me. I let my emotions win.

There would be no going back now. My people would never accept me. Likewise, remaining with the wolves isn't an option, but can I escape from their clutches? With the witches as their allies, they can easily bind me to this prison. Not to mention the binding effects of the soulmark itself....

A knock sounds on the door.

I shift in my seated position, stifling a groan as my back gives an angry creak in response. I had fallen asleep on the ground, refusing the comfort of the room's hospitality out of spite.

A knock sounds on the door once more.

"Calliope?" *Ah.* They sent the alpha. "Let's take a walk." The issued order is surprisingly strong and effective. I find myself rising from the ground without a second thought before attempting to slam on the breaks. But my feet continue to take me toward the bedroom door. I let out a growl of frustration. I should never have let Keenan mark me. It linked me to the pack and made me susceptible to the alpha's commands.

"You're a dick," I tell him flatly as I open the door. Xander spares me a small smile.

"Follow me." The order rolls over me smoothly, and my feet shuffle along accordingly beside him.

Xander takes me to the forest, leading me to a small brook that winds curiously through the trees. It's peaceful here. The sound of the water rushing past covers the gentle rustle of leaves as a breeze comes along. I would enjoy the scene more if I were alone.

"I wanted to explain to you why I sent your brother away without the ring," Xander says.

My shoulders rise and fall unenthusiastically. "It doesn't matter. It was my mistake for trusting any of you to keep your word. Wolves are notorious tricksters. It's in all the legends."

"You should know Keenan wasn't informed of the ring swap until early yesterday morning. I don't believe you managed to catch that part of our conversation," he continues smoothly. "He wasn't pleased, but the blame rests on me. I'm responsible for the well-being of this pack, and allowing your brother to leave our territory with it was not an option."

"The ring—"

"Could not be kept safe with your people. I know your argument well, Calliope. Keenan made it on your behalf, but the fact of the matter is we stole it once already. And your people have yet to secure it back from us."

"They will," I tell him seriously. "You don't know them. They won't stop until they have it. Once they learn that it's a counterfeit, JJ is the one who will face the repercussions. As will I. You've royally fucked things up, you know? You and your pack of wolves."

Xander sighs, the placating expression he wore during his little speech slipping off to a grimace. "I'm sorry for that. It wasn't our intention to cause harm, none of this was. Since we learned of Vrana's desire to acquire the ring, the conclusion made by our allies was for the ring to reside within our territory. It really is the safest place for it, Calliope. No supernatural enemy can penetrate our border with the crystal in our possession."

"The Wardens of Starlight aren't supernatural," I remind him, kicking at the soft clods of dirt near my feet. "And please stop calling me Calliope. You sound like my father." *And Wyatt.*

Xander shoots me a side-glance, a smirk treading on his lips. "Callie then," he remarks. "Be that as it may, we're still well equipped to handle your people."

"They train us like mercenaries, you know. From a young age, they teach us how to fight and defeat supernatural creatures. Dying in the name of the Wardens is an honor, so don't think for a second they won't risk it all trying to defeat you."

A long pause follows my statement before Xander continues thoughtfully. "The Wardens are human. My wolves don't harm humans and are under the strictest order not to. When the time comes—*if* the time comes—the Wardens will be subdued rather than eliminated. We'll use tranquilizer darts, standstill bullets crafted by the witches, and the witches themselves to hold them at bay."

The words are not what I expect and bring about a slew of confusion to my already fraught emotions. No doubt he's trying to make up for his act of betrayal and placate me with another lie. And for what? So I'll go running back into Keenan's arms? Become another pawn in someone else's game.

"You don't believe me?" His voice is filled with wry amusement. It captures my attention unexpectedly, for his smirk softens. "I don't blame you. Not after what happened with the ring, but that's okay. You can be mad and rage at me all you want, Callie. But no one else in this pack deserves your ire." I spare him a pointed glare, one that he returns. The alpha's mild disappointment quivers through the pack bonds and is aimed my way. I scoff to cover the feeling of remorse I feel as a result.

"I'd appreciate it if you didn't try and dictate my feelings," I tell him stiffly. The pressure of his disappointment evaporates.

"You're right," he murmurs. "I apologize. Again. But, Callie, what I said is true. I'm the only one who deserves your anger, and, well, maybe the Elder Triad from the Trinity Coven by that estimation. Not Keenan though. We made the decision and are the ones who implemented it."

A wind rustles a few leaves from their branches and into the brook. I shiver at the gentle chill in the sweeping air and wish longingly for something warmer than my thin cotton shirt. Xander rests his hand on my shoulder. I look to him in surprise as the action brings an almost immediate sense of comfort.

"You said there would be repercussions for yourself and your brother?" I nod my head along dumbly. "Would it help if you could call home?"

I stare at him flabbergasted, words caught in my throat. "What? Why? Why would you offer me that?"

"You're part of this pack, Callie, whether you like it or not, and your happiness and well-being are important to me. It's my responsibility to see that you're taken care of and safe. That extends to those that you love. If calling one of your people will help circumvent trouble your brother might encounter, then you should call home. Besides, the circumstances that brought you into my pack are largely the result of my decisions. I want to do what I can to help make your full transition into the pack be as easy and seamless as possible."

"I don't know what to say," I tell him honestly, staring at him in confusion and leaning out of his touch. The comfort it brought departs with the motion, but it has already done what it's meant to do: calm me. Soothe my irate nerves.

"Listen, Callie, I wish you and Keenan could have met under different circumstances. I wish the pack wasn't at war, because if it wasn't, and if you and Keenan did meet under different circumstance, the pack would be celebrating. Our pack is blessed with an unusual amount of wolves finding their soulmarks, and every mark found is cause for celebration. I wish we could give you two more. It's what you deserve."

"Well," I say, once I can drag the words up my throat, "we can't always get what we want. Besides, it wouldn't matter in what circumstances I met Keenan. I'm still a Warden. He's still a lycan. My family and my people will never allow it."

Xander frowns at my words. "Do they know about the soulmark?"

I let out a rough bark of laughter, shaking my head and shifting my weight as another cool breeze comes rushing through the summer day. "No. Though it might have been simpler if they did. I would have been exiled or killed sooner. Probably the latter." I chance a glance at the alpha and find his face filled with a mixture of anger and remorse. I give him a lame one-shoulder shrug as part of my reply. "It's just the way things are. Any mark of the supernatural variety upon a Warden is forbidden. It's heresy. They would never understand. They would never accept this."

Xander sighs, peering out into the forest pensively. "I suppose I'm not completely surprised by the information, though it does make me feel sick to my stomach."

"You're telling me," I retort with a scoff. We share a look, matching grim grins splitting our faces.

"When I discovered Zoelle was my soulmark, and granddaughter to one of the most formidable witches I'd yet to encounter, it wasn't exactly smooth sailing for us. Though, I doubt that would surprise anyone. It's fairly common for the supernatural to stay amongst their kind, but aligning with the witches has been the best thing that's happened to my pack. It felt forced at first, but over the months, the alliance has turned into something more. A true friendship has formed between my pack and the Trinity Coven.

"I don't know why we were all so adverse to each other in the first place. It seems ridiculous looking back on it, but that's the price we paid for listening to stories passed on from our ancestors. To holding onto old prejudices and not bothering ourselves to forge new friendships. Our alliance and friendship frighten the supernatural community because it's an oddity. But it also frightens them because it signals a change. A possibility of a different future for our kind, without the hierarchy that's in place now. Change is hard, but especially more so for those who live their lives in black and white when it's meant to be in full color."

I let out a breathy laugh, giving Xander a once-over. His hands are stuffed in his jean pockets, and the pensive look remains on his face as he stares out into the distance. "Damn," I say, "that was... mildly impressive."

Xander grants me a smile that changes his entire demeanor. He seems lighter and happier. Strong and capable. And I realize as the undertone of his gratitude reaches me through the pack bonds that he means every word he's said, that he does care for my well-being and that of all his wolves, that he won't let harm fall to the Wardens.

I offer him a sad smile. "The Wardens aren't big fans of change. Unless they pass a very rigorous inspection and is agreed upon by all sitting Council members. In *every* region. Anyway," I continue with a sigh, "the soulmark and this whole mess are really just the cherries on top of my already perilous standing with the Wardens."

"What do you mean?"

"I wasn't lying when I said they train us like mercenaries from when we are young. We're taught that eliminating the threat of supernaturals is paramount to the survival of the human race, and it's our divine purpose to do so. Not everyone wants to kill though, not everyone is cut out for it, but I was. I understood and believed in the purpose. I was good at it—I am good at it. But somewhere along the way, once I became a Stellar Warrior, I wavered. I made a huge mistake."

Xander's hand falls to my shoulder once more, and with it, that same relief and comfort, along with something else, a gentle urging through the bond to continue. I don't acknowledge the silent order, the past already slipping readily from my mouth. The proverbial flood gates open.

"We learned of a recently transitioning wendigo through our network of Shadow Scouts. Since wendigo are much easier to eliminate in the early stages of their transition from human to wendigo, only one warrior needs to be sent to take care of the problem." I take a shuddering breath, feeling my voice fill with thick emotion. "They didn't tell me it was a little girl.

And nothing can really prepare you for that, you know? For seeing something like that in person. That monsters can wear the faces of the truly innocent. When I found her, she was crying and scared.

"All I remember are those big crocodile tears and the way she was shaking. She didn't understand what was happening to her. She couldn't comprehend that this evil spirit was taking possession of her body or that soon her body would turn gaunt and frail to the point of emaciation. How her skin would stick to her bones and her eyes would sink into her unrecognizable head. That her body would turn to rot and she would become a monster. And I couldn't do it. I couldn't kill her. Not then anyway, even if it was the right thing to do."

I'm barely cognizant of the tears spilling down my cheeks as my story goes on, only that the strength of the alpha's touch seems to be the only thing keeping me grounded.

"It's all right, Callie. You did do the right thing."

I shake my head fervently. "But it wasn't," I tell him with a wet, hysterical laugh. "I hid her away, and when I went back to get her in two days' time, she was gone. I found her by chance. She'd turned faster than I anticipated and had managed to trap a small congregation in a chapel as they met for Sunday mass. She killed them all. It was a slaughterhouse, Xander. She got away from me then too, but I found her. She was with a nest of three full-fledged wendigo, and I killed them all. I *slaughtered* them. The Council removed me from the Warriors and made me a Starlight Warden because they said no Stellar Warrior could have possibly taken on that many wendigo without housing a darkness inside them. Without being a Ripper at heart."

He tugs me under his arm and into his side while I dash away my tears and take a few breaths to collect myself. "What's a Ripper, Callie?"

"It's what they call Stellar Warriors who carry the darkness inside of them. The ones who connect a little too closely with the creatures we kill. If you're lucky, you're exiled. Since my father holds a lot of weight on the Council, he was able to have me moved into a different order of the Wardens of Starlight. A lot of people didn't like that decision."

"That's a lot of pressure and stress to put on a person," he comments lightly. "Did you ever have anyone to talk to about it?"

"We're not really talkers or sharers," I explain. "We're not a lot of things."

Xander gives me a little squeeze, and I'm reminded of how much these wolves rely on physical contact to connect with one another. That, and how much I've come to crave the contact and connection in so little time.

It's turning out to be my undoing.

I pull away from Xander and place myself at arm's length away from him, gazing into the crystal-clear water of the brook. "What? No comment?"

"I believe the reason you were able to do what you do, was with an enormous sense of guilt and anger. Both of which can drive a person to do nearly impossible things. Not because of some 'darkness' inside of you. Just pent-up human emotion that came out of an already violent outlet."

My throat gives a betraying bob. "You don't think I have a darkness inside of me?"

"Maybe you do." Xander shrugs. "But maybe you don't. Either way, those lessons you've decided to do with Keenan should help. He's a good man. He's smart and levelheaded, and I'm sure he'll be able to help you."

"I'm not sure that's the best idea anymore," I confess. We stay silent for a long moment, each lost in our thoughts before Xander breaks the silence between us.

"Listen, Callie, the reason I brought you out here was to explain to you why you saw Irina with the ring, as well as to try and mend the rift between you and Keenan."

"I was curious about that particular detail," I confess. "Why not give the ring to the witches?"

He crosses his arms over his chest, assuming the stance of parent ready to lecture. I make sure to keep my listening ears on. "Irina is the fastest wolf in the pack. If trouble should arise, she'll leave with the ring immediately. She's practically as fast as a vampyré once she hits her stride. We didn't give the witches the ring because that's what they'll assume. That's where they'll go first, and Irina can slip away. Callie," the threat of an order lingers in his tone, "tell me about the dagger we found on you."

"I took a vow," I manage to say, the hidden truth of the dagger poised at the back of my tongue. I swallow uncomfortably. "I can't tell you that. Please don't make me."

"It will be all right, Callie. I don't plan on telling anyone else; this will remain between you and me. Tell me about the blade."

I suck in a hasty breath, a curl of helplessness settling in my stomach at the order I can't refuse. "It's Vogart's Blade, the Last of the Necromancers and Creator of the Vampyré. Lore has it that if the blade were to pierce the heart of a newly turned vampyré, it would change them back."

I'm not sure how I expected Xander to react to the information, but it wasn't with such stout silence. His shoulders seem to deflate from their rigid posture as the seconds pass, a look of remorse skirting his features.

"That's why you wanted it the other day. You wanted to turn your friend back." I nod my head. "But what if it didn't work? You would have—"

"Killed her?" I whisper hollowly. "I know. It's what she would want. It's what she asked me to do yesterday."

"And instead you let her feed on you?" The incredulity in his voice is hardly covered by his confusion.

I brush my hair behind my ear. "She needed help. She still needs help, and I think I can give that to her."

"I know this isn't what you want to hear, but I'd like you to consider letting me pass the dagger into Irina's protection. That way she can leave with both the ring and knife should things take a turn for the worse."

"My family will still come," I warn him. "And frankly, between all the other supernatural creatures knocking at your door, it's them that you need to be worried about the most. When they come, these woods will be painted with blood."

Xander frowns in thought. "Then I think it's for the best of everyone if you make that call to your family today."

TOO LITTLE TOO LATE

- Chapter 18 -

Xander and I return to the manor shortly after our chat, parting ways when he heads toward the garage. He instructs me to use the phone in his office, and so I go there immediately. I don't know many people's number by heart. Those that I do I can count on one hand.

"Was it 5-3 or 5-2?" I mutter to myself as I stare dumbly at the phone in my hand. I punch in the former and wait with bated breath as the other line rings.

"Hello?"

Thank God.

"Noelle? It's Callie." I can hear her sharp intake of breath followed abruptly by the rush of air over the phone's mouthpiece, along with hurried footsteps. After a minute and some indiscriminate noises, she makes her reply.

"What the hell is going on, Callie? They sent a troop out to retrieve the artifacts and look for you and JJ. You're in a lot of trouble. I shouldn't even be talking to you right now. I just hid myself in a supply closet near the observatory for heaven's sake."

I sigh and slump against the large office desk. "Short version?"

"Yes, please. And I already know it was a trap, so skip that part. Naomi and Wyatt are back, but nobody knows what happened to you or JJ. What happened to you guys?"

"JJ hid under the van and got left behind, and I used myself as bait to help the others escape. We were taken in, me by the wolves and JJ by the witches. But they sent him back, Noelle. The witches sent JJ back yesterday morning as a truce of sorts. An armistice."

"And you were left behind?"

"Yes. With Vogart's blade and the ring."

Noelle curses under her breath. "So they have both of the artifacts?" I swallow tightly at the accusation.

"Yes," I force out, "and you should know they sent JJ back with a fake ring. They told me they would send the ring as well to sweeten the deal, but it was a lie. I'm telling you because I don't want JJ to take the blame for it. Will you help him if it comes to that? Vouch for him?"

"Christ, Callie," Noelle says, taking her time to give me her response. "I will. I'll help him, but on one condition."

"Name it."

"Tell me… did you find her? Have you been able to help her?"

My throat tightens. "I found her. She's in rough shape, but, Noelle, she's okay. She's strong, and she's going to be okay." A not-so-quiet sob drifts through the phone line, and I blink back my own tears. "I told her about our plan, but she's having a tough time working her way around the vampyrés orders. I'm still going to try and save her, all right? I'm not giving up on her."

"Thank you," she says with a hiccup.

"Don't thank me yet," I joke.

Noelle lets out a weak laugh. "Anything else I should know?"

I let my mind run over the days I've been here. There is no way I'll be telling her about the soulmark, and it doesn't seem necessary to touch on Luna.

"You know about the crystal, right?"

"We overheard a conversation about a crystal, but Nova was the only one ever to spot it," she admits. "It was too deep into their territory, and Nova seeing it was a miracle in and of itself. Why?"

"It's called the Wielding Crystal of Dan Furth. Have you ever heard of it? It's created this magical border around their territory that keeps other supernatural beings out of it."

"Hmm, I don't think I know what—*oh no*."

"Noelle?" I stand up straight as I hear a small commotion in the background. There's a muffled voice, a squeal of protest, and then a door slamming shut.

Heavy panting resounds in the earpiece. "Calliope?"

Oh no. "Um... hi, Felicia."

"What the *fuck*, Calliope. Explain. *Now*." I relay an even shorter version of the story to Felicia, with plenty of apologies strewn throughout my words. "You're an idiot," she tells me savagely. "Stealing from the Wardens? Assisting the enemy? What has gotten into you, Callie? There's no going back from those crimes, and make no mistake, they are crimes."

"I know," I tell her forlornly, "but I can't change what I've done."

"What you can do is get back those artifacts and intercept the Stellar Warriors before they reach you and rain hell upon that town and its inhabitants." I feel a stone of dread hit the pit of my stomach.

"What do you mean 'rain hell'?" I rasp.

"It means that the artifacts aren't the only thing the warriors are after. They're out for blood after the latest slight, and no doubt they'll go for that pretty crystal too," she hisses back.

"Wait, wait! Slow down," I beg. "What latest slight? And what do you know about the crystal?"

Felicia makes an impatient noise, one I became familiar with at the Banks Facility and know means she's on her last nerve. "Another lycan attack. They killed a Council member, Callie. As for that crystal, well, it's extremely powerful and currently in the hands of a very powerful coven. It's messing with the balance of things, and they'll either take it or destroy it."

"But the crystal isn't hurting anyone. It's protecting people," I reason weakly, horrified over the news. I can't see Xander sending his wolves out to needlessly attack the Wardens, but the other pack might, especially if they're still working with Vrana.

"It doesn't matter, Callie." She sighs. "It doesn't matter because they're gunning for the wolves regardless. Just keep out of trouble, all right? Make yourself scarce if you can. The Borealis Matter that's running through your blood right now will last you a long while as long as you only tap into it sparingly."

"Really?"

"Yes, really," she scoffs. "Did I teach you nothing? Artifacts are routinely re-implanted with the Borealis on—"

"On a two to three-year basis," I finish. "Thank you," I whisper.

"I hate that you're in such a scrape, kid," she tells me, the aggravation still in her voice, "but I hate even more that I'm out an apprentice. You put me in a spot. So just follow my last advice and don't interfere with the Wardens. Stay out of their way. They won't go easy on you if they find you. And definitely, get away from those wolves and witches. You're going to get yourself killed if you don't." The comment makes me gulp.

"Felicia…."

She sighs over the phone. "Wyatt hasn't exactly had anything kind to say about the scenario, and Naomi doesn't have as much credibility as him."

That *dick*. "Thanks for the heads-up, Felicia. I really appreciate it. And I'm sorry, okay? I'm sorry for putting you in this position."

"Yeah, yeah," she mutters. "I hope I don't see your face around here anytime soon, Calliope."

"Bye, Felicia," I whisper back, hearing the line cut off before I even finish saying her name. "Damn," I curse aloud, running my hands through my hair.

They're coming. I knew it, but by her warning, it sounds as if they are already well on their way. They might even be here *today*, and if that's the case, I have to do something. *Innocent lives could be lost*, I think gravely, *human, wolf, and witch alike*. I have to warn Xander. They'll want to inflict pain upon their enemies, not knowing they're probably being played by Vrana. Surely, he instructed the other pack to antagonize the Wardens, knowing they won't discriminate against which wolf pack they go after.

I slam the phone down into its receiver and book it out of the study, only to run face-first into a broad chest.

"*Omph*!"

"Whoa, slow down there." I take a step back and look up at Atticus. He shoots me a flirtatious smile. "What's going on, warrior girl?"

"Now really isn't the time, Atticus," I say. "I have to get ahold of Xander or—"

"Me? I am the beta after all. What's wrong?" The frown that forms on his face doesn't suit him. "Callie, what's wrong?" The order is subtle in his voice, but it's still present.

"I think the Wardens are coming today. And they're not just in it to get the relics back, Atticus. The other pack has been causing trouble up in Alaska, and they want to hurt the pack. It's not going to be pretty. We have to do something. We have to warn the others that they're coming."

A litany of emotions flies over his face before he gives me a curt nod. "I'll find Xander and send a message to Zoelle. See if you can't find Ryatt or Keenan and let them know. They'll know what to do."

"Atticus—" He sprints off down the hallway before I can finish. My mouth closes with a snap before I follow his lead, making my way as fast as I can back outside toward the forest. Hopefully, I'll intercept a wolf out there.

I'm only a few yards from the forest line before the sun is covered by an ominous dark cloud and casts a shadow over the land. A brief look above and a deep breath later warns of an impending storm. Great. When I hear my name being shouted, I skid to a halt and turn around. Keenan is flying toward me, a look of distress on his face.

"What's wrong? What is it?" He slides to a stop in front of me, hands cupping my face as he searches for any outward marks of distress. "Atticus said to get to you immediately. That something was wrong." At the touch of his hands, I feel the full force of his concern. It's almost overwhelming and most definitely distracting.

"They're coming," I tell him with a shaky breath. "The Wardens are coming. I spoke with a friend from home—"

"When did you speak—"

"That's not important! The point is, is that I did, and I think the Wardens are closer than we anticipated. They're out for blood, Keenan. The other pack has been messing with them, which makes it personal now for the Wardens. They'll try and take out as many wolves as they can, and I think there's a chance they'll go for the crystal as well. We have to hide it."

Keenan has a sober furrow in his brow. "I don't know if we can move the crystal, but we can try. Come on, I'll take you to it. The witches should be on duty, and we're bound to run into some of the wolves on patrol."

I'm about to pull away and sprint into the forest when Keenan swoops down and claims my lips in a passionate kiss. His fingers knot themselves at the hair near the nape of my neck, tilting my head back to kiss me deeper, more fiercely than ever before. I moan into his mouth, kissing him back with equal fervor. When he pulls away, I'm gasping for air.

"I'm sorry," he breathes harshly, his hands smoothing themselves down my arms before taking my hands. "I couldn't say anything."

"I know," I tell him in a hushed voice, still trying to calm my racing heart. "It's all right. Xander and I spoke. I think I'm growing to understand the true power of an alpha order myself."

"Are you sure you're all right?" The question lingers in the air, heavy in its innuendo.

Out of habit, I chew on my bottom lip a bit nervously before cautiously nodding. "I think I'd be better than all right knowing the crystal was out of harm's way, and the witches and wolves are prepared for what's headed this way," I tell him gingerly. I don't want anyone getting hurt from the Wardens or the pack that I now find myself tied to. "Maybe something can be done to turn their wrath toward the other pack?"

Keenan shakes his head. "I'm sure the Wselfwulf's were hoping this would happen. I'd bet my life's savings that they're staying far within their territory for the next few days." We share a look of dismay. "Let's go."

With my hand still in his, we race northwest. I try to tell Keenan multiple times to run ahead of me, he is clearly the faster of us, but he refuses to leave my side.

The gesture is sweet, but stupid. Still, we run as one, racing as quickly as we can to the location of the crystal, intercepting no other wolf from the Adolphus Pack. Maybe Atticus got to Xander or Ryatt, and they told the wolves and witches to retreat?

"We need to move the crystal," Keenan announces once we arrive. He is barely out of breath while I catch mine discreetly by his side. The three women standing around the large purple and pink quartz give Keenan a dubious look.

"Not gonna happen," a woman with short red hair states. "This spot was scouted for the crystal to take root here. There's no telling what might happen to the energy border if we move it."

"It doesn't have to be moved far," I try to reason. "It just needs to be hidden. The Wardens have sent their warriors to come and take the crystal—possibly destroy it—and they'll stop at nothing until they do. Even if it means killing everyone who stands in their way."

None of the three women look particularly impressed by my speech, though the redhead does wear a more pensive look. "We can cloak it," she suggests with a mild shrug, "but we're not moving it."

"That's not good enough," I argue.

"Tough," she snaps.

"Then cloak it!" I respond heatedly. "Then get the hell out of the forest. Anybody wandering these woods will be fair game to them, and then they'll go hunting in town. You need to go back and figure out how to protect all of those people."

"Is she serious?" the brunette nearest to the crystal asks Keenan.

"Where is everyone?" he asks, his tone leaving no room for argument.

The three women pass Keenan another look of incredulity. "It's the shift," the brunette answers. "Wolves and witches are rotating out for their breaks.

No one's on the border except for us at the moment. I'm sure everyone will take a post soon. Hopefully they'll bring umbrellas. I hate running shifts in the rain."

"Keenan...." My voice trails off in warning. Something doesn't feel right. Maybe it's paranoia, but I feel like we were being watched. The skin on the back of my neck tingles, and the urge to switch on my bracers is unusually harsh.

"I'm sorry, but aren't you like, one of them?" the other brunette asks. Her hair is plaited down her back. "Or have you switched sides now?"

"Just move the fucking crystal!" I snap, lunging toward it. "Or I'll do it myself."

A burst of purple light blasts from the palm of the redhead before I have time to react. It should hit me squarely in the chest, but Keenan dodges in front of me. He grunts at the impact, stumbling backward into me. A muted cry tugs at my vocal cords as the hit vibrates through the bond. It is electrifying in the worst way.

"This isn't the time for fighting," Keenan snarls. "She's with us, and right now she's trying to save all of your lives, as well as everyone else's. Don't believe us? Then take it up with one of your elders *after* you move the crystal. They've already given the go-ahead, and we don't have time for this." This time the women look at each other with uncertainty, Keenan's forceful words seemingly doing the trick.

"Oh, hello! I didn't realize we would have visitors," Luna's sugary sweet voice turns all of our heads. In her hands, she holds a large pot with green sprouts poking their way tentatively out of the dirt. She wears a large smile, but I'm surprised to see her purple eyes a startling crystal blue and her hair a pale blonde instead of icy white. Even her skin has lost its etherealness. The witches must have given her a more powerful glamor to wear. Luna walks up to us, eyes sparkling with genuine mirth. "Isn't it a beautiful day?"

"Luna," Keenan starts, turning his body to face her, "we need to move the crystal."

His words obviously shock her for her mouth becomes ajar, bobbing up and down comically as she looks to the witches for confirmation. "Surely this cannot be done. This is the crystal's home. Here." She shifts the pot in her arms and points toward the ground upon which the crystal rests to prove her point.

"Trouble is heading our way," I tell her.

Her eyes widen, if possible, further. "Not rokama?"

My brow scrunches in confusion. "No," I speak slowly, sparing Keenan and the witches a quick glance.

"More hellspawn?"

"No," I say again, agitation creeping at the surface of my tone. "The Wardens. My people are coming."

"What are Wardens?" she asks. The pain of my fingernails in my palms does little to calm me.

"The Wardens protect ancient, magical relics. They also hunt the supernatural, and right now they're hunting all of you. And they want the crystal. We have to move it."

Luna's face pales. "Not hellspawn?"

This time I release my growl of frustration, moving out from behind Keenan's protective stance to standoff once more. The air around us crackles with energy as the witches take in my posturing. The fingerless gloves they wear let off a distinct shimmer.

"I just said it wasn't—"

Luna's finger points nervously out behind us. We turn to look. Oh no. Sickly green creatures are scattered in the near distance. Their ugly faces turned upward to sniff the air. Ears perked in the air. They slowly inch their way toward the border. From their mouths, an odd clicking and chattering sound.

"Shit," I breathe.

"It's all right, between us and the fairy, we can take them out. The others will be along shortly," the redhead reasons, turning to face off with the demons.

"If Atticus got to Xander, then no one is coming in for their shift," Keenan voices. "He'll want to keep everyone well away from the border, including all of the witches. We need to leave, now, and take the crystal."

"It's not as if it will take long," she huffs impatiently. "Come on, Luna. Show them what you're made of."

Luna shuffles uncomfortably with the load in her arms, backing up minutely. Her head moves slowly from side to side. "I can't," she says unhappily. "I've used up my magic for the day tending to the gardens and the border. Besides, I'm not overly fond of violence. Diana said I didn't have to fight anymore since it makes me uncomfortable."

My eyebrows rise to my hairline as I shoot Luna a look of disbelief. She looks back at me mildly offended, but that's not what ends up capturing my attention. It's the red dot wavering over her chest. A sharp *crack* echoes through the forest.

"Get down!" I scream, throwing myself at the fairy. She drops her potted plant with a shriek before I tackle her to the ground, releasing another cry as we land. "Are you all right?" I ask raggedly in her ear, pulling back up when I see the others begin to crowd around us out of my peripheral.

Luna shakes her head in a daze, her hand lifting to the growing spot of red inches above her heart. She opens her mouth to speak, a gurgle of blood accidentally spilling forth with a hacking cough. Panic leaks into every facet of her body. Eyes widening. Breath pitched to a frenzy. Body locking.

I press my hand dutifully against the wound. "Get back!" I shout once more over my shoulder just as another shot sounds. An instant later, a smattering of crystal shrapnel embeds itself into my calves. The shattering of the crystal lets off an angry chinking in the air.

"Take what's left of the crystal and go!" Keenan commands, but as I look back at the scene, the witches and Keenan are frozen.

The magical border lets out an angry crackle in response, brilliant crimson and violet sparks hurtling from fractures that appear by the dozen all along the magical divide. Some slowly smooth back over, while other points of fissures remain gaping open.

"Oh, Goddess." One of the witches groans in horror. "Millie, Sarah, take the crystal back to the house as fast as you can," the redhead orders.

"But, Jane!"

"Go!" she orders more harshly, sweeping her hands up in an arch. A strange mist ascends into the air from the ground, creating a wide, hazy barrier between us and the splintered border. "I'll hold them back for as long as I can. Send help." The woman with the plaited hair lets out a distressed sob, glancing back over her shoulder at the approaching figures in black still a ways out. The Wardens are here.

"Jane...." Her voice trails off only to find her next words replaced with a sharp *crack* as another bullet tries and fails to penetrate the newly erected barrier.

"Go, Sarah," Jane tells her coolly, eyes trained on the misshapen bullet lodged in the barrier, conveniently eye level with Sarah.

The two witches say not another word. Their hands rising in time as eerie words fall from their lips. The crystal quivers and rises slowly from the ground between them. They take a step, nervously eyeing the splintered barrier that wraps around their territory, but nothing happens.

"May the Goddess guide the light within you, from this world to the next," Sarah says somberly. Jane gives a jerky nod, hands shaking as another bullet crashes against her barrier.

"Tell them—"

"We will, Jane," Millie assures her, and then the two witches are off as fast as they dare go, the crystal glowing brightly between them.

"Can you get her out of here?" Jane asks, voice strained. "They're closing in too quickly. Both the hellspawn and the people in black."

"Can you move with me, Luna?" I ask hastily, and she whimpers her assent. I help her to stand, ignoring her cries as the pain becomes too much. "It's all right," I murmur to her, arm wrapped securely around her waist as she leans fully into my side. "We'll take this one step at a time and get as far—"

"Here, let me." Keenan tries to take my spot, but I push him away.

"You have to run and tell the others," I protest. "You're faster, Keenan. The witches are slowed down because they're moving the crystal, Jane is protecting us, and I have to help Luna. Which means *you* have to be the one who gets the others. You're our best chance. Go."

Jane lets out a startled cry. I stare helplessly at her misty barrier, watching in alarm as it begins to flicker. Her body visibly shakes from the effort to keep it erect. "Get the hell out of here!" Jane shouts.

"I can't just leave you here," he snarls. Our mutual terror twines together through the bond, making my next words cut all the deeper.

"You can," I shoot back. "We both know I'm right, Keenan. And if anyone has a shot at stalling them, it's me. Not you. Not Luna. Not Jane. You have to go; you just don't want to. And I get it, okay?" Emotion clots my voice. "*I get it.*"

Keenan visibly shakes at my words while I continue to hobble along with Luna. His eyes waver from brown to gold. "I can't—" Before he can say another word, he lets out a snarl of rage, twirling around and flinging something lanky and green to the ground. The hellspawn are through the border. Jane lets out a curse, and then foreign words echo through the air around us followed by a clap of what sounds like thunder. Keenan grabs the hellspawn out of midair when it dares to attack him again. It's neck twisting with Keenan's deadly hold before going limp. He drops it to the ground, panting lightly.

"Go. If I can take you on and win, those little hellions don't stand a chance." My words don't alleviate the mood, but they do get Keenan to turn and sprint off into the forest with an angry scowl.

"Hellspawn," Luna corrects me between gritted teeth as we pick up into a canter. She is considerably paler when I cast her a glance, and I note she is increasing the amount of weight she leans on me.

"Stay with me, Luna. We'll be out of range soon enough and can hide," I promise.

Luna stumbles. Her wracking cough filling the air as an ominous rustling sounds from behind us. "Can't," she chokes, falling to a knee. I twist my wrists, and the bracers ignite with their light. With little effort, I call forth the Borealis I house inside me and use my strength to maneuver us behind a thick-bodied tree.

"Don't move. Don't make a sound," I tell her quietly as I slip into a crouch. My body thrums with energy as I assess my surroundings.

Jane's cry pierces the air before abruptly cutting short. It draws a cold shiver down my back. I have nothing to protect us with, except my body. And I have absolutely no idea on how to kill the mongrels closing in on us, since I've never been taught about them. But Luna was.

"Luna," I whisper, "how do I kill them? Luna?" I gently nudge her foot, but the fairy only blinks back at me owlishly, a hand pressed weakly against her wound.

"Kill?" Tears cascade down her cheeks.

"Not you," I hiss. "*Them.*"

One of them grows bold and creeps closer. It walks on all fours like some kind of primate; back hunched and knuckles digging into the ground for support. The hellspawn's eyes are black with a filmy yellow crust around them. It doesn't look as if it sees, so much as it hears or smells.

"I could really use some kind of weapon," I mutter to myself, shifting back onto my heels. I regret leaving the manor without my butterfly knife as my vulnerability becomes starkly apparent.

"Cal-*e*." Luna stretches out her hand to me, eyes closed as her lips tremble. A sharp point presses grotesquely against the skin of her forearm, piercing it with aching slowness. I watch in muted horror as the bone-white object continues to grow and lengthen from her body in my direction. It reaches almost a foot in length before she snaps it off with a grunt of pain, eyes flaring a startling purple before returning to their glimmered state. "Kill."

I take the bone stake, swallowing past the lump in my throat and turning my attention back to our enemy. And just in time. One of the hellspawn comes out from behind the tree we hide behind, launching itself at me with a feral snarl. I roll with the impact, worming a foot between its body and myself to kick it off. It flies overhead as I tumble safely back into a crouch. I barely have time to position myself better in front of Luna before another one launches itself at me.

And then another. And another.

I can feel the darkness in me crawling forth as I knock back the vermin, one after the other. It craves death. Death granted by my hands, and before I can help myself, I snap the neck of the next hellspawn and whip it across the forest floor. My breathing comes in sharp pants as the hellspawn collect around us, their needle-like teeth protruding in crooked lines from their unhinged jaws. The darkness dares to surge forward, but with a snarl of my own, I push it back down. I will not lose myself in it. Not today. Not *now*. In my mind, a picture of a never-ending night sky filled with bright starry dots fills my thoughts. *Breathe and focus*, I chant to myself. *Don't let the darkness out.*

"Come on, you filthy bastards," I mutter as they drift forward.

A shot rings out, loud and clear through the forest, and a second later I flail backward as a jarring pain pierces my stomach. My hand darts to my stomach, but when I pull it away to see the damage, nothing is there. Still I ache. The bond between Keenan and I corrodes in agony.

"Keenan." His name is a hoarse cry on my lips before they attack, spearing me to the ground as their teeth battle each other to gnash at my body. I shriek in pain. Trying—*trying so damn hard*—and failing to escape. Luna's cries pierce the air behind me. Teeth capture a chunk of my left arm, tearing from it flesh and muscle. My scream seems to curdle as I jerk uncontrollably in pain, watching in horror as the beast devours my flesh. It triggers something inside of me, and my darkness surges to the surface. I knock a hellspawn off me and then another. But it is not enough. Not even with the Borealis helping to fuel my rage.

Pain racks through my body, to a point at which I think I may pass out, but at least Luna is no longer crying. The thought brings me little comfort knowing the reason why. A scream swells in my throat, one that scratches and aches upon its release.

Something gnaws at my ankle. Something bites deeply into my thigh. *It's too much.* A sob wracks my chest, jarring pain stemming from what seems like every part of my body as they continue their feast. I don't expect the one with its claws sunk deep into my belly to be torn away. It lets out a startled yelp, it's gnashing teeth coated in my flesh and blood. A second later, another is tossed from my body. Then another. And another. I scoot weakly backward, gasping for breath. Soft splashes of something wet land sporadically on me. Rain, I think dimly. I let my eyes drift shut, but am surprised when cool hands cradle my face gently.

"Callie? Callie, are you all right?" Nova's voice is as achingly cool as her touch, and my eyes open to see her face half covered in blisters. How fast must she have run to find me with the threat of the sun looming behind the clouds? How did she find me at all? A wet sob bursts from my mouth in reply, and she cradles me to her chest, slipping her arms under me to pull me close. "Shh," she murmurs rocking me. "Hush now. It's all right. I can help you. You just need to drink my blood, and then we can be together. Everything will be okay."

I shake my head weakly against her chest, forcing myself to push away from her. "No," I manage to get out.

Nova lets out an angry growl, her gaze darting furtively around as the forest comes alive with the sound of gunfire and the pattering rain becomes heavier. Before my eyes, her skin seems to be smoothing over, her wounds healing. "We don't have time. I can save you. Let me save you," she begs.

"Can't," comes my blood-soaked response.

Nova's eyes narrow on the fresh splatter of blood across my chin and cheeks, her eyes slipping into crimson as her nostrils flare. "But...." She must read the desperate plea in my eyes because she lets out a growl of frustration, angry tears welling in her eyes. "Fine, then take these. It will help you heal faster," she says, carefully lying me back down to take off her bracers. "They don't work for me anymore anyway, and he only let me keep them to be mean. To remind me of my old life and what I'd lost." The bracers unlock around her wrists with the correct pressure from her fingertips, and then she is slipping them onto my forearms above the other pair. The fit is tight. Uncomfortable. Yet they pale in comparison to my other injuries.

Nova helps me activate them, her eyes watching with barely veiled envy as my back bends from the culminated power. "Shhh!" Nova casts another harried look around us, her hand slapping over my mouth. "They're coming, and I can't... I can't stay. Just tell them I'm sorry. I'm sorry for everything," she says to me in a rush, hand slipping away. "He made me tell him everything. Everything about the Wardens. Everything about the relics."

My hand reaches out to grasp hers tightly, the pain in my body dulling ever so slightly. "Everything?" I gasp.

She nods her head regretfully, beginning to stand. "He knows about the blade. I'm so sorry, Callie. Please don't tell me you have it on you."

"No," I rasp, pulling myself to my elbows shakily. "Irina—" Nova's hand slaps over my mouth once more in a panic.

"Didn't you just hear what I said?" Animalistic terror frets about her words. "I have to tell him everything, Callie. Oh no." She shifts uncontrollably backward, landing clumsily on her butt. "He ordered me to... and the border is down in patches... I have to—"

"Don't." My own panic rises with the realization of what I've just done. "It's not with her. It's... it's...." But my harried excuse is no use. The tears spill forth from her eyes as she shuts them. When they open, they are a familiar brown.

"Tell my sisters I love them," she whispers raggedly, then is off in the blink of an eye. The sound of gunfire increases mere seconds after she spirits away, leaving me to deal with the aftermath.

I can't feel him, I think brokenly, trying and failing to feel Keenan through the bond. Except, there is nothing there.

It's so disturbingly bare that it rouses a pain deep in my heart. One I never knew I could feel. *I can't breathe*, I think weakly, the pain in my body once more overwhelming me. *I can't breathe*. Luna's piteous moan is the only thing keeping me from losing control. I pull myself toward her, dragging my lower half with labored breaths.

"Luna," I croak weakly, but her slumped form makes no response. Her body is littered with bite marks and angry gashes, but I can hardly tell if any are life-threatening. She's far too covered in blood. "Please," I beg, "please, wake up."

"I've got another one!" a male voice shouts, one that is vaguely familiar.

A white-hot pain spears through my middle back, as the military-issued boot makes impact. I grit my teeth against the pain, collapsing into the dirt without protest.

"Well, well, well. What do we have here?" A fistful of my hair is bunched in an angry fist before I'm yanked roughly upward onto my knees. "The little bitch, traitor," the veteran Stellar Warrior all but snarls. "Just what should I do with you?"

A rather vicious yank and my head snaps back. Throat exposed. His hot breath skirts over the delicate flesh, and my heart thunders in my ears.

"Haven't got anything to say for yourself?" He forces my head to turn toward him. *Devin Watercress, second in his class only to my brother and one to hold a grudge*. I hock the blood and phlegm clogging my airway and spit it in his face.

"Fuck you," I snarl back. He releases me in disgust, angrily wiping at his face before eyeing me with fury. I steel myself for the knockout blow that is certain to come my way when Wyatt appears out of the blue.

"Calliope." He grimaces at the sight of me, stepping between me and the other warrior. "What the hell do you think you're doing, Watercress?"

"Orders are—"

"I know what the fucking orders are, you moron. So, I'll ask you again; what the hell are you doing?" I can't see Devin's face, but I'm hopeful that it's scared shitless. It isn't wise to get on Wyatt's bad side. "Get back with the others, now. I'll take care of Calliope Sawyer."

I watch Devin's retreating figure with relief but find myself unconsciously stiffening when Wyatt crouches down next to me.

"You've really done it this time, Calliope," he tells me, "but don't worry. I'll get you out of it." He stands. Before I can make my reply, he reaches for his semiautomatic and smashes the butt of the gun against my forehead. A bursting pain eclipses all others, and then I am pulled into blissful darkness.

CROSS YOUR HEART AND HOPE TO DIE

- Chapter 19 -

Another day, another holding cell.

My body radiates an ache so deep, I'm not sure where one pain begins and another ends. Flashes of gnarled teeth and rotting breath steal into the forefront of my mind, and the urge to vomit is almost impossible to ignore. Not that there is anything in my stomach to purge. A few measured breaths resolve the minor issue, but it does little to calm my shaking nerves.

I'm back in Alaska. Back at the Banks Facility, tucked away in a cell meant for the worst of our kind. Traitors. Apostates. Thieves.

Check, check, and check.

The only balm to my wounds is that I can once again feel Keenan through the bond. He didn't die the other day, and the relief is tremendous. Even with two thousand miles between us, the bond is still there. As weak as it is, it gives me something to hold on to. It anchors me.

I'm not sure what day it is, or how long I've been here. No one has come, at least not while I've been awake. Thankfully I've been washed and put in new clothes. My wounds tended to with baseline effort.

A door opens and slams closed in the distance, and my eyes watch the long, poorly lit hallway dispassionately. The footfalls that sound are heavy. Masculine. My hands curl into fists at my side as anxiety builds in my stomach. I hope it's not Wyatt. Or worse, my father.

I suck in a sharp breath of relief when the distant figure passes under one of the working hallway lights. "JJ." I force myself to my feet, wincing in pain as I shuffle toward the bars of my cell. "You're alive. You made it." Tears blossom in my vision, and I happily blink them away.

When JJ stands before my cell bars, we reach out to each other, hands grasping onto one another as tightly as possible.

"What happened to you?" he asks, voice holding a distinct tremor. I give him the CliffsNotes version, inwardly pleased when I'm able to keep my composure the whole way through.

"What are they going to do with me?"

JJ has trouble holding my gaze, swallowing uncomfortably. "You'll go before the Council. The full Council."

My heart gives an unsteady lurch. "What?" I gasp. "The full Council? Are you sure, JJ?"

"They called them all in. The Peruvians, Argentinians, Estonians, Spaniards, Mongolians, Botswana, Moroccan, and Australians. All of the Councils, from all over the world."

"I'm in that much trouble?" I whisper.

JJ visibly swallows. "It's not just you, but there is a theory...."

I take in a shaky breath and feel my legs begin to cramp. The bite marks strewn across my body throb in tandem. "Just tell me."

"Your record was reviewed in full, Cal. You know you have marks against you for pursuing a career with the Stellar Warriors against the recommendation of the Alaskan Council, not to mention the wendigo incident. Now this? They think you're—" He cuts himself off with a shake of his head before barreling on. "—cursed. They think the root of all your disobedience comes from the darkness inside of you, and it's been working its will upon you all this time."

I pull myself from JJ's hold and slowly limp back toward the long stone bench I'm allotted. "They *honestly* think I'm cursed?" I give a hoarse laugh. They'd certainly hit the nail on the head.

"They think you should have been exiled when the Church Hill wendigo incident happened," he continues.

"Maybe I should have been."

"No," he tells me vehemently. "No, Calliope. Don't ever say that, do you understand? Our family has always been held to a higher standard because we're one of the Founding Four. There are others who've made the same mistakes, worse some still, and they're still with us today. You shouldn't be treated any differently."

"What do you think they're gonna do to me, JJ?" I ask after a long pause. "We both know this trial is all for show. It's the punishment the Council is interested in." *It's about putting me in my place*, I think, *once and for all*. "Nothing more."

JJ directs his gaze to the concrete floor. His jaw working silently, as he works out how to break the news to me. "There are… a few options. Exile, which would be the most lenient. Execution"—my heart gives a most painful lurch in my chest, chin dipping to my chest as I take in a shaky breath—"obviously not as lenient, but quick."

Our eyes meet through a shimmering gloss of tears. I give him a weak smile. "*Obviously.*"

"Or…."

JJ takes too long to respond, the discomfort on his face showing. "Or what, JJ?" I whisper.

"There has been a third proposal. An option for you to stay." Again, he stalls.

"Just tell me, all right? Just, *tell me.*"

JJ's gaze turns stony. "They'll bring in the Occult Scholars to perform an exorcism. They'll begin with the Purification Rites, then the Absolution Mantle, and finish it with a Purging."

I feel as if the floor has been pulled out from under me. And though I am seated, I find myself slumping forward, almost unable to catch myself as JJ cries out my name.

"They haven't…." My head moves dumbly from side to side. I cast my gaze back toward JJ and lick my lips. "They haven't performed an exorcism in over a hundred years. And after the last one," my words stutter along as I feel my body begin to tremble, "they deemed it too cruel. JJ—"

"Hey, hey." JJ drops to a knee and reaches out to me. "Shhh, it's going to be all right, Cal. The exorcism—"

"All right, JJ?" My wretched laughter echoes against the cold concrete walls as tears fall freely down my face. "It's not going to be *all right.* They'll waterboard me, whip and beat me without giving me a single means to protect myself, and then they'll…." The words are almost too much for me to say. For men, purging means taking poison to cleanse the body. If the man survives, the darkness is said to be rid and he can rejoin the community with all past sins forgotten and forgiven. For a woman…. "Who's the man that petitioned for the exorcism?"

I hardly recognize my voice, as flat and detached as it goes. We both know I know who it is. I just have to hear it. I have to.

"Wyatt," JJ says lowly.

"So, after I'm 'purified' and 'absolved,' they'll let him *rape me* for the *Purging*? And if his seed doesn't take—if I don't get pregnant—then it will somehow prove the darkness inside me can't be purged? How the fuck is any of that right?" My hand slaps angrily against the stone. A miserable sob wrenches from my chest at the barbaric unfairness.

JJ rubs both hands over his face, taking a few deep breaths as he straightens. "Cal, that's not all you would have to do."

"What?" I ask, aghast.

"They'll make you kill the prisoner to prove your loyalty. After losing the ring and the blade, they thought it the simplest way to demonstrate it. Of course, they'll also expect your full cooperation during the trial as well. You'll answer all their questions honestly and to the best of your knowledge."

"I can't." The words come out broken and mangled as I stare at JJ in anguish. "I can't survive that, JJ. I'd rather be dead." JJ nods stoically in response.

"If I could find some way to get you out of all this, I would. I just don't even know where to begin, Cal." Silence falls around us, enveloping us within its solitude.

"JJ," his name falls quietly from my lips, "what prisoner?"

"They snagged one of the wolves. Some big guy with a ton of tattoos. He looks like a mean son of a bitch. They're keeping him pretty heavily sedated to keep him under control."

The world tilts on its axis. I thought… I had thought….

"JJ, you have to help me get out of here. You have to help me." I surge to my feet and lunge toward the cell bars to support myself. JJ takes hold of me through the bars, eyes wide at my state of pure panic.

"Cal, I—"

"You can't let them hurt him. You can't. We have to save him. Get him out of here."

JJ's face pinches in confusion. "What the hell are you talking about, Cal. That dog took out—"

"I don't care what he's done," I tell him harshly, a burst of adrenaline rushing through my veins and keeping me upright. With a low cry, I seize JJ by the shirt and yank him forward, breathing in hard, shallow rasps. JJ bangs against the cell bars. A look of fear crossing over his face. "I don't care. You have to get us out. Do you understand me?"

I barely recognize myself in the reflection of his eyes. "Cal, calm down. This is the darkness—"

I give JJ a shake, feeling far too satisfied when he bangs once more against the cell bars. "There is no such thing as 'the darkness,' JJ. It's just some made-up story to coerce us into submission and keep us in line. Do you want to know what's real? This."

I release JJ and yank down the side of my pants to reveal a smattering of tattoos, and the one among them that is so much more.

"What the fuck are you talking about?" he barks, taking a step away from the bars.

"This." I jab at the impression of the fang. "This isn't a tattoo, JJ. I was born with it, and that man has the exact same one on him. It's—"

"A soulmark," he breathes, taking another step back. "Jesus Christ, Cal! That can't be. It can't."

"It can, and it is, JJ," I tell him, moving back to lean against the bars. "And the man they've taken as prisoner—"

"No." JJ's head moves quickly from side to side. "No."

"Yes." I don't know if it's my softly spoken insistence or the expression I wear upon my face, but

JJ quits his tremulous actions. His shoulders sinking as his face falls into a grimace.

"Cal—"

"Please, JJ. Please, I'm begging you. Help us. Find a way. You always find a way." I've never seen JJ look so torn. So defeated. I can see the tears of frustration cloud his vision.

"I…." He moves backward uncertainly, body tensing as he avoids my gaze. "I have to go, Cal."

JJ's name is a mere whisper on my lips as he turns heel and strides away. For the briefest of moments, I thought he would stay. I thought he would help. Now? Now, I am sure I've just sealed my fate.

+++

Nobody comes for me. No food is sent. Nothing. It leaves me feeling hollow inside. Hopeless. As if I'm nothing myself. There's nothing more I want than to have Keenan's arms wrapped around me, rather than my own. I've come to find solace there. A sense of security. A new home.

The pulse of his life is still weak through the bond, and now I know the true reason why. No doubt my comrades have been giving him a quicksilver tonic combined with a tranquilizer. It would guarantee his submission and his weakness. The thought brings another bout of angry tears to the surface, but I brush them determinedly away. My tears will do neither of us any good. I have to reserve all my strength for the trial to come.

Somewhere in the distance, a door opens and slams closed. I sit up a little straighter on the bench, my body screaming its protest. My wounds feel as if they're on fire, and I've never felt more tightly strung. *I need more medicine*, I think grimly. Otherwise, infection is almost guaranteed. My heart stutters to a brief stop when I hear not one, but two sets of feet make their way toward me.

It's Nathan, the guard usually stationed at the atrium, and another older guard. Both wear grim expressions.

"Calliope Sawyer," Nathan states, coming to a stop before the cell door, "we are to escort you to the Auroral Bastille. Please remove your bracers and any other tokens on your person that are the property of the Wardens." Not the observatory? No, I think to myself, it could barely fit the Alaskan Council.

"Hi to you too, Nathan," I respond lightly. "I'm glad to see you're well after that first attack."

The minuscule downward turn of his mouth expresses quite plainly his displeasure in having to be here. I'm sure I mirror it.

"Remove the bracers, Sawyer," the other guard reiterates. "You've been stripped of your titles and are required to return your gear."

Oh.

It stings more than I thought it would. The words stabbing deeply into my heart, and draining me of hope. It takes but a moment to remove both sets of bracers, my fingers lingering over the smooth metal fondly one last time before I set them down beside me and rise.

"I'm ready," I tell them, walking stiffly to the door as they open it. As I exit, each guard takes me by the upper arm to guide me forward. Thankfully Nathan is on my left side. His grip isn't nearly as tight as the other guard's and lies considerately below where the hellspawn took a bite out of me.

"We don't have all day," gripes the man on my right. "Let's not pretend you have anything better to do," I snark back. The guard whirls on me, his fist hitting my cheekbone with enough force to snap my head to the side. I collapse into Nathan, who lets out a cry of alarm.

"What the hell do you think you're doing, man?" he shouts, leaning me against the wall and stepping between us.

"What the hell am I doing?" he retorts. "She's mouthing off. Scum like her who mouth off are dealt with accordingly. She's a thief and a slut for messing around with that pack of wolves. Hell, I bet she probably planned the whole thing with them."

"Fuck you," I spit out. The man lets out a snarl and lunges toward me, but Nathan is there to stop him. He pushes him back into the intercepting hallway, not expecting the dart that suddenly appears in the man's neck.

"What the—" Nathan says with a grimace before rushing to the man's side. It's a bad idea on Nathan's part. The second he breaches the other hallway an identical dart impales itself into his neck. "—fuck." Both guards collapse within seconds of each other, and another pair of feet quickly sound.

"What are you doing here?" I ask in amazement as Noelle and Naomi round the corner.

"We don't have much time," Naomi says as her sister races back into my holding cell. "We've secured the van they were going to transport you in to the Auroral Bastille."

"What about—" I hiss in pain as Naomi maneuvers me away from the wall, her arm wrapped tightly around my waist.

"Here, help me put these on her for a moment," Noelle says once she's back at our side. A throaty cry ushers from my lips as the bracers are placed back on my arms. Both sets.

"How fast can you go?" Naomi asks. I activate the bracers and let their energy sweep through my body.

"I can keep up," I promise. Noelle looks ready to jet off, but my hand on her wrist stops them both. "Thank you."

"Just keep trying, okay? Don't give up on her," she responds after a moment, voice growing nearly as thick with emotion as mine.

"I won't. I swear it."

"Come on, they're waiting outside," Naomi tugs at my waist and we dart off through the maze of hallways and stairways. "Come on, Callie. You can do it," Naomi encourages from behind me as we traverse up another stairwell.

My body burns with the effort. "I'm trying," I pant.

"Hurry it up," Noelle calls down from above. "The cameras are on a timer and our time is almost up. We need to get to the van. *Now.*"

"Come on, Callie," Naomi cajoles, her hands giving me the boost I need. "Do it for Nova. Do it for that guy out in the van. Just push past it, Callie. You're stronger than this. Stronger than all of us."

Her words have the desired effect. Something inside me—a lightness and warmth—swims through my veins. Even as I stumble up the stairs, knocking my knees and palms painfully against the hard concrete, I keep going. For Nova and Keenan and myself.

Noelle ushers us through a heavy black door, once she has scanned the perimeter, her gun held securely out in front of her. "Follow me, in three, two, go!"

We race around the corner of the building, and there, only a hundred yards away, is a black van.

"Drive till you reach the old Lander's farm. They'll be a black truck for you to switch to. The keys are hidden in the exhaust pipe." I nod, hardly able to believe this is actually happening.

"Where is he?"

Naomi gestures in the direction of the back. "JJ put him in the back already along with a bag of some provisions. Be careful with it, all right? I put something in there that has to be handled with a lot of care. We also put that weird stake you had on you

when you arrived in there. Promise you'll be careful, okay?"
My bottom lip quivers. "I will."
Naomi throws her arms around my neck, pulling me into a fierce hug that I return with equal zeal. "She loved you, you know?" she whispers into my ear.

I nod my head once more, blinking back tears at this final goodbye. "I know," I whisper back, pulling away and out of her arms.

Noelle comes to my side and passes me a burner phone. One of those tiny Nokia's so popular in the early 2000s. "For when you see her again," she says before wrapping me in a similar hug. "Ready?"

My ragged breath sounds heavy in the air around us. The night is at its darkest, but it will only last for another hour or so. "I'm ready." The girls spare me one last glance before racing back into the building. I barely wait until their backs are turned before hobbling over to the rear of the van. I deactivate the bracers and feel the remnants of their energy linger in my cells. I can't afford to use up their power.

My hands are on the door handles when he steps out from the other side of the van. His robotic hand training a gun straight at my head. My breath catches in my throat as I slowly take a step back, hands raised weakly in the air.

"Dad." Another cautious step away from the van, and I am granted a sickening new view. JJ, lying on the ground, body unmoving. "Dad, what did you do?" He must have attacked him after he helped Keenan into the van.

"It's far past time you take responsibility for your actions, Calliope," he tells me stonily, "but to know that you manipulated your brother into helping you."

"Just... just let me check on, JJ. Okay? Please, Dad, just let me see if he's all right."

He lets out a growl of frustration as I attempt to tread cautiously toward JJ. "He'll be fine. Now, walk back to the building, Calliope. I'll be right behind you with that *thing* in the back."

The hopelessness returns full force, almost knocking the breath out of me as my father takes a determined step toward the van's back doors. Before I can think otherwise, I dodge in front of him. Plastering my back against the van doors to block his access. My father stares at me in shock, the gun in his robotic hand wavering.

"Move," he snarls.

"No, Dad. Just let me go. Let us go," I plead. He opens his mouth to speak, but I plow on. "I know I'm a disappointment to you, okay? Staying here won't change anything. No outcome of the trial will end happily for our family or me, so just let me go."

He struggles with hearing my plea, jaw tightening minutely. "Calliope—"

"Please, Dad," I beg. "I won't be a bother to you anymore. I swear. It can just be like I was never here. Like I never existed at all. I promise I won't come back. I promise I won't cause any more trouble. I'll be good."

My father shifts uncomfortably. "You don't have to do this, Calliope," he reasons. "The Council is willing to go a different route tonight. It hasn't been done in a long time, but—"

"You mean the exorcism? You would let them do that to me?"

His face turns red before running pale. "Wyatt is a respectable young man. He's far better than that beast in here could ever be for you."

I shake my head, biting down on my bottom lip hard enough to draw blood as I try to quell my growing distress. "How did you find out?" His gaze darts to JJ for a split second. "He's not a beast, Dad. He's a kind, good *man*. He's my *soulmark*."

The word makes my father's lips press together in a firm line. "You're letting your emotions get the best of you, Calliope. Empathy for these monsters will only get you hurt or killed. When will you learn, you *insolent* child?"

"I'm not going to end up like you, Dad," I keen, my eyes moving purposefully to his prosthetic. "And my emotions? My empathy? They're not a weakness. You're wrong."

I use his momentary surprise against him, calling upon the Borealis Matter inside of me to rush him and knock the gun from his hand. It takes him a moment to realize what I've done, but by then it's too late. The gun resides in my grasp, and I hold it unflinchingly in his face.

"So, this is your choice?" he says with a scowl, dropping to his knees at my gesture.

"Best damn choice I ever made," I tell him, before pistol-whipping him. He falls on his side, hands weakly rising to push himself up, before dropping to the ground in a slump.

I rush to JJ's side and spot the small, feathered dart protruding from his neck. Carefully I roll him onto his back, my fingers gently pushing back his hair. "Thank you, JJ. I love you," I whisper to his prone form.

I desperately wish to stay and make sure he wakes, but I know my time is up. If I have any hope of escaping with Keenan, I needed to leave immediately. And so, with one last parting kiss on his forehead, I stand and go.

FOREVER AND ALWAYS

- Chapter 20 -

It takes three days to get to a safe spot and for the cash we've been left to run out. Three days for Keenan to fully come out of his drug-induced state. And three days before a nasty fever takes hold of me.

Once Keenan is lucid, he finds a way to contact the pack. They reach us in less than a day. I've never been more pleased than to have a pack of wolves converge upon me. Keenan, still weakened from the high dosage of quicksilver tonic is particularly growly and possessive when Atticus has to carry me to the new vehicle.

"You came," I comment hoarsely as Atticus ducks into the car and pulls me into his lap. "Don't forget your seat belt," I mumble, feeling particularly fatigued. The combination of the wolf's higher body temperature and the beta's natural ability to ease my pain take the edge off the stress I've been feeling the past few days, as well as some of the pain.

"Seat belt." He sounds properly offended, and I stay awake long enough to look up at him in concern. But Atticus isn't upset at all. He wears the kindest smile with the tiniest, teasing crook to it. "Sweetheart, I'm a lycan. I don't need a seat belt. I am the seat belt." His arm squeezes me more tightly as if to emphasize the point, and I give a slight whine of protest. This time his displeasure is real, the smile dropping from his face fast faster than I can blink. "Don't worry. The pack's got you now, Callie. Rest." And so I do.

+++

It's too hot.

Much too hot to be comfortable, at least. I feel myself come to with a rhythmic pounding in my temples, mouth parched, and limbs aching. The room that comes into focus is not one I am familiar with. It has crisp white walls and little decor besides a large pinewood dresser.

"Where am I?" I mumble, eye alighting on a figure in the corner of the room. It is Keenan, his large frame slumped in an uncomfortable position in an unfortunate looking high-backed chair.

"You're safe," a velvet voice chimes. I turn my head sluggishly toward the opposite end of the dimly lit room. A woman with a plethora of scars hovers over a small rolling cart, her hands busy mixing something. I've seen her scars before.

"JJ. Witch," I manage to say.

"Maureen," she tells me. Maureen walks over to my bedside and pours me a small cup of water, holding it gently to my lips. When the first drop of liquid hits my tongue, I let out an appreciative moan, gulping down the water with haste. "More."

She accedes, and the process is repeated.

"Better?"

I hum in agreement.

"You should try and sleep some more, my dear," she chides in a velvety voice.

"Where am I?" I ask once more.

"You're at Mr. O'Neal's residence." *Who?* I must wear my look of confusion well, for the woman gives another kind smile and gestures in the direction of Keenan. "Your wolf."

My wolf. It has a nice ring to it. *Better than "Mr. O'Neal,"* I think dimly. I forgot O'Neal was his last name. He's always been just Keenan to me. "What day is it?"

"It's Saturday. You've been here about five days now." My lips part to speak, but Maureen holds up her hand. "Try not to speak, dear. You've been in and out for the better part of these five days with a nasty fever."

I let my eyes drift shut, nodding once more in agreement. My body seems to only know pain at the moment. From my head to my toes, there is the feeling of flames. "Hot."

Maureen fetches me another glass of water, then a glass or two of something that is most certainly *not*. I have trouble keeping it down, cringing and coughing weakly as the concoctions make their way down my throat. Thankfully, they provide instant comfort to my sorer parts and wash away some of the fog in my head.

"The bites," I croak, "are toxic."

"We've gathered," she tells me. "It took a day or two to figure out what worked best in healing you, but we've got it now. We just need to let the medicine do its work."

"Luna?"

"She's going to be just fine," comes her velvet reassurance. A small sigh issues from my lips with relief. My eyes crack open to look at Maureen tiredly. "She's a bit shaken up, but her body is different than yours. She's already mostly healed from her injuries."

"Fairy," I rasp.

Our eyes meet. "Yes. Now *sleep*."

There is something rather mesmerizing about the way she says the word "sleep." I feel as if I've been re-tucked into the bed, my pillows fluffed, and a cool touch drawn across my skin to ease the heat. It's almost like magic, and all from one simple word.

And so I do.

+++

"You can't keep me in this bed forever. You do understand that, right?" Keenan keeps his back toward me as he grabs a new shirt for the day and slips it on. The stark black of his tattoos are clearly visible through his plain white tee, as are the definitions of his muscles.

"Not forever," he agrees with a grunt.

I roll my eyes. "It's already been ten days. Ten days, Keenan."

He slams the dresser drawer closed with a bit more force than necessary, then turns to face me. "And of those ten days, you were asleep for eight of them. The witches say it's too soon for you to get out of bed. So, you're staying in bed."

I let out a groan of frustration. "I'm pretty positive I wasn't asleep for *that* long," I grumble. "Besides, I hate being cooped up inside, and if you would just give me the bracers back—which, by the way, I am still mad at you for taking them off me in the first place—then I'm sure I would heal at ten times the speed I am now." Keenan looks unimpressed at the end of my rather long-winded sentence. I'm sure I look... winded. *I am winded*, I think morosely.

"Be mad at me all you want, but technically speaking, you took them off. I'm not going to apologize for getting you to do it in one of your very *rare* states of consciousness. Besides, the witches said—"

"The witches don't know anything about them," I interrupt heatedly. "I want them back."

"Like I told you yesterday, and Maureen, and Xander, the magic doesn't work well with them on. Once you're better, I'll give them back. I swear." I avert my gaze stubbornly to the window. "You should get some rest," he tells me with a sigh, walking over to my side and tucking a piece of hair behind my ear.

"I've literally slept for a week," I tell him blandly. "I think I'll pass."

Keenan heaves another sigh before dropping a kiss atop my head. "I'll be back later," he murmurs against my hair. "I need to get back to the shop."

"Fine by me," I mutter sullenly, refusing to meet his gaze still.

"Xander's planning on coming by later today to see how you're doing," he informs me as he pulls away. "Go easy on him, okay?" The odd request turns my attention Keenan's way. "He, uh, has some news he needs to break to you."

"Okay," I respond.

Keenan departs with one last kiss, this time on my upturned lips. With little to do outside of reading the pile of cooking magazines Xander had been commissioned to bring the other day at Zoelle's insistence, I feel myself begin to doze.

"Callie?" The husky voice of the alpha lifts me from my light slumber sometime later. I come to with some cooking magazine still open on my lap, my neck stiff from the awkward position I held.

"Hi, Xander."

He stands pensively in the doorway of Keenan's bedroom, before stepping inside. He looks tired, more tired than me, if possible. His dark hair is drawn back in a messy style, with several strands daring to fall out of place. His skin, naturally warm in color, lacks its usual luster. Likewise, his green eyes are drawn, heavy with the weight of the world. He's wearing something startlingly close to Keenan—a white Henley shirt and dark wash jeans—but he doesn't do them the same justice as Keenan. This alpha might be muscular and lean, his source of power drawn from his pack, but Keenan is *strong*. In every inch of his body.

"Keenan said you had something to tell me."

Xander nods and goes and leans against the dresser opposite the king-sized bed. I worm myself up into a somewhat more comfortable sitting position, giving up as soon as I find something close to reasonable. I spot my reflection in the mirror above the dresser and pause momentarily.

I look as good as I feel—like shit. My normal glossy, dark chocolate hair is flat and greasy. A hair tie would be greatly appreciated at the moment, as well as a brush. At least with those two items I could brush my disastrous hair and braid it so it doesn't look so messy. My usual tawny skin is also deprived of its typical glow, much like Xander. Days kept out of the sun and stored away in bed fighting away death will do that to a person. It doesn't look like I have won yet though. My brown eyes hold a hurt to them, an echo of my body's sentiments.

I exhale softly. I will get better soon.

"It's about the blade and the ring." Xander's voice is oddly detached and breaks me from my reverie. It has the unnerving effect of making me uncomfortable, a fact he is quick to latch onto. "Sorry," he mumbles, straightening and composing himself into something more stoic. "They're gone, Callie."

"What's gone?" I whisper back, grasping onto hope that he isn't talking about what I think he is.

A flutter of pain crosses over his expression. "Irina and the relics."

I feel as if I've been punched in the gut. Oh God? What have I done? "This is my fault," I tell him hoarsely. Xander shakes his head firmly, but I continue. "It is. Nova saved me in the forest, and I told her. I told her that they were with her, but I didn't know she knew who Irina was. I should have known better—"

"You were being eaten alive, Callie," he reminds me. "I know all about it. You told Keenan, remember." *Had I*? I give a small shake of my head to negate the fact.

"I don't remember," I confess.

Xander strums his finger along the dresser. "Lydia said you might be a bit fuzzy about details for a while, but for the record, I know. I know, because when she questioned you, you told her what happened. You told your friend you weren't in possession of the ring or the blade, and thank God for that. There's no telling what she might have done to you if the blade or the ring *was* on you."

"She wouldn't have hurt me," I tell him defensively.

He levels me with a stern glare. "She might not have wanted to, but if Vrana ordered her to, then there would have been nothing she could have done not to." I swallow at the reprimand. "And then you told Lydia that you told your friend it was with Irina."

"Yes," I concur, feeling oddly hollow. "I'm sorry. I'm so sorry."

"You don't have anything to be sorry for."

I stare at Xander in astonishment. "Of course, I do. Your sister is gone. The relics are gone. Does that mean... does that mean he has them?"

Xander gives a curt nod, and I force myself to find some modicum of composure like the alpha. "The only one to blame is me. I should have been more vigilant regarding the Wselfwulf's activity. I should have taken your warnings more seriously the first time around. But most of all, I should never have let Irina convince me to let her guard them."

"We'll find her," I promise. "We'll find her and get the relics back."

The words I speak are spoken with confidence. We will find Irina, and we will find the relics. And after that—after that, I will find a way to save Nova. There is just one thing I need to know first. "How? How did they find her?"

The alpha leans back into the dresser, crossing his arms over his chest. "I suppose it would be better if I start at the beginning. Atticus ran into Zoelle soon after he saw you, and she called her grandmother. I was already driving over there, so when I got her call, I sped the rest of the way there. We came up with a plan quickly based on what little information we had. We were going to give them what they wanted: blood."

"How many did we lose?"

Xander gives me a reassuring smile and steps forward to place a hand on my ankle. "Not as many as you're thinking, Callie. It was thanks to your warning that it wasn't more." Xander pulls away. "We assumed that if the Wardens were going to attack, they would do so when the border was least protected."

"During a guard shift," I fill in. Xander nods.

"We held everyone back and had Diana send out the Eldritch Witches in full force, with a rather brilliant plan. Instead of truly fighting the Wardens, the witches orchestrated a grand illusion. The Wardens *thought* they were fighting the pack. They *thought* they were taking hits."

"But it was all in their heads?" Again, he nods. I find it difficult to swallow as a wave of emotion bubbles forth. "But we did lose people."

Xander's face turns sober. "We did. Jane Whitman, Mercy Hollaway, Jenny Beckman, and Kira Sanders. The Wardens fell back fully when they realized their minds were playing tricks on them, that and the hellspawn didn't feel like discriminating. They became overwhelmed quickly, and I believe once they had you and Keenan subdued, they felt it enough to retreat."

"How did Vrana find Irina?"

"It appears we underestimated Vrana. Again. He's been one step ahead of us the whole time, manipulating the entire situation. He instructed the Wselfwulf Pack to target the Wardens, and the Wardens played right into his hand in seeking revenge. When the crystal was successfully compromised and the border fractured, he got in. We don't know where he entered from, but he must have seen Irina making her getaway and stopped her. If it weren't for the rain, she would have gotten away," he comments with a menacing frown. "Regardless, he was more than aptly prepared that day to secure the ring."

"We'll get it back. We'll get them all back," I tell him again.

"We will," he says, offering me a small smile in return. "But not at this exact moment. Rest, Callie. Sleep, that's an order."

I huff in protest, feeling the weight of his command settle across my eyelids. A yawn stretches my mouth open wide, and I snuggle back into the mountain of pillows behind me unwittingly. I'm out before he leaves the room.

+++

"It's been weeks."

Keenan and I stand in his kitchen in a standoff. I hold the heavy ceramic casserole dish close to my chest, while Keenan waits expectantly with his hand outstretched.

"Just give it to me. I can put it away and you can—"

"Sit? Rest?" I growl back, shifting backward with narrowed eyes. "No fucking way. Did you not just hear what I said? It has been *weeks*, Keenan."

"And you only just got over that latest infection a week ago. You don't need to do any heavy lifting. You should take it easy, Callie."

"It was a *tiny* infection. Besides, Maureen gave me the all clear three days ago, Keenan," I argue back, "and this is not heavy lifting. It's doing the dishes!"

"You're not ready," he counters, stepping forward and into my personal space, "and you're too short to put it back above the fridge."

His hands take possession of the bottom half of the casserole dish and tug. An incredulous noise sounds from my throat, as I tug back.

"That's why Zoelle brought over a step stool yesterday. Everything in this house is made for giants! And I am not too short. I am 5'9. You're just too tall." I give a hearty tug back, succeeding in only moving myself.

"Give me the dish," he orders.

"No," I snap back. A short-lived tug-of-war ensues, ultimately resulting in the casserole dish crashing into pieces on the floor between us. "Shit." With a sigh, I sink down onto my hunches along with Keenan and begin to pick up the larger pieces.

"Let me—"

"I can—*ouch*!" I quickly pull back my hand and place my finger in my mouth. Giving Keenan an irate look, I stand and step carefully toward the sink. "I told you I could help," I mutter angrily, thrusting my hand under a cool stream of water. "If you hadn't tried to take that piece from me—"

"You wouldn't have cut yourself?" he asks dubiously, coming over to my side to check my minor wound.

"No, I wouldn't have," I argue back.

He takes hold of my hand gently, turning it to inspect the small gash along my forefinger and middle finger. "I'm sorry," he rumbles, a troubled expression on his face. He turns off the water and grabs some paper towels to press against the wound.

"You can't protect me from everything, Keenan. It's a lovely thought, but it's just not possible." He colors at my softly spoken words. Through the bond, I can feel a flare of irritation, followed closely by a swell of regret and guilt. "Keenan—"

"I'll run upstairs and get some bandages for that," he tells me, "and I'll take care of this mess, all right?" He leans forward and presses a kiss to my forehead, even though I've tilted my face accordingly to receive one on my lips. I watch him leave with a frustrated look.

True, my recovery has been a rocky one, with a few close calls throughout the three weeks I was bedridden. Though the pack and coven rallied to help my recovery through whatever means necessary, it's taken its toll on Keenan. On myself as well, if I'm being honest. I don't like being so weak, nor does Keenan. It leaves him overly protective and stressed. Now that I'm starting to feel better, I hoped the underlying tension would ease between us. *Maybe if he would talk to me about what is really bothering him*, I think sullenly to myself, *we would be in a better place.*

I maneuver around the broken ceramic and head upstairs to the master bathroom. Keenan is hunched over the sink, body stiff and the medical supplies sitting in a neat row to his left.

"Hey." My utterance snaps him to attention, and he whirls around to face me. "Are you okay?"

He says nothing, only looks at me with those soulful brown eyes, his hard jawline ticking subtly to keep his words at bay. His next movements are almost mechanical as he tends to my cuts and bandages them carefully.

"Keenan?"

He gives a shake of his head and swallows hard, stepping past me and into the bedroom. I let my anger seep through the bond and watch as he stops midstep.

"Stop walking away from me," I growl. "Talk to me, Keenan. What's wrong?"

"You're not ready," he tells me, refusing to turn and face me. "You're not strong enough yet to be doing anything."

"Keenan—"

"I know you hate it. I know you hate being stuck in bed and being stuck here." He breathes heavily, spinning around to confront me. "But if you don't give your body what it needs to heal, then you won't. You need to *rest*, Callie. Even before Maureen gave you the go-ahead, you were finding any excuse to sneak out, and we both know it didn't do you any good."

I grimace in guilt. "I do hate being in bed," I agree softly, "but I don't hate being here. Or being stuck with you. I want to be here, but, Keenan, I have to start building my strength back up. I need more than just rest to recover now. I'm ready," I stress, letting the last two words hang heavy with meaning.

"You're not, and that's okay," he tells me just as meaningfully.

"I am ready," I argue, "and it's about damn time you accept it."

My heart rate steadily increases as we hold each other's gazes in another standoff. This one I'm going to win. Before I can talk myself out of it, or Keenan can walk away, I take hold of the bottom of my shirt and lift it over my head, tossing it to the ground.

"I'm ready," I repeat, trying to give my words a more sultry edge as I peel off my leggings.

Keenan's eyes darken as they focus on me. Each sweep of his eyes draws a flush across the length of my body before his intense inspection starts to get the better of my self-esteem. Especially when his gaze lingers over my gnarled scars. My legs bear the most of them, with pinched crescent moons and long stretches of puckered pink skin. But it's my left arm that makes me the most self-conscious. A sizable piece of flesh is missing from the upper arm, leaving not only an indentation, but a constant pain I'll have to deal with for the rest of my days.

"Are you going to, you know?" I gesture impatiently toward his clothes. "All this stalling is ruining the mood."

Keenan strides toward me, a flicker of understanding crossing his features before he cups my face in his hands and kisses me.

"You're beautiful," he breathes reverently against my lips, "and brave, and I'm so damn lucky to have you in my life, Calliope. But there were so many times where I almost lost you this past month." His lips press back against mine more fiercely, a desperate moan sounding from deep inside him as he pulls me closer. I gasp when he releases my tender lips, my hands clutching his shirt so tightly I might have pierced the fabric.

"But you didn't lose me, Keenan," I utter the words against his stubbled-stained cheek, nuzzling my nose along his jawline, "and I didn't lose you. We have each other now, and that's what matters."

"I love you, Calliope Sawyer." Keenan's eyes are closed as he speaks the words, his hands languidly running through my hair, down my back, over my hips, and back up my sides. "The past month has been hell, but that day in the forest—" His voice catches for moment. "—I felt you, baby. I felt every bite and hit and claw. I felt your fear and your grief. It felt like someone took a can opener to my guts, and there was nothing I could do about it. But I can now, and sometimes I still feel that old hurt lingering inside of you. And damn, baby, I can't stand that you're in pain."

I bow my head to rest it on his chest, let his hands continue their exploration of my skin. Deftly they climb up my back and unclasp my bra, before tugging the item lightly off me. Keenan bends me backward, his head dipping toward my breasts. When his warm, full lips ensnare the rosy peak, I release a soft cry, my fingers weaving into his hair.

"You never need to feel that way again," he growls stoutly into my skin, lavishing my breast with attention. "I'm here now, and I've got you, Callie."

Keenan tugs me upward and captures my lips in another intense kiss, guiding me back toward the bed. His clothes come off in pieces as we make our way slowly toward its middle. First his shirt. Then his pants. I give an impatient tug to his boxer briefs only for him to catch my hands and bring them to his chest.

"Keenan," I utter his name on a sigh as he traces kisses down my torso tenderly. The gentle foreplay has built a kindling fire up to an almost impossible roar. I squirm beneath him, my hips lifting upward to find some relief. He groans above me, body stilling as the hard outline of his cock presses firmly against the flimsy underwear I still wear.

"Slow, Callie," he mumbles against my skin, his golden stained gaze flicking to my face as he helps me out of my panties. "We don't have to rush this, baby."

The sweet endearment makes my heart clench painfully. "I just want—" Keenan shushes me gently before removing his last article of clothing as well.

"I know what you want," he tells me confidently in a husky baritone that makes my whole body shiver. His hands help guide my legs around his large waist before teasingly running the head of his cock along my slick heat.

"Keenan." His name comes out more a whine than a growl, and his pleased smile almost makes my heart melt. He adjusts himself slowly above me, continuing his teasing motion and effortlessly driving me mad with want. His hand splays itself across my hip, thumb daringly close to my soulmark, while he rests upon his other forearm. Our eyes meet, and I am left breathless.

For though his eyes are full of want and hunger, it is not for sex. *He's hunting me.* My hands clutch at his biceps as the realization hits. Not just the man, but the wolf inside of him. All those times of patiently watching me. Of cutting things off before they got too heated and letting me decide the pace. And now the wolf finally has me in his clutches.

"I love you," I whisper shyly to him. The intensity of his regard hardly lessens at my words, but his satisfaction slips through the bond between us.

"I love you, too," he replies back heatedly, angling his hips and sliding effortlessly into me. "I'm never gonna stop—never gonna let you go," he groans. My moan is stilted by his lips slanting over mine. It has been so long, yet never has it felt so right to be with someone. To be with my soulmark. My soul mate.

As Keenan's hip rock against mine, angling himself inside me deeper with each thrust, I let out a small mewl. I can feel him so acutely. Everywhere. Not just inside and out, but all around me. His lips fall to my shoulder as he begins to pick up his pace, my hips joining in the primal rhythm and making him shudder.

"Damn, Callie," he groans against my skin, teeth nipping over the sensitive flesh as if in rebuke. "You really love me, baby?"

I pull his face toward me until it is level with my own. "Yes," I tell him firmly, just before a gasp is pulled from my lips. "Yes, don't ever doubt it. We've been through—" The words become lost as his thumb brushes over my soulmark. My hips press incessantly against his with unrestrained desire.

"Bind yourself to me," he whispers harshly against my lips. "Be mine, forever and always."

I whimper as my need grows. The heat inside me building to a crescendo around Keenan's driving thrusts. "Yes," I breathe, tilting my head submissively to the side. "I bind myself to you, Keenan. Forever and always."

The bond between us changes. It shifts, growing wider to some unfathomable depth before softening. Until there are no means to tell where one ends and the other begins. I give a soft cry. Eyes widening. Back arching. My fervent need bursting into stars before my eyes. Keenan holds me close as my climax reaches a fever pitch, driving into me with almost painful thrusts as his release shudders through him.

When we settle, he flips us around and pulls me against his side. My hand skims over the dark hair coating his chest, breathing in soft pants as my heart slowly winds down.

"What now?" I ask.

"Now?" Keenan replies, eyes slipping back to molten brown. "Now we take back what's ours."

EPILOGUE

The highest ranking among the pack gather in Xander's study at the Adolphus manor one early morning in late September: the alpha male and female, the beta, the third through the fifth, and both Quinn and me. The room holds its breath, mimicking its occupants, as the alpha male paces the room.

"It's been two months since they've been taken," he recites, words razor sharp in their delivery. "How is it that we haven't been able to find a single trace of them yet?"

It is my first meeting with the gathered group, and I watch on somewhat wearily. Everyone wears varying expressions of guilt and displeasure at the alpha's anger and disappointment. I too am shifting uncomfortably from his sentiments, but find solace in Keenan's nearness. He stands next to me, arms folded across his chest. His face held impassively as he regards the alpha.

"Ryatt? Quinn? Anything?"

Quinn shakes her head sadly. "It's like he just vanished into thin air," she responds. "His penthouse in Denver went up for sale and sold last month. His belongings moved to a storage unit. He didn't take anything with him."

"Except for Irina, Nova, and the relics," Xander growls back, slamming his palms down onto the study desk with enough force to splinter the wood. Everyone flinches, except for Keenan, at the outburst. Even me.

"Xander, we're doing everything we can," Zoelle reminds him calmly.

"Where are the witches on scrying for her?"

Zoelle's face falls. "Something is still blocking their efforts. They think Vrana is still in league with the Stormrow sorcerers, and that they've erected a blind over them so that they can't be found by magic or otherwise."

Xander's anger vibrates through the pack bonds, and again the room shifts in discomfort. It's not until the alpha takes a deep breath and straightens that the tension finally breaks.

"I don't even know where to begin to look," he murmurs.

"Are you sure she's still—" My question is cut off by an abrupt shake of the alpha's head. He turns to face us, his face impossibly hard yet torn with grief and worry.

"I can still feel her through the pack bonds. It's faint, but she's still there," he tells me tiredly.

I chew on my bottom lip for a moment. "Have you tried reaching out to others in the supernatural community?"

"I'm afraid that's a no-go, darling," Ryatt says, giving me a sidelong glance. "Our association with the witches makes us the so-called black sheep of the supernatural community."

"What about Vienna?" The eyes of the room turn toward me.

"What about Vienna?" Xander asks back softly.

I shift a bit uneasily under his regard. "It's been the seat of the power for the Ancients for the past four or five centuries, coinciding with the rise of the Hapsburg empire," I say carefully. It's obvious the room doesn't know their vampyré lore. I continue with a steady breath. "If my teachings are correct, true daylight rings secure the wearer a place in the Court of Vampyrés. He'll have to prove the ring is real and present himself to the Court, but that's just an educated guess."

"Vienna, Austria?" Quinn asks to clarify. I give a brief nod, and a smile splits across her face. "I've always wanted to go there. Divine shopping. Road trip?"

"No more road trips," Keenan and I say at the same time, sparing each other a special glance. A thrill of hope echoes across the pack bonds as Xander's grim expression softens.

"Let's make a plan," he murmurs, stepping closer to join our circle. "They've been gone for too long. It's time we get her back."

Continue reading for a sneak peek at
Mr. Vrana

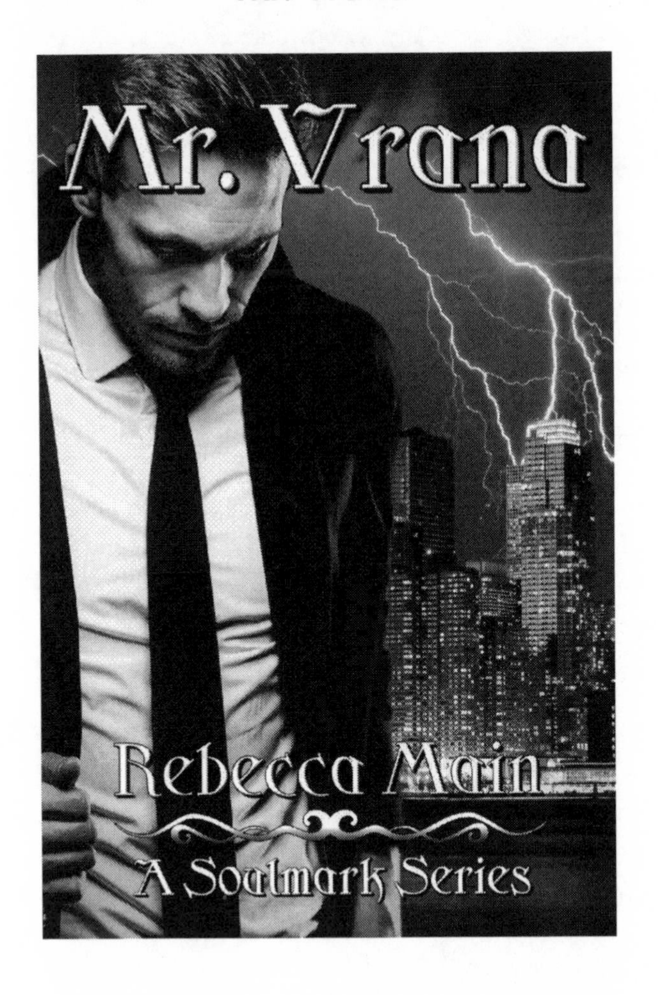

Prologue

"Say it to me again," Xander demands, his voice cutting out and back in. Reception in the forest is not good.

I take a breath to steady my irate nerves and adjust the grip on my cell phone. Though we are only half-siblings, Xander acts as if we are blood, and tends to err on the over-the-top protective side, even if I'm more than capable of the handling the mission. I can imagine him in his study, his body taut and radiating stress. If he were in the van with me now, I know he'd have my hands in his—the grip too tight for comfort and yet perfect all the same.

I release the breath with a small sigh. "I run south and stick to the forest. I don't split ways with O'Riley and Mathis until we've hit Yellowstone."

"And then?"

My fingers tighten, and the sound of the phone's plastic casing fracturing reaches both our ears. I let out another breath and remind myself that Xander is only concerned for my well-being and that of the

Adolphus pack. *Our pack.* He's just doing his job as the alpha and ensuring I know what to do. After all, if I fail, there is no telling what the consequences might be. I *must* keep the Amethyst of the Aztec and Vogart's blade out of the Wselfwulf pack's hands, as well as the vampyrés, at all costs.

"Then I keep running. I know the plan, Xander, all right? No one is getting their hands on me, the ring, or Callie's little knife." Though, little is hardly the word to describe the wicked sickle-like blade. "The car is pulling up to the drop point. I need to go."

A beat of silence, and then, "Be safe."

I swallow. The thick coating of emotion in his voice triggers a wave of uncertainty in my gut. "I will be. I won't let you down or the pack."

"Stay alive, Irina." The weight of his command, even through the phone and at this distance, is immense. I feel the burden of his words wrap around me like a vise and suck in a sharp breath to steady myself.

"I will," I say, not liking one bit the way my vision begins to cloud with tears. "I'll be back in no time, brother."

"Be smart," he whispers.

"Always." The line goes dead just as a surge of adrenaline floods the pack bonds. Something is happening north of here. A confrontation. A chase.

Our car pulls to a stop on the dirt road, and O'Riley and Mathis exit the car alongside me.

"Good luck," Valerie says from the driver's seat, before driving away back toward the real action. I watch for a moment longer than necessary to steel my nerves one final time. Rolling my shoulders back, I tilt my chin up high.

"Shall we, then?" I spare a quick glance at the towering men accompanying me on my mission. O'Riley and Mathis aren't ranked terribly high in the pack, but they are fast, which is why they were chosen to go with me.

Not as fast as me, but passable nonetheless.

"You've got everything you need?"

I nod at Mathis, mentally listing off the items in my possession. *Ring, check. Blade, check. Cash, check. Burner phone, check.*

"It's a long run to Fort Collins."

"I'm aware of the distance, Mathis. I'll make it to the Lovota pack in no time at all." O'Riley snorts at the bored expression I pass to the other man, while I stretch my legs one last time. The Lovota pack is small and tends to keep out of the disputes of the larger packs, but they made an exception for us thanks to Atticus's smooth negotiations. "Ready, boys? Let's see if you can keep up."

And then we are off. The earth disappears beneath our feet as we race along the familiar terrain of our territory. We weave through the flora with ease, soon finding ourselves near the most southern end of our land. The men flank me on either side, the sound of their breathing matching my own as our feet dig more deeply into the earth. Soon the world blurs past me in vignettes of greens and browns.

Our pace doesn't slow when the rain begins to fall. If anything, it urges us on faster. When the ground becomes slick with mud, I find myself panting from the exertion to maintain both speed and balance.

"Come on, then!" I shout over my shoulder, teetering momentarily, only to correct myself with a grin.

A clap of thunder sounds from afar, and I slow my speed to search the tree line for O'Riley. He's nowhere to be seen. My heels slam into the ground. I shoot a look over my other shoulder. No Mathis either. *Shit.*

"I was wondering when you would notice."

The velvet voice sends a shiver down my spine. I whip my head around to face the mysterious man, my ivy-colored eyes narrowing on him. He is dressed to impress with Oxford shoes, a black tailored suit, and pale blond hair swept artfully back out of his face. The rain does little to hamper his style. My active wear is a stark contrast to his outfit.

The man takes a step forward, the tilt of his lips mocking me with false sincerity.

"I wasn't expecting company," I say.

A gust of wind tosses the rain against my back and into the man's face. I don't bother to smother my smirk. Upon catching my look, he drops his facade of pleasantry. In the blink of an eye, he is in front of me, only a few feet away, well within range to strike out with his fist or feet.

"The ring, if you please."

My eyebrow hikes upward, and I shift my feet to stand shoulder width apart. "You're the vampyré?" I ask.

He inclines his head, his eyes never leaving my face. *This is the elusive Mr. Vrana*, I think, after the Amethyst of the Aztec ring so he can walk in the light. At least he isn't after Vogart's blade. The magical blade is a powerful weapon and is rumored to turn vampyrés back into humans. What would Vrana do if he got his hands on it?

"I thought you would be taller," I finish after my long and contemplative silence.

Surprise gleams behind his eyes at my unimpressed tone.

"My apologies," he murmurs. His crystalline blue eyes are fanned by thick eyelashes, enough to make a girl notice and be jealous. Lucky for me, I know precisely what devil I'm speaking with. The silver flecks in his eye give away his trade secret: his true age.

"My apologies as well," I say, adrenaline seeping into my veins as I keep my cool facade. "I'm afraid I can't give you the ring. It belongs to a friend of mine. You understand, don't you?"

He sneers. "That ring is mine." The flash of Mr. Vrana's fangs is all the warning I get before he attacks.

He moves like lightning, but I am quick enough to defend myself against his vicious assault. Until I'm not. One well-placed strike to my torso, and I become momentarily paralyzed.

Hit after hit lands, his blows pushing me back and toward the ground. I grit my teeth as another of his punches lands in my side, then another to the bottom half of my cheek. Black spots burst in symphony across my vision as I tumble to the ground. I am well versed in combat, but the vampyré is proving quickly to be out of my league.

Stay alive.

I cannot decipher whether the thought is my own or Xander's lingering command, but it is enough to keep me moving. I roll into a crouch, my hand withdrawing the blade from my side holster. The vampyré shoots me a glare, and the wolf inside of me rises to the challenge. It pushes at the bounds of its control within my body, but the lycan curse holds it back. It cannot seize control and guide my movements, nor can I shift at will to even the playing field. But I can listen to the instincts it drives into my mind and limbs.

A surge of wild abandon courses through me.

"You're not getting this ring," I say, a pant falling past my bloody lip.

The vampyré laughs humorlessly and begins to circle. He removes his jacket, tossing it onto the forest floor without care. Next, he unfastens his cufflinks, making a show of rolling up his sleeves. I watch with unease, mirroring his movements with smaller steps of my own. His skin is alabaster, even more so than mine.

"As I said before, the ring belongs to me. If you want to see your friends alive, I'd advise you to hand it over now."

My mouth opens to reply, but the words catch at the back of my throat. There, near the crease of the vampyré's elbow and half-hidden by his rolled sleeve, lies a dark impression on his skin. A mark. I school my features and inhale. The vampyré's last blow must have distorted my vision for the mark on his skin looks similar to the one upon my right wrist. Too similar.

"I'd advise you to find a different ring. Purple really isn't your color, leech."

Mr. Vrana takes my bait and hurtles toward me with incredible speed. I wait until the last possible second before diving low and striking out with the blade. The vampyré lets out a curse as the curved edge slashes through his clothing and flesh. Blood pumps through my veins at an accelerated pace at the sight, the wolf inside me howling at the small victory.

"I did offer to be lenient," he rebukes. I catch the steely undertone in his words and force my body to remain loose and at the ready. Yet when he strikes next, I am wholly unprepared. My speed is no match for his, my strength a pathetic comparison.

My back hits the forest floor, and my breath is lost in a painful *whoosh.* With a hand around my neck, Mr. Vrana keeps me pinned, the pressure of his fingers increasing with each passing second. I struggle to regain control.

Stay alive.

My lungs burn with the effort to capture the scantest of breaths, but to no avail. I lash out at his arm only to be thwarted.

"There's no use fighting it," he says, snagging my hand with the ring on it. He pries open my fist and works the ring off my middle finger. All the while, black spots begin to dot the sides of my vision.

Stay alive.

I turn wild eyes to the arm pinning me down, tracing a path toward the mark I saw before.

Stay alive.

He doesn't notice my intent, too consumed by his victory. I don't have time to second-guess myself. My hand shoots out, not to knock the ring from his hand or force away his chokehold, but to lay a hand on the mark. My soulmark…

Our reactions are instantaneous. The vampyré releases his hold on me and attempts to retreat, but my grip is ironclad. I arch my back with a mighty gasp, gulping in air like it's my first breath. It only heightens the sudden sensation of liquid fire encapsulating me. Us. The vampyré eyes me with astonishment. His lips part, and his eyes widen as he absorbs the truth.

I sink my nails further into his skin, jaw clenching as I do as my alpha commands: stay alive. "Let it be known that thy are found," I say, voice hoarse. "My soul awakened. The stars incline us, my love, and so we are sealed."

A shock of electricity draws a whimper from my throat. My body thrums with energy as some intrinsic part of me ties together with this… devil. Trembling with unexpected want, I release him. He falls to the side on his knees, staring at me aghast, before a sneer, full of hate and disgust, covers his face so completely I am at a loss for words.

"You're going to regret that," he promises darkly. His fist flies at me without restraint, and then there is only blackness.

What did you think of
Wardens of Starlight?

If you have a moment, please review Wardens of Starlight. Help other paranormal romance readers find a new story and tell them what you enjoyed most about Wardens of Starlight!

Want more?

Coven (Book 1) — *Out Now*
Midnight Scoundrel (Book 2) — *Out Now*
Wardens of Starlight (Book 3) — *Out Now*
Mr. Vrana (Book 4) — *Out Now*
Lycan Legacy (Book 5) — *February 21, 2019*
Lunaria (Book 6) — *TBA 2019*

Let's Connect!

Want to stay in the know on updates and bonus content?

Join Rebecca's Readers
rebeccamain.com

Like me on Facebook
https://www.facebook.com/AuthorRebeccaMain/

Follow me on Instagram
https://www.instagram.com/mrs_rebeccamain/

Follow me on Pinterest
https://www.pinterest.com/authorrebeccamain/

Acknowledgements

To my marvelous husband who has been there every step of the way—*thank you.* Your support and efforts to help me grow this series into something memorable is endlessly appreciated. I'm so excited to keep growing with you and to take this world by storm.

To all my friends and family, thank you for your support and putting up with my writerly ways.

A special thank you to Hot Tree Edits, especially Virginia, Randie, and Donna, for all of their help and editorial efforts, and generally whipping Wardens of Starlight into shape!

About the Author

Rebecca Main published her first romance novel—Coven (A Soulmark Series Book 1)—in June 2017 and hasn't put down her keyboard since! Quitting their respective jobs in May 2017, Rebecca and her husband now travel the world. Their calico cat, Dorcas, waits patiently for their return to become a "city" cat once more. Rebecca is an avid reader, travel-hacker enthusiast, and karaoke queen (after a shot or two). Her current writing passion is romance with a hearty dash of supernatural and paranormal thrown in for good measure.

Tear-inducing accomplishments include hitting #1 on the Amazon Top 100 list in Fantasy Romance and Paranormal Witches & Wizards, free climbing out of Belize's Crystal Cave, also known as the Mountain Cow Cave, and starting a publishing house—Via Graphia LLC—with her husband.

Made in the USA
San Bernardino, CA
20 May 2019